The Boy Who Fell from the Sky

Book One in the
House Next Door

Trilogy

By

Jule Owen

ISBN: 0993409709

ISBN 13: 978-0-9934097-0-7

www.juleowen.com

Cover design and illustration by Jule Owen

For L.S

1 FALLING

DAY EIGHT: Wednesday, 15 June 2472, Chukotka Autonomous Okrug, Siberia, Russia

At first he spins. The sky and the trees below spin too, and his stomach lurches. Then he is parallel to the horizon, arms and legs spread-eagled like a skydiver. The air pushes at his limbs. He extends and flexes his fingers, lifts his head and looks across the treetops at the breath-taking scale of the forest, the unbroken canopy of green stretching into the misty horizon and cloud-covered mountains in the distance. The assault on his senses and instincts is overwhelming. Beauty, joy, exhilaration, and terror all at once. The ground is pulling him towards it at an alarming rate.

I'm going to die, he thinks. Then, *This isn't real. This is not real.*

As the trees rush towards him, as he nears the ground, he passes close to the side of a rocky cliff face, pounding white water throttling down, and he is like a stone in the waterfall. The spray soaks him to the skin. Fighting fear, he dares glance below. There is a lake where the falling water gathers: a blue pool, pale at the edges, shading to sapphire in the centre.

I hope it's deep, he thinks as he breaks the surface, feet first.

He plunges until the water finally catches hold of him like firm hands, and he is slowed, for moments on end, still and hanging, suspended in chains of bubbles escaping to the surface. It is dark and cold. Visibility is limited to a few feet ahead. Staring into the darkness, he half-expects a monster of the deep to snatch him in its jaws or tentacles. Without even realising it, he is clawing his way towards the air, his arms reaching around and down, the pressure of the water helping him, forcing him towards the world. Light refracts on the surface, glistening and dancing.

Breaking through to his own element, he takes great gulps of air, his chest shuddering painfully, his arms thrashing. His head goes under and he swallows water; he emerges coughing and choking and thrashes some more, plunging under, panicking, until some strange, calm voice in his head tells him to stop, to be still, to lie back in the water, to trust, to get control of his breath.

Then he is suspended on the top of the sapphire pool, arms and legs outstretched like he is skydiving in reverse now, floating, waiting for his heart and the blood pulsing in his ears to quieten. The sky is a cloudless blue above him. There is a curtain of green in the corners of his eyes.

The sun is hot and already burning, but the water has chilled him, and he enjoys the sensation of his skin and his bones thawing. The water laps his ears with the wet, round, unknowable sounds of the lake. Bobbing in and out of the sounds of the forest, there's a wall of noise, of birdsong and the calls of strange animals, and he tunes in to the clamour and distinguishes whistles, clicks, buzzings, individual songs, and angry cries.

Turning his head, scanning, he spies a bank of smooth rock and swims towards it. The water is much shallower at the edges, and he is able to stand and wade onto dry land. He sits on one of the rocks and takes off his boots, drains them of water, and sets them and his socks aside to dry, flattening the sodden wool against the hot stone.

He gazes at the waterfall and the empty air above it.

There is no door. Nothing.

He has literally fallen to this place from the sky.

This must be a game, or a virtual reality world. Admittedly, it would be the most sophisticated one ever invented. It is so real. He taps the rocks with his knuckles – it hurts. It genuinely hurts. The sensation of falling, of hitting the water, of swimming, of almost drowning – well, it was remarkable. His throat is still sore from choking.

Still, this is the most obvious explanation: He has logged into Mr Lestrange's Darkroom, which happens to be playing the most remarkable virtual world ever made.

Now all he has to do is to find a way to leave.

There is no possibility of going back the way he has come. But there is no rush. It is a lovely spot, with the sunlight pouring in, the rocks hot under his skin, the sound of the birds, and the roar of the waterfall. Lying back, he closes his eyes and dozes off.

And wakes with a start.

Something disturbing – life-threatening, even – has pulled him from his dreams. But when he sits and looks around, nothing has changed except the position of the sun in the sky, which is now much farther to the east and casting longer shadows. It is still hot, and the air still sings with birds and insects.

Discomfort registers in his brain. His arms and feet are red: burnt. *Stupid*, he thinks. And he wonders again at the advanced nature of this world, making him believe he is sunburnt. Virtual world or not, his skin hurts like hell, his head is sore, and he is parched. The water in the lake, he supposes, is fresh. Wading a little into the shallows, he bends and takes a couple of tentative sips, cupping the water to his mouth with his palms. It tastes good, and he gulps more.

He ponders what he should do next. Where to start to search for the door? Remembering his view of the canopy of the forest – it stretches forever. The door might be anywhere. Or maybe Mr Lestrange will come home from wherever he has gone to and pull the plug on the game, take the skullcap off his head. That's the most likely scenario. In which case, he should make the most of this enormous playground.

If this is a VR world, he thinks, *then there should be a map.* He calls his Lenz to try the Nexus and sees a list of available networks. They are all in a strange alphabet. He tries one and is prompted for a password, and a warning message flashes. He closes it and tries the Blackweb. It is not there. He doesn't understand.

I'm really on my own.

Wading back to the shore, he sits to pull on his boots. They are dry outside but still damp on the inside. There's no choice but to put them on. His feet are swollen from the sunburn, and it hurts to pull his socks and boots onto his feet. Cursing, he ties his laces.

All around the perimeter of the lake is an unbroken wall of creeping, thriving green, with no obvious way through the jungle. He needs something to beat a path in front of him. He finds a long pole, wide enough to be substantial but thin enough to grip, breaks some smaller branches off and tests the weight of it in his hand. It's good.

The lake empties into a small river, which he decides to follow. It's bound to lead to people, to the coast or something else.

It's easier going than he imagined, although he has to veer away from the stream to walk around trees and bushes. His feet chafe in his wet boots. The pain from the sunburn on his feet and arms is persistent. It's humid.

He stops to drink again from the stream. The water pooling in his hand has bits floating in it. He swills his hand and tries again, this time scooping closer to the top where it runs faster. It tastes fine. If this was real, if he was in Elgol, hiking into the wild mountains surrounding the community, he would never be so bold, but he needs to drink. His clothes are soaked with his own sweat.

His ears are assaulted by the sounds of life all around him, but he sees only an occasional flicker of movement of birds in the trees above. Flies swarm about his face, attracted by the salt on his skin, and beyond the path he is beating for himself he is aware of small life, insects cutting leaves, crawling amongst the humus of the forest floor, gathering dying and decaying things for their food. He tries to block them from his mind.

The light is dimming, and he starts to reflect on what he will do at night for warmth and light. Although he certainly doesn't need the heat, a fire would give him light and keep animals away.

The filtered greenish sunlight in the forest suddenly curdles yellow, electricity charges the air and there is a crack of lightning and then thunder, rumbling under the ground towards him. Another round of the same and a large raindrop breaks on his nose, then another on his hand, his arm, his neck, his head.

He's experienced a lot of rainstorms in London, but this rain comes in drops so large they hurt. As the storm gains momentum, it is like whole buckets of water are being thrown over him.

Water rolls off the green, shiny leaves all around him onto the ground in rivulets and streams.

Drenched anyway by his own sweat, the rain cools him and plasters sodden cotton to his skin. Carrying on, he tries to ignore it, but drops pound on his head – it's hard on his scalp, like a persistent finger prodding him.

Eventually, he stops and searches around for somewhere to shelter. He gets under a plant with large, long leaves, but the rain comes through as the branches bow with the force of the water. He grabs a leaf and twists and yanks to snap it off – then breaks off another and another and props them against the trunk of a tree, managing to build a makeshift shelter, like a half-tepee. He just fits inside if he crouches into a ball, his knees drawn to his chin. It is not totally dry, but at least it keeps the pounding off his skull. Then he sits and waits, staring at his boots, worrying about his feet and grateful for the opportunity to rest. When he's still, they don't hurt as much.

In his peripheral vision, he catches something moving on a leaf, near his face. Something slow. The hair on the back of his neck stands. Without moving his head, he turns his eyes.

There is a spider, the size of his hand, walking across a leaf hanging beside him. It stops. It is waiting, watching, smelling, or whatever deadly jungle spiders do. He doesn't dare move. He doesn't dare breathe. Then, as silently as it arrived, it moves off into the undergrowth. He lets go of the breath he was holding.

The rain eases, then stops, and he crawls from his shelter. It's getting dark. The forest is dripping.

Even if I knew how, he thinks, *I'll never make a fire in this dampness.*

Less exuberantly, he starts to walk again, thinking *it's best to keep moving.* The stream becomes a river.

Then he hears the noise from his dream. He remembers it now: a primal, horrifying sound, a deep, guttural growl. Angry. No – beyond angry – amoral. . . . More than anything it sounds hungry.

Stopping dead in his tracks, he surveys around. Nothing. But he knows now for sure, something in the forest is watching him. He strains to detect movement, the crack of a twig, the sound of branches or leaves brushing against a body. His ears pulse with the sound of his treacherous heart, louder than the birds and the insects. Sweat drips off his nose as he stares into the forest. Leaves bob as rainwater drips from higher branches.

It's getting dark, and he doesn't want to be walking in the forest when this growling creature might come at him from anywhere.

He is standing beside a tall tree. Long, thick, sinuous vines hang from its branches. He grabs one and uses it to pull himself up, his feet walking up the side of the trunk, wincing with pain. The vine rope slips in his hand, the muscles in his shoulders and arms burn, his arms aren't strong enough.

Why didn't he spend more time playing in the holovision gym?

He loses his grip and falls. Trying again, he finds footholds between branches and in knotholes, grits his teeth, and wraps the vine partially around his arm to gain leverage. After a few falls, he climbs the tree, swearing all the way. Twenty feet up, there's a gap between the branches big enough for him to fit in if he scrunches into a ball.

He's breathing heavily; the dripping forest pelts him with drops of rain still running off leaves and branches. At first he ignores it. He rests his head on his hands, his knees drawn up to his chest, and closes his eyes. The drips are less frequent but they are large and hard. Every time he starts to feel himself drifting off to sleep, one breaks on his head or his face. After a long hour, he is wide awake staring at the sodden wood of the tree. He doesn't want to have to climb down from the tree again.

I'll never sleep like this. I have to find a way to cover myself.

Grabbing the vines, he lowers himself from the tree and collects the same kind of leaves he used earlier to shelter himself from the rain.

He finds some long strips of supple bark to tie the leaves into a bundle and climbs again, slightly more adept this time. Once he arrives and secures his seat by wedging a leg to push his body back against the trunk, he hauls his parcel after him and unties it. He lays half of the long leaves in the fork of the trunk that is acting as his bed. The rest he wedges between branches above him, making a rough kind of roof.

It's pitch dark now, and he tries to get comfortable. All around, plants and animals slither and move. He listens for a long time, his eyes open, staring into the creeping blackness.

What is this place? It can't be real, can it?

The same question churns over and over in his mind. It muddles and twists and blurs.

Finally, miraculously, he falls asleep.

2 DRAGONS IN THE BEDROOM

DAY ONE: Monday, 22 November 2055, London, England

Mathew Erlang is sitting in his bedroom watching his two dragons fighting.

They roll around one another in mid-air, tumbling over and over, their tails intertwined, writhing like snakes. The larger dragon breaks away, flies until she is almost touching the ceiling, pulls back her long neck and breathes an impressive stream of fire. Her mate is blasted with golden light, but the fire deflects off his body to an old book on the floor. Mathew half expects the paper pages to catch fire.

The dragons are two feet long, nose to tail tip, steel blue shading to black. He had stolen the design mostly from a picture by a thirteenth-century Chinese artist called Chen Rong. They are holograms, made using Gencode, a programming language he's learning for his virtual robotics course.

The male is now on the floor, examining the book pages, picking at them with his claws, puzzled because the paper doesn't move. The creature has no idea that it isn't real and that nothing it does has any effect on this world.

There's a knock at the door. It opens, and his mother, Hoshi Mori, pokes her head in. The dragons scatter, taking refuge under the bed, and then peer out, nervous but curious.

"I'm off. The car's here," she says.

The female dragon edges towards the open door, poised to retreat at the first sign of danger. Hoshi sees the dragon because Mathew has made them visible on her personal Lenz channel. Lenzes are special contact lenses everyone wears, with embedded nanoscale circuitry and processors, essential to access the ubiquitous augmented reality available through the Nexus, "the next generation of the Internet," or so it's been called for the past twenty years.

"Did you create it with your new program?" his mother asks.

"That's right," Mathew says. "There are two of them. The other one's still under the bed. I gave her more curiosity and him greater threat responses."

"Do they have names?"

He nods. "She's Yinglong. He's Shen."

"Don't spend all day playing with them, will you? The All-Day Curfew is not the same thing as a school holiday."

"I couldn't if I wanted to. I have a supervisory meeting with Professor Absolem at eleven a.m. Go. You don't want to piss off your guard."

Hoshi gives him a look, which he knows means she disapproves of his language.

"Sorry," he says. "But he is scary."

"He's there to protect me."

"Protect you or keep you prisoner?"

She rolls her eyes. "Okay, I'm going."

She starts to shut the door and then immediately opens it again.

"There's plenty of food. Don't forget to eat."

"I won't."

She leaves. Then through the door comes, "Don't let O'Malley out."

"I won't!"

The front door slams shut. He goes to the window and draws back the curtain.

There's a driverless Aegis car parked at the kerb. It's low and long, slightly taller at the boot than the pointed bonnet, the wheels jacked at the back, giving the impression of an animal ready to pounce. Its matte black body paint is exactly the same colour as the opaque windows, designed to preserve the privacy of the occupants.

Like all cars, it's self-driving, controlled by an on-board computer and a remote centralised system that manages the flow of traffic in London. It's illegal to drive unless on private land. Groups of vintage car collectors gather to manually drive, but they are a dwindling breed. The huge reduction in accidents, as well as the fact that cars can drive faster and more efficiently and passengers are free to work or watch holofilms, means most people are happy to let their cars be driven for them. Few people own their own cars anymore. They are hired on a need-to-use basis from companies like Aegis Shield.

Mathew's mother's guard stands beside the car in a dark suit, his jacket buttoned, a machine gun in his hands, passive but at the ready, calmly scanning the street. The large sunglasses are not vanity or even cliché. Mathew knows they are feeding him real-time information, allowing him to assess potential threats, data beamed from the hundreds of cameras and sensors on the road, all the publicly broadcast material from residents, and the latest intelligence from the local military police.

Visible through Mathew's Lenz, floating in the air space around the thickset man, is his profile, freely available on the Nexus.

So Mathew knows this man is called Fergus Johnson. He's thirty-eight and a senior guard with ten years' experience in domestic security, originally trained in the army. His unique security number is SD29106X, and he works for Aegis Domestic Security Services, an arm of Aegis Shield, the largest security firm in the country and the one with the government contract to police London.

Aegis's logo and its motto, "Protecting You," are floating around under the company name.

Fergus Johnson hasn't published any personal information, such as whether he is single or divorced and searching for a new partner, as people often do.

Mathew watches his mother greeting the guard. As she gets into the car, the door automatically shuts behind her. The guard surveys the road once more, slides into the front passenger seat, and the car drives away at precisely the speed limit.

O'Malley the cat, an expert at sliding in unnoticed, past legs, through open doors, is in the room. Not having Lenzes, he can't see the dragons, but they can see him. They start to stalk him. Oblivious, O'Malley saunters across the floorboards and rubs against Mathew's trousers. Mathew bends and picks him up. The cat immediately starts to purr loudly. Mathew pauses the Gencode program using verbal commands, and the dragons disappear. With O'Malley in his arms, he goes in search of breakfast.

Leibniz, their HomeAngel, is vacuuming the stairs. It senses him and stops.

"Good morning, Mathew."

"Good morning, Leibniz," he says.

Leibniz is four feet high, matte white, with a HomeAngel logo, a faux virtual badge, on its chest and a blue light where its heart should be, indicating it's on and working. When it malfunctions, the light goes red. Its face is digital, flat and simplistic, with large childlike eyes, eyebrows, and a mouth programmed to do context-sensitive expressions. It does happy, laughing, confused, and surprised. It doesn't do angry or sad.

There are many robots available for consumers to buy with much more sophisticated emotional repertoires, but most people prefer domestic robots to be functional. Besides, Leibniz is a fairly basic model. Its legs bend slightly too much at the knees, making it look odd, but it climbs stairs with surprising agility.

It has four arms that extend and retract as needed, two of which have uncannily human hands and fingers. It cooks, cleans, tidies things away, makes beds, feeds the cat, disposes of rubbish, reminds people of appointments, automatically orders and puts away groceries, does basic plumbing and electrical repairs, and answers the door. They got it as a perk from Mathew's mother's company.

Now it stands at the bottom of the stairs with one of its robot arms extended, sucking dirt from the carpet. The house is always spotless.

"Do you want me to fix you breakfast, Mathew?" Leibniz asks.

"I'll make breakfast myself, thank you, Leibniz."

"Okay, Mathew," Leibniz says and starts vacuuming again.

In the kitchen, Mathew calls up the news while he hunts in the cupboards for something natural and organic. He is trying to get his mother to buy in to the real-food movement, but she says naturally grown food is a waste of resources. Abandoning his search, he pours himself a bowl of standard lab-grown cornflakes. They don't actually taste any different from the natural, organic ones his grandmother eats. Mathew programs the SuperChef food replicator to make coffee, gets milk from the fridge and takes a seat at the kitchen table.

The Canvas is a super-thin, transparent, multimedia viewing sheet hanging from the ceiling, powered by wireless electricity, as all their devices are now. On it, he watches a report on the flood.

Looting has taken place in the houses on the river. The images on the screen cut to follow rescue workers on a boat. The boat slows as they pass partly submerged buildings. Three frogmen fall backwards into the water. A camera shakily follows them, bubbles floating to the surface. The water is murky. Bits of debris float by the lens. One of the frogmen shines a light ahead. He turns slowly to the camera and points. The camera pans around. From the gloom emerges the distinctive red and blue and white of a tube sign. It's Embankment underground station.

Next, the mayor of London, Bartholomew Dearlove, a fleshy man with pale skin and pink drinker's cheeks, is interviewed. In the interview, he promises to champion new laws to make it easier to prosecute and deter looters.

"The new Thames Barrier is in planning," he says, "and the government will spare no expense in protecting the capital city from further flooding. The Garden Party and their naive and defeatist policies of adaptation would have us abandon this great, historic city, but we want to save London, and we will save it."

Mayor Dearlove walks off, purposefully ignoring questions from journalists concerning the cost of building the new Thames Barrier and where the money will come from.

There is an interview with an angry London resident whose face looms unfocused, too close to the camera lens. "This is the fourth time in ten years the barrier has failed. Each time the government claims they will invest more, and nothing ever happens."

Mathew finishes his breakfast. Leibniz sweeps in to the kitchen with uncanny anticipation and starts tidying things away. It puts the dishes in the dishwasher and switches it on, waits the thirty seconds for the cycle to complete, and puts them away in the cupboard.

Although Mathew has only used the kitchen sink to pour a glass of water, Leibniz sets the miniature cleaner to work.

This is relatively new technology, bacterial germ-eating gloop. The little cleaning machines are hidden inside small bodies mimicking brightly coloured, friendly insects with cartoon eyes and smiley mouths, because consumer research said people didn't like the idea of barely visible, constantly morphing sludge moving around their houses. Their kitchen cleaner has a body the shape and colour of an oversized ladybird. The cleaner in the bathroom is a pink and purple polka dot snail. The ones they have permanently living in the toilets are like frogs.

His grandmother hates this technology. She says it terrifies her, and the next world war will involve similar bio-goop aimed at destroying people's immune systems. His mother says there are extremely tight controls and regulations around the use of intelligent bio-agents.

A message flashes in floating white words, hovering above the sideboard, projected via Mathew's Lenz from someone on his Allowed List. It says:

`Are you alone?`
He says, "Accept and respond" to the program in his e-Pin, the earring studs that pierce the inner part of his ears and provide audio to his Lenz.

"Okay to talk?" his grandmother, Ju Chen, asks.

She speaks to him via simultaneous translation. Her English is rudimentary, so she prefers to speak fluidly in her own language and have what she says automatically turned into idiom friends and family from her adopted nation will relate to. Mathew has heard her natural voice once or twice, but he associates her with the smooth English voice he is listening to now, calibrated and deepened slightly to account for her age.

"Yes."

"Are you watching the news?" is the next thing she says. Not "hello" or "how are you?" like normal people. But, as his mother is always telling him, his grandmother isn't normal.

"Yes, I'm watching the news."

"Did you notice they didn't interview anyone from the Garden Party?"

"I did notice, yes."

"There was no opposition point of view at all."

"Strictly speaking, the mayor did mention adaptation policy."

"You sound like your mother."

"I'm joking, Grandma."

"Oh." She takes a moment to process this and then says, "What's it like there? Are there lots of soldiers?"

"Not here. But we're a mile from the river. I haven't gone out yet because of the curfew. School is suspended, and we're doing all our lessons remotely until further notice. Not that it makes much difference anyway."

Any other adult would have called him on this, told him it was important for him to mix with kids his own age and how the social part of school was as important as the lessons. But not his grandmother. Instead, she says, "But your mother is still going in to work?"

"Yes. She can't work remotely. She needs her lab. Panacea have organised security clearance for her."

"I bet they have. Big business must go on. But how does she get in to the city? I thought the tube was flooded."

"It is. They send a car for her with an Aegis personal armed guard."

"Aegis must be rolling in money! Think of all the people they're ferrying backwards and forwards to London, now there's no public transport. Did your mum say what it was like by the river?"

"She leaves early and gets home late. We don't have much time to talk. She did mention it was bad and she felt sorry for the people living in the ruined houses with nowhere else to go."

"I saw on Psychopomp there's a lot of makeshift camps being established all across the south where people were flooded from their homes. Conditions are terrible, and the military has established cordons around them. There is nothing on the BBC, of course."

"You watch that channel?"

"Of course I do. How else am I going to know what's going on?"

"But I thought you didn't like the holovision?"

"I don't much like it. I find the Darkroom claustrophobic, but needs must."

Psychopomp is on the Blackweb, not the Nexus. He is careful not to say either of these words aloud, as it would be likely to trip the Nexus's automatic surveillance – though his grandmother saying the word 'Psychopomp' has probably already done the trick. She must know this. "How did you set it up?" he asks.

"Oh, I have friends who know these things. One young friend in particular, actually. Name of . . . No. Never mind."

Mathew shakes his head. His grandmother is something else.

She lives in Elgol, a notoriously kooky experimental living community in Scotland. It was the ancestral estate of the wife of the leader of the opposition, but she developed it into a model village to prove the viability of sustainable living, traditional farming, and low-impact technologies.

As a child he'd spent a lot of time there, staying with his grandmother alone during long summer holidays.

Time spent in Elgol always rolled along pleasantly compared to London. People took their leisure over things. Minutes and hours were stretched. And, of course, being so far north, there was the endless light, the days extending into night through the summer months. Even then, he savoured the time, some uncanny instinct telling him it was precious, glad to eke out the days before returning to school, something he always dreaded.

All Elgol community members were given chores, and as a guest he was expected to do his bit to pay his way. His grandmother worked on vegetable production, and she got him weeding, tending plants in the polytunnels, checking the water quality in the hydroponics building while the fish swam around nibbling his hand, and helping to build new no-dig beds with straw and manure he barrowed from the stables, where the farm's huge shire horses lived. It wasn't work to him. It was an adventure. London, in contrast, seemed so cooped up and claustrophobic.

On rest days, they would swim in the crystalline waters off the nearby beach or take one of the community's dinghies shore-hopping to remote coves to picnic. His grandmother let him take control of the little outboard motor, powered with recycled cooking oil converted into biodiesel.

Vividly, he recalls the smell of the fuel and the seawater, the sand, which inevitably got into his sandwiches and coffee. She would sit in the front of the boat and tell him stories of days past and how the sea used to be teeming with fish you caught with a line and hook or with nets and took home to cook and eat.

She told him there were once seals, whales, and dolphins in the bay, and the dolphins would sometimes escort the boats, skimming through the waves, so close you could reach out and touch them. It seemed strange and fantastical to him, as did many things she told him.

In the evenings he would sit with his grandmother in her wood-framed, straw-baled house, and she would read snippets to him from real paper books from her library, telling him stories of how the world used to be and why it is the way it is now, showing him pictures of extinct animals, like rhinos, tigers, and elephants.

His parents always came for the last two weeks of his stay. His father, Soren, loved to help with the projects there, connecting new solar panels or windmills, drilling wells for water, advising the community technicians on energy storage.

They all helped to build his grandmother's house, the community coming together to heft the wood poles of the A-frame and carry in the straw bales made from grass grown on the estate. They limed the walls together, and his father held the ladder as Mathew climbed up to sow seeds on his grandmother's grass roof.

He used to love going to Elgol, but now his memories are bruised and tinged with sadness.

Mathew says, "I guess the floods mean you're not coming to visit?"

"There're no trains. The lines are all flooded and broken in parts. It will take months for them to fix it. I tried to get a flight, but there's nothing affordable. I'll come as soon as things are better. I was going to send you a box of vegetables, but they'd probably be rotten by the time they got to you, if they reached you at all."

"Mum wouldn't like it anyway."

"I know. But you would. And I like to think of you getting some proper nutrition for a change instead of the frankenfood she buys."

"It's real food, Grandma. It doesn't hurt you."

"The problem is no one knows. These scientists working for corporates do things because they can, but they don't know or care what the long-term consequences will be."

"Mum's a scientist working for a corporate. So was Dad."

The word 'Dad' sticks in his throat. Two years on, and it's still painful to even mention his father. *How long will I feel like this?*

"I know, Mat."

He notes that she doesn't say, "And look where it got him," but he knows it's what she's thinking. It's what he's thinking himself.

"Mum is doing her best."

"I know that too, Mat."

"I have to go and log on at school; otherwise, I'll be registered absent for the day."

"Okay. Speak soon."

He ends the call. Leibniz tidies the cupboard Mathew disordered when he searched for his breakfast.

3 THE NAMING OF THINGS

The house is full of ghosts. Every corner of it conjures a memory of his father. For the last two years, Mathew has blocked these phantoms, walked past them and refused to see them. Now they are creeping back in as he's able to bear thinking about them for the first time.

As he walks into the Darkroom to meet his supervisor, he remembers how his father persuaded his mother to relinquish her dining room so the Darkroom could be built. He can still clearly hear his father's voice, the particular timbre of it. His father spoke excellent English, with only a hint of a Danish accent. In his mind, Mathew sees him standing in the doorway of the room saying, "This is the only place we can put it."

"Where are we going to eat?" his mother had asked.

Soren had gestured impatiently. Surrendering the dining room was a minor inconvenience to him. "Why can't we eat in the kitchen?"

"What happens when we have people over? There's not enough room."

"People will come to use the holovision."

"You can't be serious. I'll never get any of my friends to come over again."

Mathew remembers his father glancing at him, a raised eyebrow and a slight smile on his face. He remembers his mother hitting his father with the towel she had in her hands. The sound of the snap of it.

"Oh, they'll come! People chat in interactive games. It's good for Mathew. The whole world is getting them. It will help with his studies."

"Oh no . . . Don't put this on Mathew. You want the holovision for yourself."

Mathew helped his father carry the dining room furniture to the driverless van courier that had come to collect it after it had been sold via online auction. They spent a weekend painting the walls black, listening to his father's favourite classical channel on full blast, driving his mother from the house. There's still a stain on the sanded wood floor where Mathew knocked a can of paint over, and he and his father scrubbed and scrubbed, trying to remove it from the woodwork, both dreading what Hoshi would say when she got home. In the event, she didn't mention it, a sign of how angry she was over the Darkroom project.

Now the room sits in the house as a constant reminder of Soren to Hoshi and Mathew, one of the last things he did. As with all reminders of his father, Mathew is never sure if he wants it there or not.

Three years ago, the darkroom was state-of-the-art, but there are much better setups now. In fact, it's just an ordinary room, painted black and fitted with six seats, because in those days people still came around. There's an empty space at the front of the room for dynamic interaction. Hologames and holofilms are playable anywhere as part of augmented reality, but the quality of the images is often affected by material objects, so it's best to have a blank canvas to project them onto.

Plus, although people are now used to others interacting with invisible augmented reality objects in public, in much the same way people in the late twentieth century became accustomed to people apparently talking to themselves in the street when mobile phones were introduced, it isn't practical for people to run around in the street in large numbers playing war games and firing invisible weapons. After several years of chaos created by this kind of activity, it's now a minor criminal offence.

As Mathew enters the room, the system is immediately alerted to his presence and greets him. Finding his usual chair, he pulls on a skullcap, a plain plastic dome crammed with electrodes with replaceable covers. The cover on his skullcap is a fake wool cap, a bit like a kippah, the latest fashion. It's only a few weeks old. His mother bought it for him out of the blue, and he was touched and surprised. These days she is so distracted by her work.

He tells the Darkroom system to set his status to "available" and awaits an incoming call. Within seconds he is mentally transported onto a patio and into a deck chair. It is sunny, and he's suddenly warmer, as the computerised air conditioning in the Darkroom adjusts to the instructions of the program. There's a glass of lemonade in front of him on a table. Reaching for it, it occurs to him for one mentally destabilising second that Leibniz must have been instructed by the system to provide a drink. In the deck chair opposite sits his personal tutor, Professor Nan Absolem. She's wearing khaki linen trousers, a white shirt, sandals, sunglasses, and a wide-brimmed sun hat, her skullcap hidden underneath. All his other tutors run their sessions in reconstructions of their offices, sitting behind a desk.

"Hello, Mathew," she says, turning to him and smiling, holding a glass with an umbrella in it. "Cheers!"

There is a clink, and Mathew feels his glass collide with hers. He has to stop himself from resisting the created reality, from always deconstructing the haptics in his head. He needs to give in to it.

"Isn't this nice?" she says. "Better than a stuffy old office?"

"Yes, it is."

They are looking at a view of fields, a lake, and trees on a summer's day. It's a template in the system Mathew recognises but doesn't often use. People his own age always prefer dystopias and bizarre exoplanet landscapes, with strange rocky surfaces and multiple moons or suns. Mathew's dragons fly into the landscape, exploring. Nan turns her head, watching them, smiling.

"What were you working on this morning?"

"The history of artificial intelligence," he says.

"Interesting?"

"Yes. Very."

"Not distracted or upset by the All-Day Curfew? Not missing school?"

"Not especially. It's perfectly possible to do everything I do at school, at home." As soon as he's spoken, he regrets it. He knows what's coming.

"Yes, but you can't learn how to work with others at home on your own. You can't build friendships." She raises an eyebrow and smiles. Her eyes are shaded, her face unreadable.

"Ah."

"Yes. 'Ah' . . . On that note, the school thinks it's important to try to get you together with other students twice a month while the crisis continues. We've managed to arrange for transport on Thursday. You'll use the day for work on a robotics project. I'll send details through to you, but it will essentially be a group challenge to build a working robot with limited resources and time. You will be assessed on your collaboration skills. It will count towards credits."

Mathew sighs.

"What's wrong?"

"Do you honestly want me to say?"

"Yes."

"I will score badly in this exercise, and it will bring down my average."

"That's your decision, surely?"

"But it's not up to me. I know who will be in the robotics group.

27

They don't like me, and they won't allow me to collaborate."

"This exercise has remote, silent observers. They'll notice if the others are obstructive and exclude you. They will penalise the others for this, not you."

"Sure."

"They will, Mathew."

"I'd rather be getting on with other work. This won't teach me anything."

"You have to learn how to work with others, even if you don't get on with them personally."

"Right."

A pair of ducks take off from the lake, and they quack their trajectory into the sky. Mathew wonders if Nan has triggered it as a distraction. He has noticed she often does something like this when he gets emotional. The dragons take off after the ducks. He and Nan both watch.

"I love your dragons, Mathew. Well done. You've done an incredible job, engineering them to fly. You should find names for the project. My old professor of AI used to teach that when you give something a name, you gain power over it. He called it the Rumpelstiltskin Principle."

Mathew says, "I created the female first. She's called Yinglong. I think I may call it Project Yinglong."

"It's a good name. Does it mean anything?"

"Yinglong means responsive dragon."

"How appropriate."

"It was in a book my grandmother gave me. I used the pictures in it to design the way the dragons look. Yinglong is a winged dragon associated with rain and floods."

"Even better. So how is Project Yinglong coming along?"

"I took them for their first walk yesterday."

"Great. What happened?"

"Things were fine at first, but I realised there's a bit of a flaw in the way I was planning the project."

"How so?"

"I did a 3D scan of our house to create a virtual world environment for them. I used APIs for my Lenz, ePin, and skullcap, placed cheap holographic cameras around the house, and connected them all to the Gencode software.

"The dragons see virtual versions of us, scanned in real time in their world. They are holographic versions of themselves walking around in our world. I leverage the virtual reality layer in the Lenz software interface for this, so we're able to see them. In their world we're as solid as everything else. In our world they're not material. They can't interact with actual things. This creates a dissonance. The point of the project is they learn from experience. But if they don't interact with our environment, they won't learn the physics of our world. Today one of the dragons was clawing at some papers on the floor, and, of course, the papers didn't move. I could reprogram their environment, so things in their world do move when they interact with them in ours, but then they won't be synched with our world. It's incredibly obvious that this would happen, but I was so absorbed in creating the dragons as holograms, I didn't think of it. I want the dragons to be learning AIs living in my world."

"Does it really matter if there's a bit of dissonance?"

"I don't know."

Nan thinks for a moment, taking another sip of her drink. "I have a thought, and it's just a thought."

Mathew makes an ambivalent noise in response, sceptical of her "thoughts."

"A few years ago I went to Russia on a cultural exchange programme, and I met a teacher there specialising in the same field. We keep in touch via the Nexus. We were talking recently. He told me he has a pupil who's working on a virtual world project. She's focused on growing the world and building ever more complex environments mirroring our own, with fauna and flora, mountains, lakes, and seas. It's an environmental project to test complex weather systems. It supports virtual life forms like yours but doesn't have any as yet. You could copy her code onto another server and run a version with the dragons living in one of her worlds. This would give them amazing scope to learn and adapt. She's using a Gencode base that's compatible with the one you're using. I'll investigate whether you could use this work for collaborative credits instead of the robotics project. Then at least you'd feel your collaborative module is useful."

"I'd definitely like it better than playing at Lego robotics with the rugby team."

"Great. Let me make some calls."

4 THE PIANIST

It's late afternoon. Mathew surfaces from a long period of deep concentration, stretches, and goes to his window. Shen, the male dragon, lands on his shoulder and starts trying to chew his hair, snapping at air.

A sleek black autonomous car is slowly driving along the street. It comes to a halt by the kerb. A man in a dark suit, wearing sunglasses, opens the back door. He's an Aegis man much like Mathew's mother's thick-necked guard. Mathew ponders whether their corporate masters have started cloning them.

A girl gets out.

Her name is Clara Barculo. She's fifteen years old, and it's four months until her next birthday. She is single, not dating; a pupil at the Royal College of Music, her favourite thing in the world is her dog Cassie, a smooth-coated collie. He knows all this from the information hanging above her. In person, he observes that she's tall and thin, with gangly long limbs and strikingly large hands, making her seem strangely vulnerable, like a baby animal not yet grown into its body. She has long brown hair tied back tightly, a long face and nose, striking thick black eyebrows, and blue eyes.

Their neighbour Gen Lacey is a piano teacher, and Mathew has seen many pupils come and go to her house over the years, never paying much attention until now.

For a moment Clara appears to look up at his window. She sees his broadcast data, floating in the cloud of information coming from all the other residents confined to their houses in Pickervance Road, but she doesn't read it. Automatically, via his skullcap, Mathew's Lenz recognises his desire to focus in on her further. Incomprehensibly, he finds himself smiling at her, but he's standing in the shadows, and she turns away from his window and disappears from view.

Down below, a doorbell rings; there's the sound of the latch, some muffled voices, and then a door banging shut.

He's stepping from the window when something makes him turn and glance the other way, into the bay window of the house next door.

Through the darkened glass he discerns a face, pale and disembodied, staring with intensity in the direction of Clara as she enters Gen's house. The face belongs to a tall, thin man. Mathew's Lenzes adjust to the poor lighting, and the man's form slowly emerges from the shadows. Sensing Mathew there, the man snaps his gaze away from the road and directly across at him. Dark eyes in deep eye sockets drill into him analytically, machine-like. Mathew feels a chill run along his spine.

A second more, and the man is gone, leaving him wondering if he was ever there, or if it was a trick of the light.

Five minutes later, Mathew is downstairs making a snack in the kitchen when the music reaches him.

It's just a snatch at first – there are bricks and mortar in between – but those few notes hit him like a physical punch. They are so familiar to him, yet it seems like a lifetime since he last heard them. In the living room, he puts his ear to the wall. The sound is indistinct. He gets a glass from the kitchen, and Leibniz follows him all the way, asking him if he wants a drink. He shoos the robot away, crouches next to the wall, and holds the glass against it to collect the precious morsels of sound. A matrix of notes, a musical puzzle.

"Don't you feel the synapses firing in your brain?" asks his father's voice, the ghost in his head.

Mental lights are going on, memories are stirred; half of him does not want to listen. *What is this music?* He can't remember the name of the piece or the composer. His father would have told him, would have had him repeat it and tested him on it. It's shut away in tender parts of his mind. He sets his e-Pin to record. When the music stops, he plays it back to the Nexus, asks the question, and gets the response. It's Bach. The girl with the large hands and the eyebrows is playing Bach, his father's favourite composer, music he hasn't dared listen to for more than two years.

After the girl has gone, he spends his evening listening to Bach on the Nexus, researching his life and times and the highlights of his work. Using the few hours before his mother comes home, he decides to build a contraption to help him listen better, so when the girl comes back for her next lesson, he won't need to sit with a glass to his ear.

He's finishing when his mother comes through the door. It's late. Leibniz has prepared a meal according to her remote instruction. The robot is serving when Mathew comes into the kitchen.

"Hello, darling. Thank you, Leibniz," his mother says as a plate is put in front of her. She sounds tired. "How was your day?" she asks Mathew. "What did you get up to?"

"I did an AI history module and spoke to my supervisor. Oh, and Grandma rang. She's not coming."

"I assumed as much. There's no way of getting here."

"That's what she said."

She nods, staring at her plate as she slices her food.

O'Malley is under the table mewing.

"Did you feed him, Leibniz?"

"Yes, Hoshi, I fed him at seventeen hundred hours exactly. Rabbit flavour Katkins. It's the new formula, as you instructed, with concentrated amounts of synthetic taurine."

"Good. Thank you, Leibniz."

"You're welcome, Hoshi."

"He didn't eat much of it. O'Malley prefers human food," Mathew says.

"I don't know why. There's not much difference," his mother says, poking at her cultured chicken.

"Not good?" Mathew asks.

"It's fine," she says with a sigh. "I hope my mother wasn't filling your head with her enviro-political nonsense."

"Not much."

"She has nothing better to do there in that commune-thing she lives in. It's dangerous. But it's her life. You, on the other hand, have a lot to lose. You need to keep this scholarship. I don't want you engaging with any of her gibberish. Do you hear me?" she points her knife at him threateningly.

He nods. "How did your day go?" he asks to distract her. "Busy?"

"Nonstop. It's going to be this way for a while, I'm afraid."

She eats in silence for a few minutes, and then he asks, "Mum, do you know our neighbours?"

As she lifts her fork, she studies him curiously. "A few of them, yes. You know Gen. Don't you remember? She was often round here when your father was alive. We should have her over for dinner. She was very good to us when. . . . She's a nice person. I never have time to see my friends anymore." She sighs and sinks further into her chair.

"Not that house. The other side."

"You mean August Lestrange? Do you know, you've lived in this house your whole life, and this is the first time you've expressed an interest in anyone who lives on our street."

"I saw him today, staring out of his front bedroom window."

"It's not a crime, is it? You're always doing that."

"But he looks odd."

"Again, pot and kettle."

Mathew grimaces. "Thanks."

Hoshi smiles, leans across and touches his face, "You know I'm just kidding. To be honest, I haven't laid eyes on him for ages, although he's lived there since before you were born. In all those years, I think we must have spoken to him once. We used to occasionally see him in his garden, but then he put the extension on the back of the house, with the conservatory. He's a bit of a recluse."

"What does he do?"

"Oh, I don't know, some kind of historian, I think."

"A historian?"

"Don't quote me."

Hoshi has finished her dinner. Leibniz comes to take her plate.

"It's nearly midnight," Hoshi says, checking the Nexus clock in her Lenz. "We should get to bed."

Lying in bed, Mathew watches the dragons dogfight in a blur of movement under the ceiling of his bedroom, circling the light shade, lit now by the streetlights.

Thinking about the cold eyes peering at him from the bedroom window next door, he recalls the strange, immobile face, the neck snapping towards him, reptile-like, as if it sensed him there before it saw him.

Sleep washes over him, and the circular movement of the dragons lulls him. He thinks, as he falls asleep, *Lestrange doesn't even seem human.*

5 PSYCHOPOMP

DAY TWO: Tuesday, 23 November 2055, London

"My car's here," his mother says, peering around his bedroom door. "Don't let O'Malley out, will you?"

"Of course not," he says.

"And let Leibniz prepare your meals. What's the point of having him, if you don't let him help?"

"Leibniz is an 'it', not a 'he'."

"Where are the dragons?"

Mathew points to his wardrobe. Yinglong is climbing on the top. Shen is hanging from a door by a clawed foot. Mathew can switch them on and off as he wishes. These days they mostly follow him everywhere.

"They're very good. What are you working on? New project?" She gestures to the scattering of tiny electrical parts on his desk, the 3D micro-printer and nano-assembler.

"It's an acoustic amplifier microphone."

"I won't ask."

Mathew smiles.

"I'd better go. They're nudging me," she says, pointing to her eye. She means she has received a reminder message in her Lenz. "See you later."

Mathew watches his mother's car drive to the end of the road and disappear around the corner. The windows of the house next door, where Mr Lestrange lives, are dark and fathomless. O'Malley jumps onto the windowsill and butts against his hand, mewing. One of the dragons swoops at him but grasps thin air, and O'Malley purrs loudly, oblivious.

In the Darkroom, Mathew searches the Nexus for Clara Barculo, pianist, Bach, Gen Lacey, and gets the usual results: the Consort profiles, the personal web pages full of videos and photos, the official government ID records, all floating in front of him the full width of the room; he lays them out, steps back, and takes it all in.

Gen Lacey is Genevieve Lacey of the Royal Academy of Music. Clara Barculo is a fifteen-year-old piano prodigy, known in particular for her interpretation of Bach's keyboard masterpieces.

He finds a holofilm of Clara performing in the Wigmore Hall and runs it.

Suddenly, he's in the audience, rows of seats behind him with enough virtual individuals to fill the room, mostly wearing evening dress. They cough, shift in their seats, and fiddle with their programmes. Someone comes in late and makes the people behind Mathew stand. In front of Mathew's seat a stage appears, with waist-high dark wood panelling on the back wall and two doors. He raises his eyes and sees the distinctive mural of the Soul of Music in the cupola.

A grand piano materialises.

There is a moment's silence and then applause.

Clara comes onto the stage in a simple black dress, her hair piled on her head. Someone in the audience whistles. She takes a small, nervous bow as the applause dies, sits, and abruptly starts to play. She is so close, so real, he feels he could reach out and touch her.

Her large hands no longer look awkward; they fly across the keys, so fast and fluidly it is barely possible to see them. The span of her hands reaches across unfeasible distances. Her arms are bare, and Mathew notices for the first time how muscled they are. A strand of hair breaks away from the bundle upon her head and falls on her shoulder. She doesn't even seem to notice. Her face wears an extraordinary expression of peaceful concentration. She is somewhere else, lost in her head, and the concert hall and the audience have disappeared for her. He recognises the experience of being transported by an utterly absorbing task; he has felt it himself. He watches the whole thing; but it is just one piece, and too soon the holofilm clip ends. The piano and the audience fade.

Still in his seat, he uses an encrypted script to open Charybdis, the main software portal to the Blackweb. His mother doesn't know he accesses the Blackweb in the house. It's not exactly illegal, but it's the sort of thing she would class as dangerous, not least because the government propaganda endlessly bangs on about how insecure it is and how much criminal activity happens on it. Mathew doesn't believe the propaganda, not all of it anyway.

The Blackweb is the alternative Internet, created on a matrix of independent networks. The authorities find it harder to snoop on than the Nexus. It was founded by people who didn't want the web to be entirely under corporate and government control. The establishment says those rich enough to launch satellites to provide an alternative Internet infrastructure must be criminals, which is probably partly true. People on the Blackweb say corporates and governments own the Nexus, and everything people do on it is watched and recorded. His mother wouldn't approve of what he is planning to watch.

He initiates Psychopomp.

A seated figure appears in the centre of the Darkroom, hands on its lap, feet flat on the floor, head bowed. It has the head of a donkey. Not a pantomime donkey but a real living, breathing donkey, with rotating ears reacting to sudden noises, long eyelashes, and huge black eyes. Its body is human: a young woman. She is called Nicola

Bottom, although it isn't her real name.

There are sometimes other commentators, including a man called the Snout, sporting a pig's head, who's famous for leaking state information and exposing corruption; a rabbit-headed girl called Snug; a skinny, tall man of indeterminate age with the head of a starling, called Starveling. There is also a commentator who wears Venetian style masks or whose many faces are masks – it's difficult to tell which, if any, are real. His name is Peter Quince, and he does political satire and exposes personal hypocrisy and corruption. Along with the Snout, he is the main reason Psychopomp is always moving its headquarters and has a complex system of access. It's the subject of innumerable undefended lawsuits. No one knows who the Psychopomp are. Their critics often complain about their theatricals, saying it undermines their message, but Mathew, like many others, thinks it's part of their appeal.

Nicola Bottom is wearing a summer dress, white plimsolls, and ankle socks. She raises her eyes, and it feels to Mathew like she is staring him directly in the eye, addressing him personally. "Today we have an exclusive interview with Cadmus Silverwood, leader of the Garden Party," she says.

Cadmus Silverwood magically appears from nowhere in a chair next to the donkey girl. He is a silver-haired man, thin and spry-looking, his face youthful although he's in his eighties. Hardly anyone seems old anymore; no one stoops or shuffles, and no one gets dementia. There are members of the House of Lords and CEOs well over a hundred years of age, but then some people joke that this was always the case, at least in their attitudes.

"Cadmus, thank you for joining us."

"A pleasure," he says, not in the least disconcerted by the idea of talking to a half-donkey in a dress.

"You were not always a politician."

"I don't like to think of myself as a politician now, to be honest."

"But you lead a political party, and you nearly won a general election. Some people say, you did win a general election, but the vote was rigged. What are you, if you're not a politician?"

"A frustrated man, father, scientist, citizen of the world, who wouldn't stand on the sidelines any longer. I spent many years being angry with governments and their policies, puzzled about why no one was doing anything. Then I woke one morning and realised I couldn't reasonably expect others to solve problems I wasn't willing to deal with myself."

"And what is frustrating you?"

"An age-old thing – the inevitable ascendancy of the rich and powerful, the one-sided battle to protect their interests at the expense of the rest of us."

"You say this is an age-old inevitable thing. Why do you think things will change now?"

"I have to believe, because of what is at stake. It used to be human lives and morality at stake, now it's all life on the planet. We're facing the extinction of human life."

"You think it will come to that?"

"Yes, I do."

"Wow. Okay. I want to know why you think that, but first can we take a step back? We'd like to hear the story of your life before you founded the Garden Party and why you think you're qualified to say these things?"

"Years ago, I worked for NASA. My work there led me to become a climate scientist, gradually being dragged into policy meetings with international institutions, trying to get commitments to a reduction in the global dependence on fossil fuels and greenhouse gas emissions."

The donkey says, "That's top of mind for everyone right now, as this is the fourth time London has been flooded in ten years. Floodwaters are not retreating from increasingly large areas of southern England. The US, Europe, and major coastal cities around the world, including Shanghai, have suffered similar fates. This summer, the US was hit again and again by mega hurricanes on the Gulf Coast and Eastern Seaboard, and we've experienced unprecedented super storms in Europe, plus other extreme weather, including severe droughts and water shortages.

"But our leaders claim it is all in hand. They have given tax breaks to various private initiatives investing billions in carbon fixation technologies, artificial induction systems, and precipitation control. They say this policy is a great success."

Cadmus interrupts, "Forgive me, but I wonder if any of the people made homeless last week after years of promises feel like things are under control? Many of the technologies the government has poured billions into may actually be making things worse. The problem is we simply don't know."

"And what is your solution?"

"Adapt. Stop pouring money down the drain trying to defend cities and towns inevitably to be drowned. Retreat and build for what we know is coming in the future: even more extreme weather, sea level rise, more storms, rain, heat, water shortages, crop failures."

"And you're not against fusion power, GM food, or even lab-grown food?"

"Not at all. We need to leverage all our human strengths to survive into the future, including technology and innovation. We are technological animals. We need electricity. We need food. Given what has happened to the climate and to our water supply and the population, we simply cannot sustain people using naturally grown food. People will starve if we rely on traditional agriculture."

"Isn't Elgol experimenting with traditional agriculture?"

"Elgol is my wife's project, not mine, but you will find a range of technologies being trialled there. You have to understand, we have a different agenda from the corporations producing food, energy, and managing the environment. We aren't driven by profit. We are driven by the desire for our species to survive and to live as harmoniously as possible within the complex systems comprising our world. Because we are not driven by profit, we do not drive innovations to market before they are properly tested. We don't make claims for our products beyond their capabilities. We don't use technologies we even suspect may be harmful to humans, to other living creatures, or to the environment."

"Let's turn to the election. Your party took a case to court, claiming evidence there was widespread vote rigging, corruption, and coercion."

"I'm afraid I'm unable to comment."

"Why?"

"Because the court not only ruled in the Universal Popular Party's favour, it issued an injunction against me, which stipulates I can't speak of this matter in public."

"Some people say the judges who heard the case were bought."

"I've no comment on what others said or say. I will be violating the injunction if I talk."

"You will be arrested?"

"Yes."

"We have reports saying you're being watched. You are under effective house arrest."

"I try to live my life as normal, but yes, I do have an unofficial armed guard – but none of us have any privacy anymore. Every communication channel is being intercepted."

"Not this one."

"Of course this one, from time to time. Some of us get away with privacy if we have the right technology, know-how, and luck, but it's becoming harder and harder. When the government introduces its new national biological identity system . . ."

"This is the bioID passport? In the run-up to the debate on bioIDs, the government hailed them as a great step forward and said they will make life more convenient: fewer queues when travelling across borders; less financial fraud, as you will be able to use it as authentication for your bank account, to get paid and pay bills, and manage all digital accounts. You will even be able to use it as the means of security for your house. Why is this a bad thing?"

"The government is made of men. All men are frail. You should never give all your power to another human being. If we allow this thing to happen, it will mean no person in this country will have a private moment from this day forward. The minute you displease anyone happening to be in authority, you are at risk of becoming persona non grata. Your bioID will literally be marked. When they introduce this, the government will be able to track your movements day and night. Combined with what is already being tracked about you through your medibot, it will know everything about you. It will know where you go, who you talk to, what you say, what you watch, what you read, and how you feel about it."

"But medibot data is private, according to the terms and conditions of the agreement with Panacea."

Cadmus laughs, "Panacea has been passing people's medical data to the government for years."

"That may be so, but having a full bioID is still a long way off, surely? The bill to introduce it was only just rejected in Parliament."

"It will happen anyway. We're heading for war, and when that happens, the government will declare a state of emergency. With its new powers, it will steam-roller in the legislation to turn you into a node on a network . . ."

"Why do you say we're heading for war?"

"All the signs have been there for a long time. The Japanese have fixed their gaze beyond their own geography and population in order to get the resources they need to remain preeminent in the world economy. They have been economically and politically aggressive in their region for years – especially in China and Korea. The Chinese have naturally resented this, and there is, of course, historical animosity there, as well. The Americans have done what they always do and have agitated against the Chinese in order to maintain, depending on how you look at it, a balance of power, or chaos, in order to ensure American world dominance.

"The world wrote off the Russians after their collapse in the twenty-twenties. They were always overplaying their hand because they felt so threatened. But for a long time geopolitical analysts advising governments failed to factor in what would happen to

Russia when the climate changed. Probably because years ago, you will remember, there used to be so much climate change scepticism. The West underestimated Russia.

"Initially they were as badly hit as the Americans, especially with uncontrollable forest fires, drought destroying their agriculture and threatening lives as millions struggled with heat waves in the South, much in the same way southern Europe has suffered. Turkey took advantage of their weakness in the Caucasus, and they lost all control over their old Soviet satellites. But then the sea routes in Siberia, previously blocked by ice, became clear for their war and merchant ships. Even if the world's fresh water resources are massively depleted, the Russians have a quarter of what is left – and although they've lost their agricultural land, they have enormous new territory in the north now available to them for food production.

"They want what they have always wanted. To control access to the Black Sea and to put as many buffer states between themselves and Western Europe as possible. Now, I think their ambitions may be greater, but they may have acted a bit prematurely. These are well-known facts available to any citizen of this or any democratic country. There are many published works on the subject. If the rumours about the new Battlestar are correct, then it will be a huge provocation to the Russians and the Chinese. It will be a huge miscalculation on behalf of the USA. That is why I say war is coming."

6 MR LESTRANGE

Still in the Darkroom, Mathew closes Psychopomp and calls a virtual space he created himself.

He is on a vast ocean, in a small wooden sailing boat. The Darkroom chair moves appropriately, so he feels like he's floating. It's night, and he steers the boat by the stars. The pattern he has placed in the constellations leads to his destination. The wind catches the sails, and he moves through the water, the only sounds water lapping at the bottom of the boat and the canvas flapping. After a few minutes, he sees land on the horizon. A small island, an oasis of yellow sand, a single palm tree. He runs the boat ashore and climbs out, in the Darkroom, standing, stepping forward. He kneels under the tree and digs in the sand with his hands, uncovering an old wood and leather trunk. When he has cleared enough sand away, he takes a key from his pocket and unlocks the large brass padlock that hangs from the clasp on the lid and throws the trunk open. Inside there are documents, old books, which he takes out and places on the sand and then goes back to his seat.

In reality, the documents are digital artefacts concerning his father, kept in a place as secret as he knows how to make it. He could not explain why he feels the need to hide these things, but ever since his father died, he has wanted to protect them, as if a sixth sense tells him they are not entirely safe in the open.

Mostly they are photos and videos. But there is the order of service from his father's funeral, condolence letters from family friends and relatives. Mathew also has a collection of news articles on the solar island in the North Sea which his father was visiting when the cyclone hit and scattered the solar energy station, and the 131 men and women working on it, like match wood.

No one survived.

He has letters from Helios Energy, his father's company, documents easily pilfered from his mother's not especially secure personal drive: one regretfully confirming his father's death, another informing them that his life insurance was unfortunately limited by a clause in the policy, and then a further letter disclaiming any further responsibility for Mathew and his mother. There had been a court case in which the disaster victims' families sued for compensation, but the judge ruled the storm was an act of God, for which the company was not responsible.

Mathew scrolls through these documents and finds a video of Elgol, two summers ago, the last summer holiday before his father was killed. The video is of Mathew and his grandmother. She hasn't changed at all. He himself is so much younger, happy and carefree. He feels a pang of jealousy and resentment towards the boy in the video, who doesn't know what's coming, how his life is going to be changed forever. They are in his grandmother's garden, making a trellis. The frame is flat on the floor, half constructed. He's holding the wood while his grandmother hammers.

His father asks from behind the camera in his Lenz, "What are you doing?"

Ju Chen says, "What does it look like? Switch that off and come and do something useful. You're letting your son do all the work!"

The camera in his father's eye pans around. Hoshi is sitting on a bench under the kitchen window reading in the shade of the flowering honeysuckle, which casts shadows across her eyes.

Mathew hears his own idiotic laughter off-screen. His father is pulling faces at his mother. She grabs her Paper and walks away. She doesn't smile. Before the video ends, his father's pleading voice says, "Hoshi. Hoshi, come on . . ." and the video terminates.

That last summer before his father died, his parents did nothing but row.

It's four o'clock. Back in his bedroom, Mathew goes to his window.

A car comes smoothly to a stop outside Gen Lacey's house. The girl, Clara, is on the pavement. She wears a calm, impassive expression, but her eyes scan the road. Like most people these days, she's on her guard. Mathew knows she can't see his face, but she glances in his direction, perhaps scanning his broadcast data. Her hair is around her shoulders. She brushes a strand of it from her eyes with one large, long-fingered hand, tucking it behind an ear. She pauses only a moment. It's too hot to linger. Then she disappears from sight.

Mathew looks across to the bay window of the house next door and for a second time sees the man with the deep-set eyes, staring at the space Clara Barculo occupied a moment before. Again Lestrange's head snaps to the side, and those dark, dead eyes bore into Mathew like they are drilling for oil. In the next heartbeat, he steps back into the shadows of the room.

Mr Lestrange is watching the pianist, Mathew is sure of it now. But why? And should he tell her? What would he say?

He goes downstairs, realising with surprise that he's shaking.

With O'Malley butting against him and the dragons dive-bombing him as he kneels on the floor, he installs his tiny amplifier in the front room, in a gap behind the skirting boards, under a loose flap of wallpaper. It's a place his mother is unlikely to discover and Leibniz is unlikely to disturb while cleaning.

It's rigged so the audio stream comes through to his e-Pin. He

47

switches on the feed now, setting it to record, so he'll be able to listen to the music again afterwards. The amplifier is so sensitive it detects footsteps in Gen's house. The hinge of an inner door squeaks, and he imagines Gen Lacey and her student entering the front room, where he knows she keeps her grand piano.

"Was your journey okay?" Gen asks.

"Yes, fine. The car cuts across town. We take a bit of a detour, but there are fewer cars on the road than normal, so it takes the same time as the direct route nearer the river. I didn't notice anything too unusual, except no one's about, there's no people walking around. It's like Sunday morning all day, every day."

"How are your parents coping?"

"Oh, they're fine. Since they're teachers, they're stuck at home, doing their supervision and lesson authoring from there. I think they're enjoying it, actually."

"I have to say, it doesn't make a huge amount of difference to me, either. Now what do you want to work on today?"

"I'm struggling with the opening piece."

"Honestly, Clara, I think you're worrying over nothing. You still have plenty of time to prepare, and the way you're playing, there's very little work to do."

"The expression isn't right," the girl says. "Technically, it's fine, but it's not what I want to say."

"Why don't you start? I'll listen, and then we'll discuss."

Mathew sits on the floor with his back to the wall, the sound coming from the amplifier. His head resting against the wallpaper, he closes his eyes. O'Malley climbs into his lap and falls asleep.

Memories of his father flood back, in particular his love of classical piano music. For the past two years it has felt dangerous to listen to any kind of music, to do anything to rouse emotion. He has avoided films and games with stories of fathers and tales of storms and disasters. It shouldn't surprise him that he hasn't been able to listen to music he closely associates with his father. But now, as his memory of his father recedes, he wants to pull him back. The fear of losing him forever is greater than the fear of feeling.

When he was five or six years old, his father sat him down and made him listen to Chopin's Nocturnes and Beethoven's Moonlight Sonata. Afterwards he listened to these pieces over and over, until they wore into him. Searching for the melodies, straining to find whatever meaning his father found in them. Soren loved a wide range of composers, but most of all, he loved Bach. Bach, he told Mathew, is the mathematician's music. It's the music of logic, of science. "This music feeds your brain, Mathew."

The music is all Mathew lets in for the next hour, broken only by discussions between Clara and her teacher. Clara's anxious search for her own version of perfection is at odds with the sublime emotions the music generates.

Listening, absorbed in her playing, he is calm.

He's so lost in the place in his head where the music has sent him, it takes him a moment to realise Clara has stopped playing and is saying goodbye to Gen.

He scrambles up and gets to the window in time to watch her disappear into her car, the Aegis guard shutting the door.

The guard scans around the road and then suddenly glares directly at Mathew.

He receives an incoming message from the guard, not encrypted. Open. The equivalent of shouting, it says:

`Haven't you got something better to do, weirdo?`

The guard grins or snarls, it's hard to tell which, and then gets into the front seat.

Mathew steps back as if slapped.

The autonomous vehicle does a mathematically precise three-point turn and drives away. The passenger window winds down and Mathew watches Clara, who must have also received the message, craning her head to search for the "weirdo" the guard yelled at. She does not catch sight of him, but she will have seen his name and broadcast data again.

He is angry, embarrassed, flustered, and, because of this, he has forgotten about Mr Lestrange, but as he turns away from the window, he catches a glimpse of a shadowy figure retreating from the light in the semi-darkness of the house next door.

Mr Lestrange is far weirder than I am. It's much creepier for a grown man to be staring at a fifteen-year-old from his bedroom window than it is for me to do it. So why did the guard confront me and not him?

Then he realises. The guard didn't confront Lestrange because his surveillance gear didn't detect him.

Later, as he sits with his mother while she eats her late-night supper, she notices his faraway look. "Penny for them," she says.

"Mr Lestrange."

"Him again. What has prompted this?"

"We know nothing about him. Don't you think it's odd?"

His mother raises an eyebrow. "No. I don't think it's odd at all that you don't know him."

"Before the curfew, did he leave the house?"

"I don't know, Mathew. I leave early in the morning and come back late at night. You're more likely to have run into him than I am."

"I don't remember ever seeing him."

"Do you remember noticing Gen walking down the street?"

Mathew frowns. "I'm sure I do."

"Gen's a bad example. You've known her since you were a baby. Do you know Mary in the house opposite?"

Mathew shakes his head. "I didn't even know there was a Mary opposite."

"Well, then."

"But you notice people. You must have spoken to Mr Lestrange

50

at some point, over the garden fence or in the porch. Do you remember what he's like?"

She searches her memory, "D'you know? I couldn't tell you."

"But you met him, didn't you?"

"I think that was your father."

"You've never met him?"

"Come to think of it, I don't think I ever have."

7 EVA ASLANOVA'S VIRTUAL WORLD

"Don't let O'Malley out," Hoshi says, shutting the door behind her.

"I won't!" he shouts after her.

Mathew shoves off his bedclothes, goes to the window, and watches his mother's car pull away and disappear around the end of the road.

The sun is already beating down, melting the tarmac. The doors of the houses on Pickervance Road are all shut, and the street is deserted and still, as it has been each day of the All-Day Curfew. The silence is interrupted only by the black Aegis cars coming to take the few people who have city passes to and from work and the Hydroponic City and Techno Food delivery trucks bringing supplies to the housebound residents.

In the kitchen, Mathew allows Leibniz to make him breakfast, while he watches a report on the Canvas on the multinational Vulcan Energy and Power Services – VEPS, for short – mining Helium 3 on the moon for use in the still experimental nuclear fusion power stations on earth.

The newsreader says, "VEPS has bought a 15 per cent stake in the part-privately financed NATO Battlestar Space Security System, or B3S, earth's first line of defence against asteroid bombardment. VEPS's board justified the investment to shareholders, saying the Battlestar would be used to displace incoming moon-bound asteroids, on course to hit the VEPS Moonbase, now permanently manned. A spokesperson representing both companies said the additional investment would partly fund the development of a further Battlestar."

Mathew laughs, remembering what Cadmus Silverwood had said in the Psychopomp report about rumours of a new Battlestar. He and everyone else on the face of the planet knows the main purpose of the Battlestars is to control satellite-based rocket launchers that are targeted at strategic locations on earth.

They are there to keep everyone in his or her place.

Mathew vaguely thinks about what Silverwood said about the war.

Leibniz clears the dishes.

Mathew has an appointment in the Darkroom. Nan Absolem has arranged a meeting with the Russian girl who builds virtual worlds.

Eva Aslanova is slightly younger than Mathew. She is so blonde her fine hair is almost white, as white as her skin. In the Darkroom she sits in an armchair made to seem enormous by her tiny frame. She frowns constantly, and doing so over many years has actually made creases in her forehead. He is unable to raise a smile from her, but he thinks he catches something sparkling in her eyes as she watches the dragons fly around the room.

"Why did you make dragons?" she asks him. There's only a tiny delay when speaking via simultaneous translation. Eva doesn't speak a word of English, and Mathew certainly isn't confident speaking Russian. "It strikes me as . . ." she begins.

"Frivolous?"

"I was going to say childish."

Shame the auto-translate function doesn't work on manners and cultural differences, Mathew thinks. Eva is mercilessly direct.

"I wanted to make them real. Dragons have a different meaning in my father and grandmother's cultures. My mother is Japanese, my grandmother is Chinese. My father was Danish."

"Was?"

"He's dead."

Eva doesn't say "I'm sorry" or react in any way to this news. Mathew feels relieved and grateful because it means he doesn't have to reply, "It's okay," as he normally does. Because it isn't. It isn't okay at all.

"In my father's culture dragons are evil creatures that kill and terrify people. They have to be defeated by a brave warrior. In my grandmother's culture they are mystical and lucky: They protect us and save us. My grandmother is always trying to teach me Chinese culture because she thinks I will never learn to appreciate it living here. She thinks I'll forget my roots."

"You are a foreigner in the country you live in."

"No."

"You said your grandmother thinks you are forgetting who you are."

"It may be what my grandmother thinks, but it's not what I think. I'm British."

Eva accepts this, or is too bored to pursue it. "I understand why you wanted to make the dragons now," she says, and Mathew considers it strange she thinks he'd appreciate her approval, but in a way he does. She asks, "Why is your mother Japanese and your grandmother Chinese?"

"My grandfather, my mother's father, was a Japanese businessman. He moved to China for a job and never left."

"And how did your mother and grandmother come to England?"

"My mother came here on an internship. She works for Panacea's biotechnology division. They have offices in China and in most major cities worldwide. She wanted to visit England, because her secondary subject at college was English. She only intended to come for a year, but she met my father, and they fell in love and got married. Her company helped with the visa arrangements, and so she stayed."

"And why is your grandmother living in England?"

"She lives in Scotland now, but she came a few years after my mother, when my grandfather died, to get away from the trouble in China caused by drought and flooding. My mother invited her for a long holiday, and they managed to get her indefinite leave to remain on compassionate grounds."

"Do you miss your father?"

"Of course I do! What kind of question is that?"

"It's a valid question. Just because he was your father it doesn't mean you liked him. I loathe mine. I wouldn't care if he wasn't here anymore. My brothers are all he cares about. They are all stupid and are still struggling to pass their foundation exams even though they are older than me. He's a Neanderthal and thinks women don't need to be educated and they're only fit to be wives."

"So how come you are able to program and study?"

"I have a good teacher, and my mother isn't as docile as my father thinks she is."

"Why are you building a virtual world?"

"Because I can, because it has all kinds of practical uses. It's officially an environmental project. I'm building worlds and running climate models in them to test the impact of pollution on the world's ecological systems. But I originally just wanted to build a world with no people in it."

"Really?"

"Yes, really. Haven't you ever wished you could have the world to yourself for a while? Haven't you ever wished there were vast expanses of an unpopulated world for you to explore alone?"

"Now you come to mention it, it is appealing."

"Exactly."

"But then, you won't want my dragons wandering around in your world."

"It's not an issue, is it? The whole point of my project is that I replicate my worlds for scenario testing. We'll mirror my world, and you can have two or more, as many as you like, parallel versions of it. Versions to split off and do different things with. Whatever you imagine. I don't mind if we clone one of my worlds for you to use. I think it might be interesting."

"What happens when you add new territories? Would they synch to my version?"

"Yes. Your dragons will have an ever-expanding world to live in, rather than being confined to your house. And you'll be able to meet your dragons there – and me as well, if you like."

"I'd like it very much, Eva Aslanova."

"It appears we have a project, Mathew Erlang."

Eva invites Mathew into her world. He gets the demigod tour rather than the human pedestrian perspective, to give him a sense of the scale of it. As he sits in the comfort of his Darkroom seat, his brain is stimulated by the skullcap, and his senses are assaulted and fooled by the complex coordinated technologies in the Darkroom. Eva takes his hand and flies him over fields, great empty plains, forests, deserts, seas, lakes, mountains, ancient dead snow-topped and active volcanoes. They dive under water and skim the colour-shock of coral reefs. Finally, she brings him to rest on a mountainside. They are staring across a valley, a deep gorge cut into the landscape, velveteen with green and studded with trees. Fluffy white clouds cast shadows moving ship-like across the land.

He's done this kind of thing before. Eva's world isn't unique, but there is something different, something pristine and innocent, plus, if he wants it, he'll have a version all to himself

8 O'MALLEY ESCAPES

Number nineteen and number twenty-one Pickervance Road are houses nestling against one another. They are part of two rows of Victorian terraces with elaborate bay windows and tiled porches, set back from the road, with short redbrick paths, flower borders, and garden walls.

Their front doors are right next to one another, making it all the more surprising that Mathew's parents had never got to know Mr Lestrange. It also means that when Mathew puts his acoustic amplifier to the party wall between his and Mr Lestrange's house, he's recording whatever is going on in the hallway of the house next door, which appears to be nothing very much at all.

Mathew tries several places, upstairs and down, in the hope he might catch Mr Lestrange having an e-Pin conversation whilst wandering in his house, but he is greeted with nothing but silence.

He sits on the staircase with his amplifier on his knees. It's possible Lestrange has soundproofed the party walls. He goes upstairs. The corner of his bedroom is only a couple of feet away from Mr Lestrange's bay window. What if he attaches his amplifier to the wall? Then he'd be able to listen directly into the room.

The window in Mathew's bedroom hasn't opened in years. Given the climate and the permanent need for either air conditioning or heating, hardly anyone opens their windows these days. Mathew climbs onto a chair he fetches from the kitchen and manages to force the window ajar. He has fashioned a kind of hook attached to the wire he wraps round the amplifier, intending this to fasten to the pipe clips on the drainpipe running between their two houses. Leaning precariously, he manages to fix the amplifier in place, but as he gets back in through the window, trying to thread the wire with him, he slips, the stool going from under his feet. Grabbing the window ledge before he falls, he dislodges the precariously attached amplifier and sends the whole thing hurtling into the olive tree growing next to the front room windows.

"Damn!" He drops to the floorboards and jogs downstairs, taking his stool with him.

First he goes into the garden to try and retrieve the amplifier from the tree, but he can't reach it. It's stuck in the crook of two branches growing against the side of the house. He realises he would be able to get at it if he stretched from the window in the front room.

Downstairs, he thumps the window open. It is as stuck as the one upstairs, but he manages to force it and leans across to grab the amplifier. As he does, O'Malley, whom he's totally forgotten about, bounds off the window ledge onto his shoulder and out through the window. Mathew drops the amplifier.

"Damn cat!" he says.

He opens the front door and goes into the street. As always, the heat hits him like a wall.

O'Malley has disappeared.

In the garden he starts searching on his hands and knees under the juniper and rosemary bushes.

"O'Malley? O'Malley!" he calls, increasingly loudly, half-expecting the entire neighbourhood to come and tell him to get indoors. It crosses his mind that he may be breaking the terms of the All-Day Curfew. "O'Malley?" he says again. O'Malley's distinct mew calls back to him, more half-strangled duck than cat. "Good boy, come here. Come on."

"Mew," says O'Malley, but he doesn't appear.

Mathew thinks the meow is coming from Gen Lacey's garden, and he peers over the fence separating their properties.

"O'Malley, come here," he says, aiming his voice at the garden.

"Mao," O'Malley says, but this time Mathew catches something moving in the bushes on the far side of Gen's path.

His bare feet burn on the pavement as he heads for Gen's garden gate. Wondering if he should knock before he searches through her shrubbery, he decides he doesn't have time and will explain if she comes. He gets on his hands and knees and starts lifting branches. In the corner of the wall, under a laurel bush, O'Malley's turquoise eyes glimmer. Mathew pats the soil in front of him, "Come on, come on." Finding a broken twig, he starts waving it in front of the cat. O'Malley obligingly responds and swats at the stick with his paw. Mathew slowly draws the waving stick towards him, and O'Malley edges forward.

"Don't move or I'll blow your bloody brains out!"

Somehow Mathew is now face down, with his cheek ignominiously pressed onto a hot paving stone, his arm painfully pinned behind his back, a heavy weight pressing on his spine and something hard, metal, and definitely life-threatening pushed into the side of his head.

"ID!" barks what Mathew assumes to be the man kneeling on him.

"What?" Mathew says, struggling to breathe.

"Where is your ID card?" the man punctuates each word with additional pressure from his knee, so Mathew involuntarily finds himself groaning.

"It's in the house."

"What's it doing there? All citizens must carry their ID at all times with them during the All-Day Curfew."

"I didn't think I'd need it to hunt for my cat."

"Your what?"

"My cat escaped."

"There's no cat."

"He's under there." Mathew tries to lift his arm to point but the man slams him against the paving stone hard.

"What on earth is going on?"

This is another voice. A woman. A voice of reason.

Mathew's eyes, at ground level, see a pair of women's shoes.

"Why on earth are you kneeling on my neighbour's son and pointing a gun at his head? Are you mad?" It's Gen Lacey.

"Please stand back. This boy is wandering around without ID during a government curfew, a criminal offence under the Special Measures Act 2042. This same boy I observed wearing Lenzes and spying on my client yesterday, which is not only highly suspicious behaviour, it is also a criminal offence under the Personal Privacy Act 2035."

Gen says, "He's Mathew Erlang, an educational apprentice to Hermes Link and son of Hoshi Mori, senior researcher at Panacea. I don't think anyone would be especially happy if you arrested him."

"I am making an arrest until his identity is vouched for."

"I *am* vouching for his identity. I have told you who he is. Please listen. I live here. You have seen me each day for the last year. So you should be able to vouch for *my* identity, at least."

"Please don't abuse me, madam. I am authorised to use my weapon."

"I'm not abusing you. I'm helping you. You are assaulting a sixteen-year-old boy out searching for his cat, and I am trying to get you to stop before you do something you will regret."

"Maow," O'Malley says.

"What was that?" the guard asks.

"My cat," Mathew says.

Mathew still can't turn his head but hears a third voice, a strange but calm, soothing voice. It says, "I think we should stop this now."

The metal is lifted from the side of Mathew's head. The knee is removed from his chest. He turns on the pavement, onto his back, and gapes up. Briefly registering Clara staring imperiously down at him, his eyes are drawn to Mr Lestrange. He has the muzzle of the machine gun in his hand and is gently handing it back to the guard, who now has a puzzled but soft look on his face. Mr Lestrange actually takes the guard's hand in his and places the muzzle of the gun there, wrapping his fingers around it. "I think you should go back to your car now. Come back at five o'clock to collect Clara."

"Right." The guard hesitates for a moment and then retreats to the car, glancing over his shoulder, bemused. They watch from Gen's garden as the car drives away.

Gen hurries to Mathew and helps him to his feet. "Are you okay?" she asks.

O'Malley comes from under the bushes and rubs against his ankles. Mathew bends and picks him up. "I'm fine," he says.

O'Malley starts to purr loudly.

Mr Lestrange is tall and thin, dressed conservatively but not oddly. His face is long, his skin pale, almost translucent, the skin of someone rarely touched by the sun. He is clean-shaven and of an indeterminate age. His eyes are dark and framed by extraordinarily long, thick eyelashes.

Mathew realises too late that he is staring open-mouthed.

Mr Lestrange has something in his hand. Mathew doesn't know where it came from because he didn't notice it when he was talking to the guard. It's his acoustic amplifier and a tangle of wire. Mr Lestrange hands it to him silently, with the faintest hint of a smile.

Gen Lacey has opened the front door and is guiding Clara through it.

"Mathew, come in for a minute. I'll make you some hot tea. You must be in shock."

Mathew is still staring at Mr Lestrange. Indiscernibly, he urges Mathew forward, so he finds himself walking towards Gen Lacey's beckoning hand without consciously planning to.

"This is my fault. I'm sorry. But I think it will be alright," Mr

Lestrange says as if talking to himself.

Mathew is distracted by Gen, who's ushering him into the house and helping him with his complicated burden of the cat and a bundle of wires.

He turns back again, but Mr Lestrange has disappeared through his own front door.

Clara and Mathew are in Gen Lacey's large front room. Gen doesn't have a HomeAngel – she says the Royal College of Music doesn't have the budget – so she has gone off to make the tea herself. They are sitting on either end of the sofa, something Mathew is grateful for because as they walked in, he realised Clara is taller than him.

They are both staring at the grand piano. He glances across at her. She has a long nose and freckles, three dark moles on her cheek.

"So you were watching me?" she asks.

Mathew feels unwell. "No."

"Why did the guard say you were watching me then?"

"The man's a psycho. You saw him."

"He takes care of me when I travel and is nothing but nice to me."

"Your nice man had me pinned to the floor with a gun to my head."

"It was quite extreme," Clara admits.

"Yes, it *felt* quite extreme."

"But he must have had a reason. What were you doing sneaking around like that?"

"I was searching for him," he says nodding in the direction of O'Malley, who jumps onto the piano stool. He explores the room, his legs retracted to short stumps in fear, his neck extended in curiosity, starting back as he encounters each new thing. Mathew gets up and retrieves him before he jumps onto the piano.

"It's a pretty cat," Clara says. "Is it a Siamese?"

"His name is O'Malley, and he's half-Siamese," Mathew says.

"Oh, it's a he. Isn't he allowed into the garden?"

"Used to be, but he has to stay in now because of the birds."

"The birds?"

"The government passed a law making it illegal to kill birds and included a house cat clause. So he's now shut away in the house all the time and doesn't understand, and he's always trying to run away."

O'Malley is straining to get at Clara. She extends one of her long hands and strokes him. Mathew is holding O'Malley back.

"It's okay, I love animals," she says.

Released, the cat climbs onto her lap and starts to purr like he has a motor.

"He likes you," Mathew says, wanting to tell her how much he enjoys listening to her playing, but he doesn't know how to begin.

She says, "You're the weirdo."

"What?"

"Yesterday the guard said someone was watching me, and it was you. He called you a weirdo."

"I happened to be at my window when you arrived. I wasn't watching you. Alright?"

"Why would he say that then?"

Mathew hesitates. "It might have appeared like I was watching you."

She raises an eyebrow and assesses him sceptically. "Right," she says. "Whatever you do that makes him think that, can you stop, please? I'm too spooked out by everything going on at the moment with the government. My parents are on some frickin watch list, and the last thing I need is a teenaged stalker."

Mathew's face colours purple. "I am not watching you, but if you want to know the truth, the man who lives next door to me, the one you just met, has been at his window each time you came and went ever since I've been home from school, and your awesome guard hasn't even noticed."

"You're making it up."

"If you don't believe me, come and see. When you've finished your lesson here, come round and I'll show you." He stands.

Gen comes through the door with a tray of tea. She glances between the two of them curiously. "Everything alright here?" she says.

"Fine," Clara says, smiling brightly.

"How are you?" Gen asks, frowning at Mathew with concern. "Why don't you sit down?"

"I'm fine," Mathew says. "I should be going."

"Stay and have some tea, at least."

Mathew shakes his head. "I've disturbed your lesson. I should leave."

"I should call your mother," Gen says.

"No, please don't. She's so busy. She'd worry and come home, and there's nothing she can do."

"I'll make a complaint. That guard was crazy," Gen says.

"There's no need," Mathew says.

"When I was young, the police weren't thugs," Gen says. "They didn't have guns, and the whole country understood why. These days, I'm sure they hire a lot of these men straight from the criminal courts. Convicted criminals get the choice of joining the army or the security services rather than prison time."

"Do you think Mr Lestrange works for the police?" Mathew asks Gen.

"Mr Lestrange?! Why on earth do you ask that?"

"Because he is always watching people."

"Like you, you mean?" Clara says.

Gen says, "Clara, I am sure Mathew wasn't watching you. Not intentionally, anyway. And Mr Lestrange isn't a policeman. He's some kind of historian."

"That's what my mum says."

"He's got an impressive library, you know, of old-fashioned paper books."

"How do you know? Were you in his house?"

"Yes. Once. When I was doing my stint as neighbourhood watch organiser. You know, it rotates around all the adults in the street. Even your mum has done it. The local police were doing a sweep of houses, the usual thing, people harbouring illegal immigrants, and I had to accompany the police around the houses to make sure they didn't damage anything while they searched."

"What was his house like?"

"Like this one. Actually, no, more like yours. He has a Darkroom, I don't. But his front room is this wonderful library, full of beautifully bound books. History books, he said."

"But there was nothing odd? No strange equipment?"

"I didn't notice anything, no. I think he's fairly ordinary. People always think people living on their own and who keep to themselves, are suspect, but he's harmless."

"I don't think he's harmless at all."

"Why?"

"Because of the way the guard reacted to him. When you spoke to him, the guard was getting angrier. When Mr Lestrange spoke to him, he immediately backed down."

"Perhaps it was a man thing?"

"Perhaps . . . but I don't think so. It was odd."

"The entire thing was odd," Gen says. "How did O'Malley escape, anyway?"

"Through the living room window. I had dropped . . . something in the tree. It's a long story . . ."

"Is that the thing you dropped?" Clara asks, pointing to the amplifier and the wire bundle in Mathew's arms.

"Yes," he says.

"What is it?"

"It's an amplifier."

"Mathew is a science scholar," Gen explains to Clara.

"I'd really better go," he says. "I'm sorry to have disturbed you. Come on, O'Malley," he says to the cat. O'Malley is happily curled on Clara's lap and doesn't want to move. Mathew isn't sure how to retrieve him. Clara scoops him into her arms and offers him to

Mathew.

· "Thank you," Mathew says. She doesn't meet his eyes.

Gen stands and shows Mathew to the door. "Don't let go of him until you get in the house."

"I won't," he says. "I'm hanging on for dear life."

Back in his room, Mathew finds Mr Lestrange playing on his mind as he works on the amplifier. He decides it's too much trouble to fix the amplifier so finds a new design with hooks built in. While it's printing, he starts to search on the Nexus for Mr Lestrange.

The Nexus is so ubiquitous, even the most tech-averse person is on it somewhere. But Mr Lestrange is not on the electoral register. He's not a member of any social network. Lestrange the historian hasn't published any academic papers. There's no Professor Lestrange registered as teaching at any school or university, in London or internationally. There are no random photos, either, taken by a colleague, friend, or family member and tagged. It's impossible that someone hasn't captured him on camera or film or commented on him somewhere. Mathew tries every variation of Lestrange's name he can think of, tries searching for his address, but as far as the Nexus is concerned, Lestrange doesn't exist.

The 3D printer has completed its run. Mathew tests the new amplifier and connects again in the living room, ready for Clara's lesson the next day.

At nine o'clock, just as he's finishing, he receives an alert from the social network Consort, a connection request. He hardly ever uses Consort. It's a cross between a school playground and a human meat market, full of tribes, shallow relationships, and vapid content. He'd like to terminate his account but doing so is tantamount to dying online. And, bizarrely, the account is unofficially required for college and employment applications.

Requests come in from random people all the time, and he ignores most of them – they barely register with him – but Clara's name catches his eye.

"Accept," he says.

Clara is there online, waiting.

"Thanks," she says. "I wasn't sure you'd accept."

"Why did you think that?"

"Because of the way I spoke to you. I was rude."

"Yes, you were."

She pauses and then says, "Anyway, after you left, Gen and I chatted. So I wanted to apologise and to explain."

"You don't have to." He's wondering what Gen said, guessing she told Clara about his father and now she is sorry for him. He hopes not.

"I want to. Please let me."

"Go ahead." His voice comes out colder than he means it to.

"Not here," she says. "Can I come and see you sometime, in your house?"

"Sure. Just come after your lesson. I'm stuck here, remember."

Later, Mathew logs onto the Blackweb and searches for Mr Lestrange using MUUT, the Blackweb search engine. His search returns zero results.

I need help, he thinks.

9 DROWNED LONDON

DAY THREE: Wednesday, 24 November 2055, London

Most of the Thames bridges are closed. The tunnels are all flooded. There are only a few options for getting across the river, to reach Mathew's school.

Nan Absolem has arranged for a car to come and collect him. It's an Aegis car, like the one his Mother and Clara travel in. It comes with a guard, too. Mathew gingerly steps past him, as he gets into the back.

One dragon zips inside in front of him, but the guard shuts the door on the other. There is nothing stopping the dragon from getting into the car, but it believes it is left behind. Mathew opens the window slightly and the dragon squeezes in. The guard, sitting in the front, opens the glass panel separating them, glances over his shoulder, and says, "Alright?"

"Yes, fine," Mathew says. "I was just testing the windows."

"Right," the guard says, sniffing as he turns back to face the road.

Mathew has the black fake-leather upholstered seats in the main body of the car to himself. Like all cars, this one is arranged inside like a mini-living room, with two two-seater sofas facing one another and a coffee table, which doubles as a holovision, in between.

The backs of the doors and windows are made from unbreakable glass and act as screens. Right now they surround Mathew with a forest scene – a lake, trees, and a blue sky – but they are connected to the Nexus and can display any web page, TV channel, or video. He changes the display so he can see the world outside, and the forest melts away to reveal houses, pavements, and the road. The view is only one way. Aegis assumes its customers want anonymity.

Most cars don't have a front seat at all. The only reason the Aegis cars have seats in the front is because they come with armed guards. The security company found that its clients were unable to relax sitting in the back of a car next to a man with a machine gun balanced on his knees.

Normally, Mathew would get to school using public transport, but all the tubes and train lines are shut. This has happened before – the flood, the transport system being brought to a standstill – but when it did, he went to a school nearer his house and he walked.

They leave Pickervance Road. All the shops and cafes on the high street are shut. Some are boarded up against looters coming from the riverside and the makeshift camp in the park and on the common. One or two of the shops look like they've been looted. There's an armed policeman walking to and fro along the pavement. He guards whatever remains of the stock and the robotic shop assistants. People rarely work in shops anymore. All the shops are owned by corporates and are fully automated.

Mathew's mother had described the camp, but he found it impossible to imagine. They drive past it now, and he's unprepared for what he sees.

Tents, tarpaulins, and makeshift shelters cover the whole of Blackheath. Litter blows across the patchwork of grass and mud remains of the ancient common, collecting in piles. People sit on the edge of the road looking shell-shocked; others stand around between the tents. There is a long queue at a pipe with a tap at the end attached to a wooden stake. People are waiting with buckets and old milk cartons, bowls, and containers of all kinds. There's another long queue at a bank of Portaloos. A sign above one marquee says, "Food supplies," but there's nothing but a table and some empty boxes.

The flooding happened ten days ago. On the news the prime minister assured his interviewer that the government would provide food, shelter, and water to all the flood victims, and that they would be re-homed within a week. There would be no repeat of what happened during previous floods, when people were without shelter for months and there was rioting and even an outbreak of cholera.

The world rolls on like a film from behind the tinted glass screens of Mathew's car. He has to tell himself, this is real; this could be me.

They turn and drive across the common, towards the park. There are people on the road. The car slows, and its on-board computer registers the obstacle and sounds a horn, driving forward all the time. Most of the people scatter. One man in a suit that's crumpled like it's been slept in for the last ten nights turns and kicks the car, swearing angrily. A policeman marches towards him. Mathew turns to the back window to see what happens next, but the car drives away down the hill, and the man and the policeman are gone.

They wind their way down to the river. The flood level is dropping, and people whose houses were swamped are clearing the mess as the water retreats from their homes. Mattresses are pulled over walls to dry. Piles of ruined household things lie around with detritus from the river – branches, leaves, sodden paper, fabric, cans, bottles, and sludge. The car pauses while people walk across the road carrying a table, and Mathew gazes straight into the eyes of an old woman sitting on the wall of her house. It's as if she's staring at him, and he has to remind himself that she wouldn't be able to see through the tinted glass. She wears an expression of total despair. Mathew wants to open his door and help, but the car drives on.

Down one of the streets, next to some half-flooded factory buildings, there's a makeshift ferry. Like Aegis, many entrepreneurial people are finding ways of benefitting from the disaster.

The car stops, and the guard does a quick check of the area, walking to the water's edge to talk to the ferryman, before he comes back to open Mathew's door.

"Go with that man," he says, pointing. "You'll be safe. The boat will take you to the Embankment. There'll be another car waiting for you there."

Mathew looks at the ferryman, a man in his twenties, small but muscled and heavily tattooed. He isn't confident about going with this man and glances back uncertainly at his guard, now the most reassuring figure imaginable.

"We have a tracker on you," the guard says. "We know where you are at all times. We'll be waiting for you when you come back this afternoon."

"The boat's this way," says the ferryman. Mathew has no choice but to follow.

A small number of people are waiting in a makeshift shelter by the water's edge. They are "respectable" people in suits and clean clothes. Mathew finds himself thinking he will be safe with these people. The group is silent. They are as shocked and uncomfortable as he is. The stench from the river is overpowering, and many of them are holding their ties or t-shirts across their mouth and nose. When the riverside streets of London flooded, so did the sewers.

The group is waiting for Mathew.

At the water's edge a boat, forty feet long and half as wide, sits low in the water. In the back stands a guard in black combats, a machine gun hanging from his arm casually, like a kit bag or a coat. The ferryman steadies a rickety wooden walkway leading onto the boat and helps the passengers on. On the deck an assortment of plastic and wooden chairs, crates and boxes serve as seats.

When they have all found somewhere to sit, a young boy, from the look of him the ferryman's brother, or perhaps even his son, hands them all umbrellas, mostly old-fashioned black ones. "To keep the sun off," the boy says. It's a novel idea of service, Mathew thinks, opening his gratefully. It's already hot. His umbrella has a broken spoke.

The ferryman starts the engine. The boy pulls in the wooden ramp, then runs to the front of the boat and jumps off onto dry land. He pushes the boat into the water until he is waist deep and then heaves himself up, head first, his legs dangling in the air. Mathew doesn't want to think about what the boy was wading in. He finds himself pulling his t-shirt over his nose, like the others, and breathes in the clean detergent smell.

The boat powers away from the shore and heads into the centre of the river, racing along, the current behind them.

Mathew has travelled along the river many times in ferryboats in better times, but the Thames is transformed. It was never a pretty river. It was always too powerful and at high tide slightly disturbing, like a wild animal running through the heart of civilisation. Now it is positively feral, spreading its arms anywhere to grab at the land.

The Royal Naval College is half-submerged, buildings sunk beneath the thick brown water lapping through broken windows and tugging on sodden curtains. The old tea clipper, the Cutty Sark, is on one final voyage, its glass skirt shattered by the force of the incoming water, steel ties worked loose. It sails again along the Thames, a ghost ship, rigging flapping, its Muntz metal bottom glistening in the sunshine as it cuts through the muddy sludge of the river. The wooden sailor climbing on its mast surveys the surrounding devastation, facing north across the river to the strange, newly formed wetlands of the Isle of Dogs.

The South Dock Marina and Greenland Dock have been breached, boats sunk and broken against their moorings, some broken free, wild horses in the incoming tidal surge, untapped now by the overrun Thames Barrier downriver.

Northwards, Canary Wharf is a sunken forest of skyscrapers, the bright day reflected in the newly formed lake washing the panes of the glass sides of the first four stories. It's a city of mirrors floating in the sky.

As they travel on, the boatman expertly dodging flotsam, they see more crew-less yachts cut loose from London's many marinas, along with uprooted trees, branches, park benches, and furniture washed from riverside homes. The boatman pushes larger objects away with a long oar.

Then he cuts the engine, and they watch him push away a strange bundle. It turns in the water, and Mathew sees it is a distended corpse, made bloated and grotesque by days in the river.

"Shouldn't we pull it out?" someone says.

The boatman turns and grins. "Do ya want it sittin' wif ya?"

The one voice of conscience is silenced, and no one else speaks.

The body is taken into the current, just another piece of flood debris, and they power away from it, the smell lingering long enough for them all to find it hard to forget.

They pass a block of flats where people have made a camp on the roof, a fire burning smokily away. A boat is tethered to the wall, and someone is returning via the unsubmerged part of a fire escape. Then Mathew notices that many waterside rooftops have people on them, with improvised shelters built to protect them from the rain and the sun. Even though it is November, the sun is harsh.

"Why do they stay?" one of the passengers asks a companion.

"Nowhere else to go. Or to protect their stuff. There's so much looting. Who knows what you would do if this happened to you."

"The river's miles from my house. It will never happen to me."

A police boat powers past them, disappearing around the bend of the river. When they reach it again, the police are pulling three men and a woman into the boat, all handcuffed.

"Looters," someone says.

"Wouldn't like to be in their shoes."

"What will happen to them, do you think?"

"Who cares?"

They pass Wapping and progress under Tower Bridge, both spans of the bascule up. Water laps high on the walls of the Tower of London. They continue under London Bridge and Southwark Bridge and just scrape under the Millennium Bridge. They watch other, taller boats pulling to the side and offloading their passengers.

"The water level must be dropping at last," the talkative passenger says. "We couldn't travel this far on Monday."

Victoria Embankment is flooded, as are the lower floors of all the buildings on it. They have to pull in before Westminster Bridge, a part of the river their ferryman says is impassable, so they make their way along Northumberland Avenue, branch off by Craven Street and stop next to the Playhouse Theatre. The boy jumps off at the waterline, pulls in and steadies the boat. The ferryman stops the engine and puts down the plank.

Mathew sees a number of cars waiting at the top of the lane with their armed men, broadcasting the names of the people they're waiting for, type hanging above their heads. There are a number of real policemen amongst them.

The passengers begin filing off. Mathew walks slowly along the road until he spots a floating tag reading "Erlang." The guard reads Mathew's Nexus information but still wants to check his ID card, examining it critically and scanning the chip before opening the car door.

It takes a while for the road to clear of cars. Once away from the river, the familiar streets are relatively everyday, except there are far fewer pedestrians and there are piles of sandbags around the doorways of the buildings nearest the waterline.

At Trafalgar Square things are different. Whitehall is blockaded.

There are army vehicles parked in the street and packs of soldiers, some in exoskeletons. They are standing still, poised, but if needed they are capable of running twice as fast as the fastest man and crushing human bones with their robotic hands.

Surveillance robots, black metal dogs without faces, patrol the area, sniffing for explosives or people. When they move from one area to the next, they bound with an uncanny gait.

He glances above, noticing movement. A couple of drones fly over the roof of the National Gallery.

They start to drive along Charing Cross Road and sit for a while in traffic. Through the glass separating Mathew from the guard he hears a sudden flurry of noise. The guard speaks to the on-board computer, turns, pulls back the glass plate, and says to Mathew, "We're going to take a detour. Nothing to worry about." This immediately makes Mathew anxious.

The car swings off to the right. They head along St Martin's Lane. As they get to Seven Dials, Mathew peers along Cranbourn Street.

There are people everywhere, and many of them are throwing things. A car is on fire, and furniture is piled in the road, also alight. An armoured police van drives into the pile of burning furniture, sending it flying, knocking people aside. There's the sound of gunfire.

Mathew's car turns sharply onto Garrick Street away from the disturbance. As they drive away, he hears an explosion. They drive along Floral Street. Covent Garden is deserted. The guard turns back to Mathew, grinning, "Told you. Safe as houses."

Five minutes later, they park in front of Mathew's school. He walks up the steps, shaky and unnerved. There are guards here too, checking people's ID. As they move through the doors, he joins the line, thinking he'd never expected to be grateful to come into this building.

10 ROBOT BUILDING

They are sitting in a windowless room facing a large Canvas screen. When the students are all assembled, a video starts to play, providing their challenge instructions. Some people start to write notes on their personal Paper devices, their super-thin portable computer interfaces. Mathew doesn't bother. He switches off his dragons in order to concentrate.

The challenge is to build any kind of robot, but extra points will be awarded to the group for originality and planning.

Mathew knows the room is well scattered with cameras and that the real purpose of the exercise is to test how each individual scores against the academy's latest template for leadership and teamwork. The criteria change depending on the academic staff involved. It's impossible to discover who is setting and assessing the test, so it's impossible to game the system.

Mathew hates these exercises.

He scans the room and recognises all of the fifteen assembled, including Alison Gai and Kaleb Merryfield, his physics partner, but his heart sinks when he spots Theo Arkam.

He realises his arms are folded across his chest, and this appears defensive. Arkam is contemplating him with a slight smile and an ironic twinkle. He is sitting back in his chair with his arms behind his head.

"Great way to start, Erling," he says. "Awesome body language."

"It's Erlang, as you know. And likewise," Mathew says, nodding at Arkam's posture. "Not to mention awesome interpersonal skills." But he isn't as cocky as he sounds.

"I'm so sorry for getting your name wrong," Arkam says. His voice sounds genuinely contrite, but there's a hard glint in his eyes. "I was almost right." He suddenly turns to the rest of the room. "Right, team, shall we get started? Is that alright with you, Mathew? Are you ready? There are fifteen of us. Shall we split into five teams of three and brainstorm high-level ideas for fifteen minutes? We then each come back with a pitch and vote in a ballot on the best one?"

"Are there some instructions I missed appointing you leader, or did you appoint yourself?" Mathew asks.

"It was a suggestion in the absence of any alternatives."

"There wasn't a chance for anyone to offer any alternatives, was there?"

"He's right, Arkam," Alison says.

"You want to debate how to run the session?"

"I think it would be in the spirit of the exercise," Alison says.

"Okay. How do you want to run the session, Erling?"

"Erlang. It shouldn't be a debate between you and me. Why don't you ask some of the other people here?"

Arkam glares at Mathew, but he says to the room, "Suggestions?"

Kaleb says, "Why don't we brainstorm ideas all together first? That way we'll use the big group to bounce ideas off each other. Then we build a shortlist of the best five and afterwards we split into teams to build proposals we pitch to each other. We vote for the best, and then we make a plan, divide the work, and split into teams to complete."

"Sounds complicated. Any other suggestions?" Arkam says.

There are no other suggestions.

"Not sure what the point of this was," Arkam says testily.

Mathew says to those around the table, "Simple show of hands. Those for Arkam's approach?"

Five hands tentatively rise, including Arkam's and that of his best friend, Oliver Thyer.

"Those for Merryfield's?"

Ten hands go up, including Mathew's.

"Merryfield's method has it, I think."

"This is stupid," Arkam says. "My idea was clearly better. You just voted against it because you like Merryfield better."

"Are you for real?" Alison asks Arkam.

Mathew catches Alison's eye and, trying not to smile, turns to ask Merryfield, "Do you want to run the brainstorming session?"

"I . . ." Merryfield is flustered. "Okay. . . ." He stands awkwardly and walks in front of the Canvas, grabbing the digital pen in the clip at the side. He swipes to get a clean whiteboard. "I think we should start by listing any and all thoughts. There are no silly ideas. I'll write them down. What kind of robot could we build?"

"Cyborg," Alison says.

"Great," Arkam sneers. "How appropriate."

Thyer guffaws.

"There are no stupid ideas," Merryfield says, scribbling "Cyborg."

"Some of us have implanted e-Pins. We all have medibots, making us forms of cyborg. It's not impossible," Alison says.

"I agree, Alison," Arkam says, straight-faced. "There's a lot of evidence of cyborgs, even in this room." He glares at Thyer. "Oli, stop sniggering," he says. "Gai made a good point."

"Exoskeleton?"

"Great idea," Merryfield says, capturing it. "There are different variants."

"For paraplegics."

"For soldiers and policemen."

"For VR games."

"Base jumping."

Merryfield scribbles them all down. "What else?"

"Helperbots. HomeAngels, carers for the sick."

"Guide dogs."

"Sniffer dogs."

"Bomb disposal robots."

"Military drones that defuse bombs."

"Space walkers to fix broken parts on space stations. Mars and moon rovers to identify Helium 3 deposits."

"Exoplanet explorers."

Mathew says, "There's small stuff. Insectibots. Pollinators. Beebots. Spybots."

"Cyborg spy rats."

"Or mice. They're smaller."

"Cockroaches."

"Animated morphing intelligent goop that moves between gaps in walls."

"Cool. I like it."

"So do I."

"This is getting stupider by the minute," Arkam says. "How are we going to make 'goop'?"

"Kitchen cleaners are intelligent goop – they can't be hard to make. Our medibots are built with intelligent viruses, right? There's nothing in the scope here concerning sticking to machine parts. Why should we stick to things we have all done before?" Mathew says.

"Because we're good at them," says Arkam.

"And what will we learn?"

"You think you're here to learn?" Arkam is smiling at Mathew. He shakes his head. "I thought you were supposed to be smart."

Merryfield says, "At this stage we should pool all our ideas and not discuss how we're going to do them. Anything else?"

"We haven't got soldierbots."

"Okay, what next?" Arkam says. "We need five ideas."

Merryfield splits the Canvas screen so their ideas are on the left and there is a blank screen on the right. "We need a framework to narrow them. Any suggestions?"

"How long will they take?"

Merryfield writes, "Time."

"Do we have the materials?"

"Is it possible to make the materials? Or get them easily?"

"Do we have the knowledge?" Arkam says.

"How easy would it be to learn?"

"Is it fun?"

"Is it useful?"

Merryfield creates a grid reading, "Time, Materials, Knowledge, Fun, and Useful" at the top. He draws lines down and across. The computer immediately interprets what he wants to do and creates a table.

"Let's go through the list, shall we? Let's score them. One is most positive, five is most negative. Lowest score wins. How feasible is an exoskeleton?"

"It would probably take us a while, because it's fairly complex."

"It depends on how ambitious we are. I think it's not beyond us to build something supporting muscle power in legs, for instance. It also scores pretty high on usefulness."

"Shall we list the different types of exoskeleton for scoring?"

"We've only got today, you know," Arkam says.

"You're right, Arkam," Merryfield says. "Let's limit this session to half an hour."

"If this session is half an hour, how long is the next stage? And the one after?"

Merryfield gapes mutely at Arkam.

Arkam turns to Mathew. "You're quiet, Erling. Have you left us for the duration?" Mathew is doing something on his Paper. "Are you able to spare some time to join us and offer some time-management tips?"

Mathew says, "Just a moment." He finishes something and then smiles at Arkam.

Arkam is watching him. Mathew points to the Canvas screen. "Accept, will you, Merryfield?" Mathew says as a dialog box pops up with a message saying, "A friend is trying to share your screen. Accept. Deny." Mathew says, "Move the new window to the left where you have the score chart."

"You've made a neater version of Merryfield's chart. Well done!" Arkam says with sarcastic enthusiasm.

"Look at your Papers. I've sent you a voting app. It contains all of Merryfield's options. You have to go through line by line and score each option. The average accumulated scores will appear on the Canvas as you vote." Mathew turns to Arkam. "Quicker and more democratic."

Arkam snorts, but he unscrolls his Paper and opens the app. The voting is done in a few minutes. They have five candidates. The lower body exoskeleton for paraplegics, the guide dog, the spybot, the moon rover, and the military drone.

"Now what, Mr Organiser?" Arkam says. "Shall we split into teams and discuss?"

Merryfield either doesn't detect the sarcasm or chooses to ignore it. Mathew decides Merryfield is a better person than he is. "Yes. Great idea, Arkam. Let's split into five teams of three, based on where we're sitting."

"I'd like to do the spybot," Mathew says.

"Does that work for you? Are you happy to work with Erlang?" Arkam asks the two people sitting next to Mathew. They nod.

"We're the moon rover," Alison says after a whispered conference with the two nearest her.

"As we're staking claims, we're the military drone," Arkam says.

Jane Wilson, who is sitting next to Arkam, says, "I want to work on the exoskeleton."

"I'll swap with you," Oliver Thyer says.

"Guide dog," another student says.

"Good," says Merryfield. "Half an hour from now, we report. You need designs, plans for execution, and a pitch. We'll meet, hear the pitches, and vote anonymously, Mathew, if you don't mind creating another voting app?"

"Not at all."

"The winning team will lead the project and allocate work. We break for lunch at 12:30. We'll spend the afternoon building the robot."

They split into their teams and scatter around the room, taking their chairs.

Mathew is with Wyatt Yerby and Lydia Dowd. He gets an extra chair and snaps his Paper to the back of it.

"Any ideas?" Wyatt asks.

"We base our spybot on a pre-existing model. We'll download plans from the Nexus and adapt them. It will save a lot of time," Mathew says.

"Shouldn't we be worried we might plagiarise something?" Lydia says.

"None of these ideas are particularly original. What do they expect us to do in a day?" Wyatt says.

They both look at Mathew, who says, "I think you're both right. We need to offer an original spin on an existing idea."

"Fantastic. But what?"

"What if we use something not meant to spy for spying?" Mathew asks.

"Like what?" Wyatt says.

"What small robot is used for practical purposes?" says Lydia.

"Medibots?" Wyatt suggests.

"I love the idea, but we'll probably not get it past the practicality committee," Lydia says.

Mathew says, "There's beebots."

"Erm . . ." Wyatt frowns.

Mathew persists, "Crop pollinators. What farmers use these days instead of bees."

"Okay . . ."

"They're small enough to squeeze through keyholes and walk

under doors. There are also thousands of free templates on the Nexus. We download one of these and use plans for a more conventional spybot to add recording capabilities to the beebot."

"It's very simple," Lydia says.

"And that's a problem because . . . ?"

"Seven votes for the drone. Ha!" Arkam says, his eyes shining in triumph, gazing directly at Mathew as he speaks. "Seven votes wins it."

All morning Arkam has been the head of the practicality committee. When Mathew questions the feasibility of building a drone plane with operational arms able to grasp and lift in one afternoon, everyone believes Arkam when he says, "I would not champion an idea I don't believe would work."

Mathew knows this is a lie. Arkam simply doesn't want the afternoon going on the way of the morning, with other people taking control. With his idea selected, it means he will spend the afternoon telling others what to do with perfect legitimacy.

"Why don't you work on the arms?" Arkam says to Mathew, as he allocates work after lunch.

"I've no idea how to build arms on a perfectly aerodynamic object without ruining the aerodynamics. The arms will destabilise the front of the plane. I told you so earlier when I said this project won't work."

"So negative!" Arkam says. "We need total commitment here. We need to work together. I don't want you poisoning the atmosphere and demoralising the rest of the team. Buck up."

They are asked to leave at 5:30. School security comes to tell them a fleet of Aegis cars is waiting to take them home.

Mathew hasn't managed to make aerodynamic arms for the drone.

"Let's hope they grade us on our teamwork and leadership skills, rather than productivity, hey, Erling?" Arkam says, catching Mathew as he takes the stairs towards the exit. He puts his hand on Mathew's arm, stops him, and turns him slightly, bending his head to look him in the eye. "I thought as much," he says. "Why are your eyes blue, Erling? You're not Caucasian."

Mathew shakes him off, saying. "They aren't. My Lenzes are."

"Are you still wearing Lenzes? I've moved on to X-eyte Wear. The natural look is more in now, you know. Changing your eye colour is a bit suspect." Mathew doesn't say anything. It takes a moment, and then it clicks for Arkam. "They weren't bought for you, were they? They belonged to your dad."

Mathew sighs. "What do you care?"

"Touchy. Very touchy. Your father was Soren Erlang, wasn't he? The Soren Erlang."

"Why? And what do you mean, the Soren Erlang?"

Arkam shrugs. "No reason. Just curious."

"What do you mean?"

"Look it up, Erling. Look it up."

"Look it up where?"

But Arkam doesn't respond. Mathew watches him skip down the last few steps and across the lobby.

Bastard, he thinks.

The journey in the car to the river is punctuated by blocked roads and detours.

Someone throws a bottle at the car as they drive through Covent Garden. It makes a surprisingly violent noise. The guard swears loudly, but the car doesn't slow. It keeps on driving, accelerating away from the trouble. The guard cranes his neck around, identifies the perpetrator, someone in the faceless mass behind a police barricade. It will all be on dronevision anyway.

The car drops Mathew by the Playhouse Theatre. The same people he travelled with in the morning are standing waiting. There's the same boat, the same ferryman, the same guard at the back, and the same boy wading in the filthy river to bring the boat in to shore.

The boat trip is slightly less unnerving the second time around. Mathew thinks it is possible to get used to anything. The people on the rooftops, their fires, and their makeshift shelters aren't a surprise. The front-row view of the drowning ancient city isn't so shocking.

The car and his guard from the morning are waiting for him at Greenwich. Sitting in its roomy back, Mathew sends an ETA to Leibniz as they crawl slowly up the hill, past the stuff hung to dry and the people in their tents and shacks on the common.

Mathew turns the dragons back on for light relief. They are bewildered. The last thing they remember is being in the school lobby.

As the dragons play around him, Mathew rolls out his Paper and displays the beebot design he'd worked on in class. He rotates it with his finger and makes some small adjustments. He thinks about Mr Lestrange, his lack of Nexus records, the meek way Clara's psychotic guard retreated, the acoustic amplifier. He thinks about Clara and her parents and her fear and anger over being watched.

Closing his eyes for a moment, he sees Mr Lestrange once again through the window of the upstairs bay window in Pickervance Road. Why is he watching her? Something tells him that if he can find a way into Mr Lestrange's house, he'll find the answer.

A meal is waiting in the kitchen when he gets home. Leibniz has set the table. Mathew sits as a plate of food and a drink are put in front of him. O'Malley is rubbing around his legs, mewing loudly, wanting attention after being home alone all day.

Grasping his knife and fork, Mathew says, "Thank you, Leibniz. I appreciate it."

"You're welcome, Mathew."

Mathew knows he is talking to a complex computer program and not a person, but it seems rude not to thank Leibniz. "I made robots today," he says.

"I am a robot, Mathew," Leibniz replies.

Mathew thoughtfully scrutinises his machine. He says, "I know you are. But what does it feel like to be a robot?"

But Leibniz just blinks. The light on its chest panel indicates thought cycles quickly, in the way it does when it's crashing, and then turns red.

Mathew sighs, "Cancel conversation." When that doesn't work, he says, "Reboot."

Leibniz's lights go off. When it starts again, it immediately goes off to wash the dishes.

On the Canvas, there's a report of a suspected terrorist attack on crops in Texas by Mexican separatists. They have destroyed hundreds of thousands of acres of specially designed drought-tolerant crops aimed at easing the latest food crisis in the southern US.

The governor of Texas is interviewed. He says, "This is a particularly cynical and evil act, given the humanitarian crisis we have here right now. But those responsible should know we will not be intimidated and will stand against them using any means necessary."

Amongst those interviewed in the report is Minister Eben O'Hingerty, founder of the Edenist movement, whose activists were first thought to be responsible for the sabotage.

O'Hingerty says, "We are against these genetically modified crops. They are an abomination in the sight of the Lord. They are an example of the extreme arrogance of today's scientists wanting to play God, when they know no more than children. We believe these kinds of monstrous experiments with nature will have dire consequences for all of humankind. At this time in human history, when nature is teaching us all what happens when men interfere with laws laid down by God, we should know better. But the Edenist movement operates within the law and the democratic process. We condemn this sabotage as a terrorist act and are at one with the government in standing against these separatists. We offer our full support to the police in hunting down the culprits."

Mathew is imagining what his grandmother will say when she sees the BBC showing an interview with the leader of the Edenist movement whilst boycotting the leader of the Garden Party. He makes a mental note to ask her.

When his mother comes home, they sit in silence in the kitchen. When she asks him what he's done all day, he starts to tell her about his trip to town and his robotics class. Normally, she would quiz him, but she just nods, gazing at her food, prodding at it with her fork.

"Mum, can I ask you something, or are you too tired to talk?"

She straightens herself, guilty. "No. Of course not. You can ask me anything."

"How did Grandma get to Elgol?"

His mother raises an eyebrow. "Being at home alone is giving you too much time to think. But if you really want to know, she was invited to join when she was living in London."

"She lived with us?"

"Yes, when she first came to England, she lived here for eighteen months. Don't you remember?"

He shakes his head.

"You were little, I suppose. She was told there was a plot available at Elgol by someone she met at a Garden Party meeting."

"She was in the Garden Party?"

"Yes, Mat, we all supported the Garden Party. Grandma, your dad, me. A long time ago."

"You did?"

"Yes."

"And now?"

"Things have changed."

"You've changed?"

"Perhaps."

"But not Grandma?"

"She was always a bit stronger in her views than me. But you have to remember what she went through in China."

"What did she go through in China?"

"Drought. Famine. Riots. Awful things."

"My car drove across the common this morning. That's pretty awful."

"Yes, it is. But it could be much worse."

He struggles to imagine how. He says, "Don't you worry, with her so far away?"

"Of course. But to be honest, I think she's safer there than we are here."

"Even considering what's happened to Cadmus Silverwood and the opposition?"

"Yes, even considering that."

Hoshi stands, and Leibniz moves in to take her plates. She extends her hand to Mathew, "Come on, we should get some sleep."

11 THE FIRST SPACE WAR

DAY FOUR: Thursday, 25 November 2055, London

Mathew is dreaming of his father.

They are on holiday in Elgol, at the beach. It is one of those endless summer days. The heat shimmers over the sand. In the dream, he is grown, older than he is now, but his father and mother are young. The three of them are standing waist-deep in water, throwing a ball around in a circle. His mother is laughing, splashing water at his father. Mathew is happy. His grandmother is sitting on the beach with his Japanese grandfather, who's wearing sunglasses and a business suit and is reading a paper book, even though he is dead and Mathew has never met him. His Danish grandparents are walking away along the water's edge; their backs retreat and blur with the heat haze on the horizon.

There is someone else there too, not in sight, a stranger.

"Come and play ball," Mathew's father says to the stranger.

The familiar, disembodied voice says, "Carry on. I'll watch. Don't let me disturb you."

There is a strange, distracting noise that doesn't belong. It's trying to pull him away, but he doesn't want to leave the dream because he wants to stay with his dad. He wants to ignore the noise, wants it to go away.

Awake suddenly, eyes open, he hears it clearly. It says, "Mathew!"

It's his mother outside his door. Not her normal morning voice. She is stressed, worried.

Something is wrong.

He climbs carefully over O'Malley, asleep next to him, clambers free of the bed, his foot catching in a sheet. He stumbles over to the door and opens it.

"What is it? What's happened?"

His mother is pale, shocked, disbelieving.

"Have you heard the news?"

"No. I was asleep."

"Come and see," she says, and she leaves him to follow.

He is close behind her all the way to the kitchen. She sits on a chair, her eyes on the Canvas.

The prime minister is being interviewed. Text is cycling fast across the bottom of the screen. "US Battlestars destroyed. Hypersonic aircraft attack US and allied military bases worldwide."

The prime minister is standing on the steps of 10 Downing Street, surrounded by reporters. He's saying, "I have spoken to the president of the United States and the leaders of NATO and can confirm that at 2200 hours GMT last night the NATO Battlestars Heracles, Pallas, and Polemos were destroyed by enemy missiles. The Battlestars were in the process of being evacuated when they were hit. Ninety-seven crew are unaccounted for at this time. The Japanese moon base and space station were active in assisting the survivors. In addition, the RAF and USAF have told me that hypersonic craft have attacked bases on British soil at Lakenheath, Mildenhall, Croughton, Molesworth, Welford, Menwith Hill, Fairford, and Alconbury. Similar attacks were reported at bases in Belgium, Cyprus, Germany, Portugal, Norway, Spain, Italy, Turkey, Poland, India, Korea, and Japan. This is an entirely unprovoked attack against the US, Britain, and our allies. It is with a profoundly heavy heart that I have to tell you, as of last night we are at war with China and Russia."

His mother stands and walks away from the Canvas to take a call.

"Of course," she says. "I understand. Yes."

She hangs up and studies Mathew's face.

He says, "They want you in at work?"

"Yes. Will you be okay?"

"Yes."

"Don't leave the house."

"I wasn't planning to anyway."

"Good."

"I'll call to check on you later."

"I'll be fine. Don't worry."

After his mother has left, he calls his grandmother. She sounds relieved to hear from him.

"Mathew! I was going to call. Are you okay?"

"Of course we are."

"I was worried sick."

"They attacked military bases. Not towns. Not cities."

"For now. But god knows what will happen next. If things escalate, London is a short flight from Moscow. Is your mother there? I'd like to speak to her."

"No, she went into work."

"That company of hers has no conscience. They'll have her working overtime now. Listen, Mathew, you should come and stay with me until this situation ends."

"I won't leave Mum."

"It would probably help her to know you will be safe."

"No. I'm sorry. I can't leave her."

"Hopefully this will be sorted quickly. I heard the German prime minister is chairing talks between the US and China today. I think the US is probably bluffing the negotiations to buy some time while they plan a counterattack."

Mathew says, "Cadmus Silverwood warned this would happen."

"Yes, he did."

Mathew pauses and then says, "You know, you mentioned your friend who helped set the alternative service up for you?"

"Did I?"

"Only in passing. Not specifically."

"Oh. Good. I worry what I do and don't say sometimes. It's my age, I think. Or maybe I've always been this way. What do you want with my friend?"

"Do you think he would help me?"

"What kind of help? You said everything is fine."

"It's just something I'd like to research. It's a bit unorthodox."

"Nothing serious, though, Mat?"

"I don't think so."

"Nothing that will get you into trouble?"

"No," he says definitely.

"Now I am worried."

"Please."

She sighs. "I'll find out if my friend is available for a chat."

"Thanks, Grandma."

"You're not going to get me in trouble with your mother, are you?"

"No."

"Good. I don't want to give her any excuse to make it difficult for me to talk to you."

"She's too busy to notice, anyhow."

"I'm sure that's not true. I've got to go. The milkman is here wanting his barter veg. He has wonderful cream."

Mathew laughs, "Okay. Speak soon."

Mathew is glued to the Canvas, watching the war coverage on the news, with O'Malley sitting in his lap. There is little new information and mostly commentary. He is considering going to find out what people are saying on the Blackweb and Psychopomp when Leibniz appears in front of him holding a tray containing an elaborate non-alcoholic cocktail, including a pineapple chunk on a cocktail stick.

"You have an appointment now, Mathew. Your supervisory meeting with Nan Absolem."

"I'd totally forgotten! Is it in the Darkroom?"

"Yes, Mathew."

He meets Nan Absolem on a beach. She is lying on a deck chair, dressed in a sarong, wearing sunglasses and a sunhat. Waves crash into the shore behind her.

"Isn't this nice? Some might consider it a little self-indulgent under the circumstances, but I think we must raise our spirits in difficult times," she says, smiling broadly. "You seem a little tense. Is it the news?"

"No. It's not the news," Mathew says, although, in fact, he is unnerved by it.

"What is it then? The collaboration session yesterday? You needn't worry. It wasn't that bad."

"Thanks."

"You were doing well in the morning."

"Until I pitched the beebot. Yes, I know."

"At least you know. Do you want to talk through what went wrong?"

"No, it's okay. I met with Eva Aslanova."

"Yes. My Russian colleague told me. And?"

"I think we'd work well together."

"So do we."

"Have you spoken to anyone at the school about me using the Yinglong project towards my collaborative credits if I work with Eva?"

"Mathew, it might be difficult now, given the political situation," Nan says.

"Of course. I didn't think."

"I don't know what the school and the education board will say. I'm assuming the situation with Russia means there will be restrictions. I need to ask. I hope you'll continue to work together."

"I do too."

"Is there anything wrong?"

He says, "No, I'm absolutely fine. Although the journey to school was unnerving." This at least was true.

"You're not the only one to say so. We were discussing whether to continue the collaborative module via the holovision for the time being."

"That would be better."

"Yes, it might be sensible. Now shall we talk through your study plan? How's the AI module going?"

Mathew is grateful for the strict timetable his learning schedule keeps him to. He needs to complete a certain number of elective courses a day to keep on track. Inspired by the robot project, he completes a course on the use of bacteria to build circuits, challenging enough for him to block Mr Lestrange, his father, and the war from his mind.

At four o'clock he is at the window watching Clara slide out of the back seat of her car. She gazes at his window, spots him, smiles and raises her hand. He raises his own hand in response and smiles back.

"Hi, Mathew," she messages publicly for the benefit of the guard.

"Hi," Mathew returns.

The guard shakes his head, getting back into the car.

She steps onto the pavement and says, "Where were you yesterday?"

"I had to go in to school."

"That sucks."

"Yeah. Did you miss me?" He can hardly believe what he's saying.

He watches her smile, but she says, "Are you okay for me to come over, like we discussed? Can I come after my lesson?"

"Yeah, come," he says.

Clara disappears from view below the window frame. He hears the doorbell and then the door slam.

Mathew refocuses on the house next door, fully expecting to

come face to face with Mr Lestrange. He is surprised and strangely disappointed when he doesn't. He adjusts the zoom on his Lenz to "tele." But Mr Lestrange is not there.

As he's searching for his neighbour, the acoustic amplifier automatically switches on, detecting noise from Gen Lacey's house. Clara's music starts streaming into his room, which makes him think of her on the stage at the Wigmore Hall and her absorption in playing, her face transcendent. He is drawn downstairs to the living room, where he knows she is sitting only a few feet away from him, on the other side of the wall, playing Gen's grand piano.

Sitting on the floor, with his back to the wall, he closes his eyes.

She is playing something gorgeous and sad he hasn't heard before. When she's finished, she and Gen discuss adding it to the programme of an upcoming concert. Their voices are so familiar and close. They have nothing to do with his school or his family or anything causing him pain. More than anything right now, he wants to be back in Gen's front room talking to Clara.

It occurs to him just before she arrives that he should make some kind of attempt to clean his room. He runs upstairs and frantically shoves clothes into the washing basket and bits of electronics into a drawer, and instructs Leibniz to give the room a quick hoover and polish. The doorbell rings, and he runs downstairs, tripping on the top step and nearly falling.

Straightening himself, he takes a deep breath and then walks more slowly and opens the door.

Strangely, when they are face to face, he's startled to actually see her there and stands struck dumb for a few seconds longer than either of them is comfortable with.

She smiles awkwardly. "Hi," she says. "Can I come in?"

"What? Oh. Yeah. Come in," he stands back to let her pass and closes the door behind her. "Won't your guard have a meltdown about you visiting me?"

"He seemed fine about it."

"I would have thought he'd be even more paranoid, now we're at war."

"God, the war! It doesn't seem real to me."

"Me neither."

There's another awkward pause. They are staring at one another. She has noticed his blue Lenzes, he realises, and is probably thinking much the same thing that Arkam did, but perhaps with a little less malice. Her eyes are naturally blue. He knows he should speak and thrashes around in his head for something to say. "Do you want a drink?" he asks finally.

She shakes her head. "I can't be too long. The guard . . ."

"Oh, right. Yes." He puts his hands in his pockets, pulls them out, and wraps them round his body, then realises this is defensive, and holds them in front of him awkwardly. "Shall we go upstairs?"

She nods. He starts to move and then says, "After you."

"I don't know where we're going," she says.

"Oh, yeah. Right," he says.

Reaching his bedroom door, he quickly shoos Leibniz out of the room.

"Don't make him go," Clara says. "I've never seen a HomeAngel before. I've only seen the commercial ones."

"They're not much different," Mathew says, but he calls Leibniz back to meet Clara.

"It must be cool having one of these," she says, smiling as Mathew tells Leibniz that Clara likes it, and Leibniz blushes. It is a corny basic programme, but it amuses most people.

Clara says, "We have the bathroom and kitchen cleaners like everyone else, robot vacuum cleaners and floor mops, and of course a replicator, but we can't afford a HomeAngel."

"Hardly anyone can. They're given as corporate perks, mainly. My mum works for Panacea."

"Lucky you. I take it your health insurance is free, as well."

"I guess." Mathew opens the door to his bedroom. As Clara follows, he's relieved to note that Leibniz has done a good job of cleaning.

"Nice room," Clara says, peering around. "Very tidy."

Mathew thinks he catches a mischievous glint in her eye, but she walks over to his desk and the window before he can be sure. He follows her and stares across at Lestrange's bay window. There's no one there.

"He normally stands there," he says.

"When did you first notice him watching me?"

"Monday."

"Perhaps it was just a coincidence?"

"He was there when you arrived and left on Monday, Tuesday, and Wednesday. I wasn't here yesterday."

"But not now. Was he there when I got here?"

"No. Perhaps he's realised we know he's watching."

"Are you sure he was watching me?"

"What do you mean?"

"Perhaps he was watching someone else on the street. Someone who isn't here now."

"He was definitely watching you."

They both scan the empty room of the house next door for a few moments. She says, "So I wanted to explain to you about why I was so angry the other day. I didn't want to do it on Consort for obvious reasons. I told you before, my parents are being watched and harassed. I wasn't joking."

"Watched by who?"

"Some government agency. The Secret Intelligence Service, probably."

"But how do you know they're watching them?"

"It's been going on for the last three years. Maybe more. They started to notice about three years ago. Little things. For instance, they were overcharged for car hire. There were fines for late payments of taxes and utility bills. Salary payments went missing. We'd get sudden inexplicable power and Nexus blackouts at home. These things didn't happen all at once, but in a steady trickle, and they were always sorted. The money was always refunded. Errors always corrected. There were always apologies. But it required lots of time and effort to resolve each of these incidents, and it was incredibly stressful and unnerving."

"Why did this happen? What did your parents do?"

Her smile is twisted. "My dad was a Garden Party activist. In his day job he teaches politics, but in his spare time he wrote for this online journal. He was investigating claims that the Popular Party was imprisoning opposition members without trial and disappearing some of them.

"At first when the strange things started to happen, my parents were defiant, but it wore them down. So my dad stopped doing his investigation, he stopped writing for the journal. They even cancelled their memberships to the Garden Party. Things did get better, but last month we came home and the back bedroom window was open. You know as well as I do, no one opens windows anymore. We certainly didn't open it. So you might understand why, when I'm told someone is watching me, I might be a bit jumpy."

Mathew doesn't know what to say. After a long pause he says, "Clara, I'm sorry."

"Please don't be. I'm the one who should be sorry. But you do understand a little bit now, don't you?"

"Yes, yes. Of course I do."

"Unfortunately, these days I think everyone is watching us. I'm totally paranoid."

"No. No, you're not. You're absolutely right."

"I should be going," she says.

"Okay."

"Thanks for letting me explain. And sorry once again for being so rude."

He shakes his head. "Doesn't matter."

They walk downstairs. "I'm going to find out about him," he says. "I'm going to find out about Lestrange."

She frowns. "Don't do anything stupid," she says, opening the door and walking into the heat. "Remember what happened to my parents."

12 THE BEEBOT

After Clara has gone, Mathew sits for a while on the bottom step of the stairs with O'Malley butting against his knees and climbing on and off his lap as if to protest against this unusual arrangement.

A message comes to him, floating above his face. It says:

`Special offer! Free technical support. Say 'Yes' to connect.`

"Ignore," Mathew says brusquely. He and his mother are unlisted for advertising.

`This is an offer you shouldn't ignore! Please say 'Yes' to connect.`

The words float above him like a swarm of gnats, and he knocks them away with his hand. They disperse and regroup, undeterred.

"Oh, for . . ." Mathew is exasperated. "System. Please check privacy settings."

A menu appears before him, and the settings are as they should be. The system should only receive messages from their allow list or flag a warning before any unsolicited messages get through.

Mathew says out loud, "Okay. Whoever you are, how are you

screwing with our privacy settings?"

This offer was forwarded by a family member. Please say 'Yes' to connect.

Then the penny drops. It is the help he's asked his grandmother for. "Yes," he says.

A Charybdis Blackweb session opens.

"Hi, I'm Wooden Soldier. A mutual friend said you wanted to connect?"

"Yes! Thanks. I'm Mathew. I didn't get it."

"No problem, but no real names here, please. We like to keep the environment clean and secure. I'll assign you a handle for the duration of the call. You will be Tin Drum."

"Okay. I've never actually spoken to anyone on the Blackweb before."

"It's best if you don't use that word."

"Oh. Yes. I thought we were safe here."

"It's not like using the Nexus. You're not listened to all the time, but as you never know who or what is listening, you should behave as if you are. What do you need help with?"

"Are you any good at searching?"

"For?"

"For people with no presence on the Nexus."

"It's an interesting request. Who is it you want to search for?"

"My neighbour."

"What's he done?"

"I think he may be a government spy."

"Whoa! Why do you think that?"

"Because no one knows him, he never leaves the house, and every day of the curfew I've caught him spying on Clara."

"No names. Let's call her Goshawk. Who is she?"

"She comes for piano lessons next door."

"Is there some reason the government would be interested in her?"

"No. I don't think so, anyway."

"Then why do you think he's spying on her?"

"Because I see him watching Cl – I mean Goshawk – each afternoon. He's got an intense stare."

"Maybe he's just a perv."

"Maybe. Isn't that as bad? Also, her parents were Garden Party members."

"Whoa! Man, you really need to watch your language. Seriously. How long has your watchful friend lived there?"

"I don't know. All my life. I guess sixteen years. Maybe more."

"How long has Goshawk been coming for piano lessons?"

"I've no idea. Maybe a couple of years, at most."

"If he's really a spy, it's unlikely it's Goshawk he's spying on, if he's spying at all. It's more likely someone living in your road. Or you. Have you thought of that?"

"No. I hadn't."

"From what I know about our mutual friend, I'd say it's a possibility."

"What do you mean?"

"You must know."

"No, I don't. Enlighten me."

"Best not talk about it here. Have a think about it. So why do you say he has no presence on the Nexus?"

"There's no record of him on the Nexus. I checked."

"That is strange. But a spy would normally have a record – a squeaky clean false identity provided by the government. Perhaps he's anti-tech. There's a movement, you know. Our mutual friend is part of it. Respect to them."

"If he was anti-tech, he'd probably be a radical, wouldn't he?"

"Ouch. Language, man. I'm not joking, Tin Drum. He could be anyone. But given your family background it's probably worth investigating. I told our mutual friend I would help. I'll boost encryption for this next bit. Hang on. One, two, three. Okay. We have sixty seconds. What's his real name?"

"August Lestrange."

"Let's call him Ithaca. I'll try. Next time you get an advert . . ."

"I'll read it. Thanks, Wooden Soldier."

"No problem, Tin Drum."

After Wooden Soldier logs off, Mathew sits for a while thinking about Mr Lestrange. Then he remembers the beebot. It's waiting ready on his Paper. Using the 3D printer in his mother's office, he can print a more flexible range of materials at finer resolution than on the one in his bedroom. While it's printing, he sits in the kitchen watching the news and eats a meal prepared by Leibniz.

The newsreader is reporting a deadlock at the talks in Munich, when she suddenly looks surprised. A faint smile passes across her face before she recovers her composure.

She says, "News just in: The US has successfully completed a daring counterattack. We have footage, yes, released from Washington, actual footage of some of the action. I have, via satellite link from Washington, Commander Brian Kips. Commander, I understand you will talk us through what happened."

"Yes, ma'am. Yesterday, when our bases were attacked, we were able to trace where the attacks were launched from. Many of the aircraft on the ground at our bases were destroyed, but we did get some away. Fortunately, we also have a number of mobile bases for hypersonic aircraft and missiles. We needed a little time to coordinate, but this morning we managed to deploy significant resources against our enemies and destroy not only those bases we know were responsible for the attacks on our servicemen and women, but many other key military targets as well, including intelligence command centres. We believe this action was necessary to disable any further attempts at aggression against us and our allies."

The film footage was taken from the hypersonic planes and has been slowed considerably. It shows one explosion after another.

"Commander Kips, please stay with us. We have more breaking news. We have reports that the Chinese moon base, space station, and several military satellites have been destroyed. Are you able to comment, Commander?"

"I believe that is true information."

"Will you confirm the US received support from Japan in this operation?"

"I am not able to confirm at this time, although, as you know, Japan is one of the nations under attack by China and Russia. They have the right to defend themselves."

The printer in his mother's office beeps. The beebot is ready.

It is the length and width of a little fingernail, scaled slightly from the blueprint of the agricultural version. It's beautiful in its miniature perfection, complete with compound eyes, antennae, thorax, and proboscis but no sting.

He carries it on his fingertip to the kitchen.

To control the beebot he uses an off-the-shelf plug-in for the hologame environment. Sitting in the Darkroom, he can drive the beebot using controls designed for a flight simulator game, and he's inside the beebot. His perspective is beebot scale, and through its eyes the world is huge.

He takes off and flies around Leibniz in the kitchen. Through the tiny cameras on the front of the machine, Leibniz is the size of a skyscraper.

He flies his spying machine along the kitchen counter, above the kitchen table. Landing on top of the Canvas, he grasps onto the wafer-thin membrane with the tiny claspers at the end of the beebot's feet, and then he takes off again.

As he circles the kitchen, the dragons go after him, swatting at the robot insect. If they were able to make contact, they'd send it plummeting from the air, but their efforts are futile. Looping around in insect-like randomness, he makes the dragons hurtle off and crash. When they recover and come back, he tries to engage in a genuine dogfight with them, improving his mastery of the controls.

He flies into the hallway, takes a tour around the living room, back again into the hall, and then directly up the stairwell, dragons in tow. Bringing the beebot to rest on the landing carpet, he walks under his mother's bedroom door, does a circuit around her bedroom, and then hovers by the keyhole, managing to land next to it and walk through to the other side.

After a few hours of flying the beebot around the house, he's ready for its real mission.

Later, he sits with his mother, watching the news.

Saul Justice, the prime minister, is being interviewed, announcing new security measures to be rushed through Parliament that day.

"Today, Parliament declared a state of emergency and passed legislation to help the emergency government make provisions for public safety and the preservation of our country, now we are at war. It will allow us to maintain public order and to manage the control of food, energy, water, and other things essential for us to carry on as normally as possible as a community in these exceptional times. Britain has a long and proud democracy, and it is always regrettable when we as citizens have to relinquish some power, but I can assure you my greatest priority is your safety, and I will do everything necessary to protect this country and its people."

"What does that mean?" Mathew asks his mother.

"I don't know," she says. "I expect we'll find out soon enough."

13 BOOKS THAT WRITE THEMSELVES

DAY FIVE: Friday, 26 November 2055, London

After his mother leaves for work and Mathew has had breakfast and checked into school, the beebot gets one more test flight around the house. Then he takes it to the front door, places it gently on the tiles in the porch, and goes to the Darkroom and logs in. A beebot-eye holographic view of the front garden materialises in front of him.

Flying the little machine upwards, he avoids the olive tree and moves above the rooftops of the houses on Pickervance Road.

It hasn't occurred to him that anything would be different. As his mother requested, he's stayed in the house. But things are different now.

Through the eyes of his tiny robot, he sees military helicopters swarming across London. Soldiers are standing by anti-aircraft guns on the top of a block of flats nearby. At the end of the street, there's a roadblock and yet more soldiers. It crosses his mind that they are likely to have surveillance equipment capable of recognising his beebot.

Flying towards number twenty-one, he hovers around the front door, searching for a keyhole. Many people nostalgically keep legacy keyholes, even though keys are obsolete. A few years ago there was a fashion for having keyholes fitted on doors that didn't have them.

Number 21 doesn't have a keyhole. There's no quaint, old-fashioned letterbox to be wedged open, either. The door is flush in its frame. Manoeuvring the beebot around the walls of the house, he surveys the lower floor. The back is sealed by the conservatory; there's no way in there.

He flies to the roof. Some of these old houses have gaps around the eaves, as he knows well, because a few years ago there was a wasp's nest in their own loft. He spends several minutes searching for a way in before it strikes him the house has a chimney. There's no way of knowing whether the chimney is blocked off or not, unless he goes down. For a few minutes he circles the red clay top of the chimney, peering into the darkness.

The beebot isn't fitted with lights or infrared vision. As he starts to descend, he's blind, but he's able to use the intelligent software bundled with the package he's downloaded to auto-drive the beebot by bouncing radar off the brickwork. If he'd tried to drive himself, he would have become disorientated and likely crashed the little robot into the side of the chimney.

As it happens, Mr Lestrange hasn't blocked off his chimney, and the beebot comes into the light, flying into a room. He loops around the light fitting and lowers the beebot onto the uncarpeted floor, then turns it slowly on its feet to get a 360° view of the room.

It's a bedroom. There's a double bed with tree-trunk-sized wooden legs, a wardrobe, and a sideboard the height of the Shard in relation to the beebot. It's a normal bedroom, except it's meticulously clean and tidy, as though no one uses it.

Flying the beebot around the room, he notices that the wardrobe door is slightly ajar, and he squeezes into it. It's full of clothes, neatly hung, unworn, and like new. Carefully, he edges free again, flies to the door, and walks under it.

The floorboards on the landing shine, cleaner than those in Mathew's own house and surgically spotless. Perhaps Mr Lestrange has a newer model HomeAngel.

He scutters along the hallway with tiny, quick bee feet and under the door of the bedroom at the front of the house, the one with the bay window, where Lestrange watches Clara.

This is much like the back bedroom, with all the normal bedroom furniture, and immaculate and unlived in. There are no personal possessions lying around, no worn clothes lying across chairs, no hairbrushes, Papers, ePinz, or spare Lenzes.

But these must be spare rooms. Mr Lestrange lives alone, and this is a big house for a single person. He walks back under the door and takes a quick tour of the bathroom, buzzing through the open door, noting the absence of cleaning robots and the pristine state of the sink, the toilet, and the shower.

There's another bedroom, the third and last. This room is empty but for an upholstered armchair and a telescope on a stand pointing towards an unadorned up-and-down sash fenestration, the size of a cathedral window from the perspective of the beebot. It has a view across the back garden.

The house is a mirror image of his own, with the kitchen at the back, a front room, and a dining room. The kitchen extends into a conservatory containing some plants, orange and lemon trees, and a number of orchids on a small, low table. The kitchen is modern, containing the usual SuperChef Replicator food maker, sink, waste disposal unit, cupboards for storage, dining table and chairs, and fridge.

Winging to where the old dining room is in his house, he crawls under the door into blackness. It's a Darkroom, like his, with a couple of chairs. There are small boxes in the top corners of the room and at various points around the sides, containing cameras; standard equipment.

There's only one room left. He crawls under the door to the

front room. In its dimensions, it's exactly like the room in Gen Lacey's house and the mirror image of his own front room, with large, light bay windows at the front. But this room doesn't have a sofa, armchairs, or a Canvas like most lounges.

It's a library. The walls are fitted from floor to ceiling with bookshelves filled to bursting with old paper books of the type people rarely keep in their houses anymore, unless they are special presents, like the Chinese books Ju Chen bought Mathew for his last birthday. It's a lot like his grandmother's library in Elgol.

The beebot flies alongside the shelves, its eyes combing decorative book spines, some colourful, some with elaborate bindings and gold-leaf lettering. From their titles, they are history books, ordered by chronology from the farthest bottom right corner of the room, climbing through the centuries along each shelf section. He flies past strange words: Palaeolithic, Neolithic, Mesopotamia, Harappan, Egypt, Kingdom of Kush, Indus Valley, Vedic, Xia, Shang, Sassanid, Delian League, Maurya, Gupta, Dravidian, Aksumite. The letters are huge compared to the beebot.

Then there are more familiar words, like Greece, Rome, Byzantium, Ottoman, Mayan, and Aztecs. From things his grandmother has told him, he recognises the Qin and the Han. The book's subjects become more familiar: the Dark Ages, the Middle Ages, the Holy Roman Empire, the Renaissance, the Enlightenment, the French and Russian Revolutions, the Industrial Revolution, the First and Second World Wars, the Cold War, Information Age, Globalisation, the World Council. It's like he is flying along human history itself. Then he notices something that stops him in his tracks.

Launching from the shelf, he circles the beebot around the room to go back and survey it again.

But he hasn't imagined it.

There on the shelf is a book with the title "World War III."

Landing the beebot, he stops for a moment to make sure he's recording. As he does so, the door to the room swings open and Mr Lestrange hurries to the table standing in the bay window. There's a book lying there. He opens the cover and bends over it. Carefully, Mathew takes off from the shelf and flies to the table, hovering above Mr Lestrange's head. From here he is able to take in the book, adjusting the focus of the beebot's eyes and zooming in on the page.

Lestrange's eyes are staring at the words on the left page. The beebot follows his gaze.

The words are rewriting themselves as Lestrange reads. The old words turn red, a line runs through them, the letters waver for a moment and then disappear as new letters and words appear. The beebot focuses in further.

Mathew reads:

```
Mathew Erlang focuses the beebot cameras on the words
in the book and starts to read what is written, profoundly
shaken to realise he is reading about himself.
```

Mr Lestrange's gaze peels from the book and turns around. Mathew watches as Lestrange's hand reaches towards the beebot, blocking his view of the room. He doesn't have time to react. In the Darkroom, his video feed suddenly goes dark.

Mathew sits in his chair for several moments. What he has witnessed is impossible, and he's stunned, not trusting his own eyes. Then he remembers he recorded it all, and he reboots the system to recover the file, and sets it to play.

There's nothing but static.

Thinking he may have loaded the file incorrectly, he tries again. Still receiving static, he initiates a routine to check for errors on the file. The file appears to be fine. He keeps trying, unable to process the fact that he has no way of knowing whether he saw something irrational or is losing his mind. As he sits there, trying the same things over and over in different order, something small comes into the room. It takes a circuit and then lands on the back of his hand.

It's the beebot.

Someone else has taken control of it. Text flashes fleetingly in front of Mathew, one word at a time. It says:

```
I think this is yours. It's a nice little robot, Mathew.
Why don't you use it to talk to Clara? She'll like it, I'll
bet.
Best regards,
Your neighbour.
```

In the Darkroom, Mathew's head is spinning, his brain struggling to process the words that just floated in front of him.

Then he's interrupted by a Consort message from Clara.

"Hi. It's me."

"Hey, there!"

"What are you up to?"

"I've just been visiting my neighbour."

"What?!"

"Not in person."

"I don't get it."

"I can't explain here. I'll tell you when you come round again."

As soon as he has hung up from talking to Clara, he's pinged again, this time via Charybdis.

```
Mathew. It is me: the girl building you a world. I will
ring your holophone on the Blackweb via a scrambled line in
half a minute. Please accept my call.
```

Mathew waits for thirty long seconds, and then the request comes through. Household security systems kick in:

```
Unverifiable call. Maybe a virus or a spam call. Warning.
Advise not to accept.
```

Mathew accepts the call. Eva appears before him sitting on the edge of her armchair. She seems nervous.

"I can't speak long," she says. "My father is at home, and he will kill me if he discovers I am calling you.

111

"We live on Tverskaya Street in Moscow, and yesterday there was a huge military parade. The usual thing with tanks and missiles, but there were also soldiers in exoskeletons and proper robot soldiers, seven or eight feet tall. They congregated in Red Square by the Kremlin. There were a lot of politicians and endless boring speeches; it was all over the TV. It was ridiculous.

"Anyway, the Kremlin is closing shared services with enemy states. They haven't shut ordinary Nexus connections yet, but I think that will happen within a day or so. They have shut down the servers I have with you, and I was issued with a warning. The whole country has gone insane."

"Eva, I am so sorry. The last thing I want to do is get you into trouble," Mathew says.

"Not at all. You are not the problem. Anyway, I wanted to ask you, given your government is probably as mad in its own way, if you still wanted to continue. It will take me a day or so, but I'm pretty sure I will be able to build the world on servers on the Blackweb. I have all the code copied to offline storage. I'll understand if you think it's too dangerous, but I suddenly feel more like doing this than ever. Do you think I'm a lunatic?"

"Yes."

Eva looks crestfallen.

Mathew says, "But so am I. Let's do it anyway."

Eva and her armchair have gone. The room is dark and then . . .

```
Offer  extended.  Unbelievable  value.  Absolutely  free
technical stuff. Say 'Yes' to accept. Why wouldn't you?
```

"Accept," Mathew says. "Hello, Wooden Soldier."

"Please call me No Right Turn. You're Hard Shoulder."

"Okay, No Right Turn."

"Greetings, Hard Shoulder. I have news."

"Great. I hope it wasn't risky."

"No! A little bit of hacking. So many organisations claim to have quantum security, but opening government and corporate records is as easy as opening the fridge. As it happens, you were right. Mr Lestrange of 21 Pickervance Road doesn't exist or, at least, not in a normal way."

"I'm listening."

"He does have a social security number."

Mathew is disappointed. "How is that not existing?"

"Wait a minute. Patience. There are also medibot records, an ID card, a bank account, and a passport.

"Well, it sounds to me like he does exist."

"All of his records are registered as current, but none were updated in the last sixteen years. His bank account hasn't been touched; it's accumulated interest, though. He's wealthy. It's amazing what compound interest does with time. There are no deposits or withdrawals registered; he's not left the country, although his passport was auto-renewed, as was his ID card, the usual in-person interview waived. The weirdest thing is his medibot data. It's absolutely normal."

"Why is that weird?"

"No one's medibot information is absolutely normal, unless the data is fabricated. Your man truly doesn't exist, Hard Shoulder. If it's okay with you, I'm going to examine his home network, try and get in and see if that reveals anything interesting."

"Are you sure you want to? What if you get caught?"

"Na, no bother. I'm curious now, anyway."

When his mother gets home, he's sitting in the kitchen, staring at the beebot he's placed on the table in front of him. Mr Lestrange and his library have got to him.

Hoshi is dazed with tiredness and preoccupied, but then, she always is these days. Leibniz serves her dinner, and she starts to eat in silence, intent on her food.

After a while, she looks up, remembering herself, and says to Mathew, "How was your day? You did stay in, didn't you?"

"Yes, I stayed in."

She nods slightly and carries on eating.

"So what did you do all day all alone in the house with no school? Were you working on your dragons?"

"Actually, I was working on that," he indicates with his head the little adapted crop pollinator.

"What is it?"

"A beebot."

"A what?"

"Here. Hold your hand flat." He carefully places it on her palm. "It's a miniature robot. I had the idea in our group class on Thursday. It doesn't seem much, but I'm able to fly it using software in the Darkroom. It has inbuilt cameras."

"It's amazing. So tiny."

"Actually, it's a 3D print of an industrial model for pollinating crops from a blueprint on the Nexus. I made it a little prettier and added the cameras."

She puts the beebot back in his palm. "It's wonderful, but isn't it work? Shouldn't you be doing something different on your day off?"

"I enjoy doing these things."

"Did you exercise? Did you go for a run using the holovision?"

Mathew shakes his head. "I was too busy."

"I'm not sure this curfew is good for you. You need to do some exercise – otherwise, we'll be having our GP ringing up wanting to review your medibot records, threatening to cancel your insurance. At least, play an active game or something. Anything to get you moving."

"Okay, I will. I promise."

"Did you do anything else? Speak to anyone?"

Mathew recalls Eva and Wooden Soldier. "No," he says.

"I hope this curfew is over soon and we can get back to normal. You need to see people."

"Do you think it likely now, with the war?"

She sighs, "No. No, I don't."

14 CHIPS

DAY SIX: Saturday, 27 November 2055, London

It's his mother's car and his mother's thick-necked guard. Mathew and Hoshi sit in the back facing one another across the table. The dragons are curled up, piled on top of each other on Mathew's lap. One of them is growling in its sleep.

"We're lucky to be called so soon," Hoshi says. "The longer people have to wait to get their biochip, the more difficult it'll be for them."

"I suppose Panacea arranged it for you?"

They stop at the newly erected roadblock at the end of their street while the police check their ID cards and speak to the driver. Then they leave Pickervance Road and pass the boarded-up shops. There is newly broken glass on the pavements.

The common is a hive of activity, with military vehicles, and police vans parked all over the place and people being herded from their shacks and makeshift shelters into buses and other vehicles.

"Where do you think they're taking them?" Mathew asks his mother, but she shakes her head.

A mile from their house, there's a makeshift passport office in tents and marquees on land belonging to Woolwich Artillery. They are dropped at the gates to the barracks and directed through the barbed-wire-topped chain-link fence to join a long queue of people.

They make it inside. A woman in uniform takes their ID cards, scans a list on her Paper, and checks them in.

She smiles at them reassuringly. "No need to worry. Everything is in order. Please take a seat."

She waves them through into the tent, where there's a waiting area. They sit at the back. A digital numbering system summons each person in the queue in turn via their Lenz. One by one people are called and disappear through a flap in the tent into another room.

Mathew and Hoshi wait their turn.

He sees Clara online using Consort and pings a message to her.

"Being chipped," he says.

"Ouch. I have my appointment next week. Are you okay?"

"Not sure."

"Call me later if you want to chat."

"Thanks."

"No problem."

Suddenly there are raised voices in the next room. Two of the soldiers standing to one side in the waiting room glance at one another and rush through the tent flap. A few minutes later they burst into view with a struggling man grasped between them.

"You are fascists!" the man is shouting, his voice hysterical. "This is fascism! You cannot do this! Let go of me!"

He slips free, but the soldiers immediately grab him again. They struggle, and he falls to the floor; one of them sits on him, and the other one ties his hands behind his back.

"Bastards!" the man spits, between his teeth. His red, angry face is squashed on the ground. Mathew remembers the guard in front of Gen Lacey's house and feels sick to his stomach.

Swearing and protesting, the man is taken from the tent. A little later, one of the soldiers is standing near Mathew's seat. Mathew leans across and whispers to him, "The man you arrested, what did he do?"

The soldier smiles at him, good-humoured enough, conspiratorial. "Least said, soonest mended, eh?"

Mathew's mother's number is called. She stands and smiles at him. "Don't worry. It will all be fine," she says and disappears through the tent flap.

A few minutes later, his own number floats before him with an invitation to join the main tent. A soldier lifts the tent flap for him. There is another tent beyond, partitioned into three rows of interview booths, separated by tall freestanding panels. As he's led to his booth, he passes his mother seated in front of a table, a man in a suit talking to her and working away at a Paper, a woman in a lab coat standing to one side, preparing something on the top of a tall trolley. He's urged forward and directed into a booth with another woman in a lab coat and another man behind a desk.

The man lifts his gaze, unsmiling, and stares at Mathew with suspicious, appraising eyes for a moment past politeness, and then says, "You are Mathew Erlang?"

"Yes."

"Sit down." The man turns to his Paper and starts to work at it. "ID card," he says, staring at his screen.

Mathew pulls his ID card from his pocket and places it on the desk. Still focusing his eyes on his Paper, the man grasps it, scans it with a barcode reader, and then puts it through a shredder.

"Nurse," the man says.

"Roll up your sleeve," the nurse says to Mathew. She is no friendlier than the man behind the desk. She is cold in her uniform. Her skin has goose bumps. The weather is turning, as it does, suddenly and with no warning. There's no heating in the tents.

The nurse has a needle attached to a wire, which in turn is attached to a machine on the top of the trolley. She swabs Mathew's arm roughly and plunges the needle into his median cubital vein.

The machine makes a series of beeps.

"Confirmed," the nurse says.

"Congratulations," the man behind the desk says, glaring at Mathew from his Paper. "You are who you say you are. You're lucky you have medibots. Your mother's corporate healthcare plan, I suppose. It makes this whole process a lot quicker."

The nurse presses a cotton pad with disinfectant onto the puncture wound on the inside of Mathew's arm and puts his fingers across it, indicating he should hold it there.

"I'm going to ask you some questions, while the nurse prepares your chip," the man says. "You are not British."

"I am British. I was born here."

"You don't look British."

"You mean I'm not white? Neither are the majority of the population."

The man is smiling slightly. "Your father was Danish. Your mother is of mixed Chinese and Japanese lineage."

"Yes."

"The Chinese connection is worrying, don't you think? Given the war?"

"My mother is a British citizen."

"I know. But she was born in China. It must be confusing for you both, this war."

"In what way?"

"Who to support. Who do you support?"

"I live here."

"That's an evasive answer."

"I am British."

"Don't think me rude, but I won't be the last person asking you these questions. A better response would be, 'I support Britain, America, and her allies and will do all in my power to ensure they win this war.' Something along those lines."

Anger rises within him. He thinks of the man being pinned to the floor in the waiting room and the guard attacking him in Gen

Lacey's garden. Taking a long controlled breath, he tries to suppress the blood flushing from his neck to his face.

"I believe in this country," Mathew says.

The nurse takes the wad of cotton from Mathew's arm, replaces it with another, and covers it with a plaster. "Bend forward." She moves him so his head is bowed and loosens his shirt from around his neck, pulling back the material. He tries to turn to watch what she is doing. She forces his head forwards, firmly. "You'll experience a small sting," she says.

Something cold presses against his skin, and then there is a hard punch and a sensation something like an insect bite. He draws his breath sharply between his teeth.

"All done," the nurse says.

"Congratulations," the man across the desk says again. "Welcome to the world of the living. Your bioID is active immediately. You will find it has a number of useful purposes, apart from allowing you to continue to live in your home. There's information on our web site, as well as a store where you can buy compatible applications and appliances. You may go," the man says, smiling a small, pained smile.

Mathew walks back to the waiting room, where his mother is sitting. He draws his fingers across the back of his neck, where there is a spreading numbness. There's also a small lump there, like the lump in O'Malley's neck, where he has his ID chip.

"Okay?" his mother says, standing.

Nodding his response, but he's not sure at all.

Back in his room, Mathew is sitting on his bed with his back to the wall recalling the morning. He can feel the chip under his skin, or at least he imagines he can. Somewhere in an office building, in a grey cubicle overhung with bad strip lighting, an SIS workstation running complex algorithms is registering his new bioID and assimilating all the data that's available about him, making connections, categorising, assessing, and rating him for risk. A computer has recorded his movements back from Woolwich. It knows he's now sitting in his bedroom. It knows when he logs on to the Nexus. It knows that his heart is beating a little too fast, that he is anxious, agitated. But it doesn't know, yet, what he is thinking and what he is planning to do.

As he stares at the rotating lunar landscape cycling on the far wall of his room, a message materialises in front of him. An advert for security software:

```
Act quickly to take advantage of this once-in-a-lifetime
offer!
```

"Accept," Mathew says, smiling. "Who am I today?"

"You're Difficult Child – I'm Sleeper. I have news."

"I'm all ears."

"Ithaca is unhackable. I know this will not especially impress you, but it impresses me. At first, I thought there wasn't even a network there. There is a fairly normal one, however, and something else, something beyond any kind of technology I've ever seen; and it's all rolled in a kind of wrapper like an opaque, slick, wet ball. Once you think you have a handle on it, it slips through your fingers, but not in any brutal kind of way. It's a curious thing. It's like it smiles at you before it goes. It's way beyond me. I'd like to get some other friends to check it out. Are you okay with that?"

"Go for it," Mathew says.

He pings Clara. "Back home," he says.

"How was it?"

"Horrible."

"Does it hurt?"

"Not much. It just makes me feel terrible. Like I'm no longer in control of myself."

"You never were."

"I guess. I have news about our friend. Can you come over tomorrow?"

"Yes, for a short while."

Later, Mathew and Hoshi are sitting in the kitchen watching the Canvas. They have eaten. A newsreader is announcing that the government is investigating plans to ban the Blackweb.

His mother studies him and says, "I don't want to know what you're up to. I don't want you to explain, but please be careful." She rises slowly. "I'm exhausted. I'm going to have an early night for once." She leaves the room and climbs the stairs slowly, wearily.

While Leibniz is cleaning around him, a written message comes through on his Lenz. It's from an unknown sender. It says:

> Don't believe everything you hear. Trust what you know. Remember the Nexus is physically in the control of the SIS. The Blackweb is not. Learn to use quantum key distribution. Photons generate an encryption key and anyone intercepting the key touches the photons. They can't find you without telling you they are searching for you. Work with people you trust to create a maze to play in. They will never find you.

"Who is this?" Mathew messages back.

But there is no response.

15 LETTING GO THE DRAGONS

DAY SEVEN: Sunday, 28 November 2055, London

Mathew wakes early and lies awake pondering the dragons and Project Yinglong. Still in his bedclothes, he sits at his desk and works on some fixes to align with Eva's code base. Building a little routine, he addresses the bulk of differences in syntax and edits the rest by hand. It's easier than he anticipated. He's decided to upload an updated version of the dragons' code base to Eva's world, so the dragons can grow, breed, and evolve.

His mother says her goodbyes through the door.

"Is O'Malley in there with you?"

"Yes, he's here."

"Don't let him out," she says.

"I won't!" he replies with slightly less conviction than he used to have.

After breakfast, he wanders aimlessly around the house, finds himself in the Darkroom and logs on to the Blackweb, where he discovers Eva present. He sends her a message.

"Can you talk?"

Her armchair materialises in the Darkroom. She has her legs

curled up in it and appears as comfortable as O'Malley does in his bed upstairs.

"How's the robot soldier rally going?" he asks.

"They've taken their sabre rattling on tour. It's in St Petersburg now. TV's still full of it, though. Good news is my dad has gone. He's a propagandist or journalist, take your pick, for one of our state-sponsored channels. He's gone to cover the circus, and I'm home alone."

"Great! Because the dragons are ready to be released."

"Good to know. Your world awaits you."

"Our government is threatening to close the Blackweb."

"Yes, ours too. But it's all talk."

"Yes, you said so last night."

"No, I didn't."

"Quantum key distribution. Remember?"

"I know it's one of the reasons they're going to have trouble shutting us down, but I didn't message you last night."

"Someone did. It came through on the Blackweb as an anonymous message. I thought it was you."

"Nope."

"That's odd."

"Why?"

"Because I don't know who else it could be." He thinks of his hacker friend. "Or maybe I do . . ."

"It could be a scatter message from some of the people on Psychopomp or MUUT reassuring their user base. They might be worried people will be frightened off the service. There are some things you should be doing, if you don't know already, to set traps around your connection and also to jump to random locations. I've virtualised all my data and hidden it dispersed in different places. The virtual worlds I'll create for you will be literally no place. But the first one is set up, so we should go."

"If you give me access, I'll upload the Yinglong code."

"Doing so now. Get your bits done and then meet me here in

five minutes. I've established some additional security. It represents itself visually to you, and I want to show you how to get through it."

He receives a location and then an invitation to a holosession and pulls on his skullcap. He doesn't sit, having a notion this session will be interactive.

After a few moments of darkness, foliage begins to grow all around him. At first, a single leaf sprouts from the Darkroom floor, curling upwards on a thickening stem, then others grow from the ceiling, crawling across the back wall. He has to move his foot as tendrils grasp at his ankle. Moving through the spreading green, he brushes leaves and branches from his face. Then before him is a large wooden door at the top of some grey steps in a high stone wall. The door has a round rusted iron handle. He tries to open it, but it's locked.

"You need to do this." Eva is suddenly beside him: a diminutive person, her head barely reaches his shoulder. He likes that she hasn't chosen to appear as an avatar. Or perhaps she has. He supposes he wouldn't know. She runs her hand along the wall. "Three across, fourteen down."

"Pi."

She smiles. "We'll keep changing it."

The brick comes loose. She retrieves a large key.

"There's no keyhole," he says.

She pulls a knife from a belt around her waist he hasn't noticed before.

"You have one too," she says.

He looks down at his waist. So he has.

She cuts her finger and smears a symbol on the door. It's the Greek letter gamma. "Again, we'll change it regularly."

A lock appears.

"How did you do that?" he says.

"It's reading my bioID."

"You got those too, huh?"

"We've had them for ages. There were never any civil liberties to speak of in Russia, remember."

"I suppose not."

"I'll enable it for you too, so you can come in on your own, anytime you like. We'll need to exchange a bit of data after this session."

Eva puts the key in the lock, and the door swings open.

They step into a large open space. A fertile grassland spreads before them, spotted with moss-covered granite rocks, rolling to mountains, skirted by forests. It is a lush alpine world.

"This is amazing, Eva," Mathew says.

They start to walk.

"The dragons are over there," Eva says, pointing.

He sees two crates, the sort used to transport animals, with wooden plank sides and bars at the front. As they approach, he spots the dragons, larger and wilder than the ones he has in the house. They're restless in the confined space and come towards them to the front of their crates, biting at the bars.

"You should let them go," Eva says.

"Yes." Mathew climbs onto one of the crates, the one housing the female, and raises the bars. She comes crashing out, stretching her wings, breathing fire. The grass in front of her singes black. In this world her actions do have consequences. Mathew is grateful it's only his virtual body that's vulnerable to harm. The female looks back toward her mate and lets go a tinnitus-inducing screech.

Mathew climbs onto the second crate and frees the male. In keeping with his programming, the second dragon leaves the crate more cautiously, sniffing at the unfamiliar grass, and spooking when Mathew jumps off the box.

The two dragons go to one another, bashing heads and wrapping necks. The female surveys acres of sky with her red and gold eyes. She beats her wings and lifts off, whirling around, climbing higher and higher above their heads, catching thermals. The little male clumsily follows after her.

They watch for a while as the dragons fly into the distance, their bodies illuminating periodically with fire.

"I think you may have a few forest fires on your hands," Mathew says.

Eva shrugs. "Hey, it's your world," she says. Then, turning and nodding in the direction of the forest behind them, she says, "I built you a hut, in case you wanted to come in here and explore and watch them for real, as it were, and stay for a while. There's real weather in this world, you know, and it's not always nice. Of course, you may prefer to watch them on your Paper."

She leads the way to a little copse. Sheltered amongst the trees is a small wooden house. They go inside. It's furnished rustically, with a log fire blazing in a wood burner, a rug on a rough wood floor, and a rocking chair with a blanket.

"It's a Russian hunting lodge," she says.

"I love it," Mathew says. "Thank you, Eva."

"It's the only house in any of my worlds. If you go through this door here, there's a shortcut back to reality."

He follows her through and finds himself back in the Darkroom, facing her in her armchair.

"Well, that was fun!" she says. "I'd better run. Let's keep in touch. If you want to discuss the world, or the dragons, or anything else, let me know."

"I will, for sure."

At four o'clock he's standing at his bedroom window. Clara's car makes its appearance in spite of the newly erected roadblocks, and he wonders if she's chipped too by now.

Mr Lestrange does not appear in his bay window. He thinks about what Wooden Soldier / No Right Turn / Sleeper said about Lestrange's home network being impenetrable and hopes his hacker friends are having some luck.

Mathew turns his gaze back to the road. Clara is staring right at him. She holds up her hand, half a salute, half a solidarity wave, and he mimics her gesture. She smiles and he smiles back, and then she disappears.

Automatically, he turns from the window and runs down the stairs. Clara's car is just turning out of the street.

Mathew steps over to the front door of the house next door. There is no bell, so he knocks and waits. Time passes. The door remains closed. He knocks again, louder. The door stays firmly shut in the sphynx-like house.

He looks at the window. The curtains are drawn. He's never noticed them drawn before, but then he's never really paid attention. He tries one last time.

"Mr Lestrange!" he says loudly to the unresponsive door. He opens the Nexus and searches for the house in the freely available directory, but then, of course, it isn't there. Lestrange has never broadcast any data. It's like his house is sealed. Whatever is in there, he really doesn't want anyone knowing about it.

Mathew glances over his shoulder. Across the line of garden walls, he can see the roadblock at the end of Pickervance Road. A couple of the soldiers are staring his way. He decides on a tactical retreat and goes back inside his own house.

Clara comes at five. They go to his room. He offers her his seat at his desk, sits on the edge of his bed, and gives her a summary of what he and his hacker friend have done to find out about Mr Lestrange.

"He might just have been out," she says when he tells her about knocking on his door.

"I don't think so. I don't think he goes out. Cars don't visit his house. I've never seen him on the street. It's so frustrating. His house is just there, through that wall. Last night I was lying awake thinking maybe I should just break in."

"You're not going to do that! Seriously?"

"No. Of course not."

She turns to scan the bay window. "You haven't seen him in the window again?"

Mathew shakes his head.

Her eyes drop to his desk, and she sees the beebot. "What's this?" she says. "Is this the thing you sent down his chimney?" She glances at him. He nods. She says, "Can I pick it up?"

"Yeah, you can't break it. It's pretty tough."

"It's so small!" She turns it over in her hand.

"We need a way to talk to one another," he says. "Privately, without fear of being listened to."

"Can't I just come here?" she asks, smiling cheekily.

He smiles, then blushes and coughs. "You can."

They both laugh.

Then he says, "But we can't really chat on Consort. It would be good if we could chat the way I talk to Wooden Soldier."

"I hate Consort anyway. It's a meat market."

"Exactly. And Nexus is mainlined to SIS. I wanted to talk to you privately because of what you said about your parents."

"So what do you suggest?"

"Guess."

"Wow… The Blackweb? No! Isn't that illegal?"

"Actually, it's not illegal. The prime minister is only threatening to outlaw it. He hasn't done it yet."

"But it's full of criminals and terrorists, isn't it?"

"I've never met any, if it is. But then I haven't used it long, to be honest."

"Won't SIS track us using it?"

"It's a lot harder for them to monitor us on the Blackweb than on the Nexus. But if you're worried, I won't do it."

"Actually, I think it's kind of exciting."

He smiles. She smiles.

"But I wouldn't know how to start. How do you even access it, anyway?"

He examines the beebot again and remembers Mr Lestrange's message, *Why don't you use it to talk to Clara?* He says, "I have an idea, but I don't know if I can make it work."

"What is it?"

"I might be able to turn the beebot into a Blackweb communication device."

"My guard is pinging me," she says, standing up.

He shows her downstairs. At the door, they reach for the latch at the same time, feel a sudden spark of electricity, and withdraw their hands like they've been bitten.

"Sorry!" they say at the same time and laugh.

He steps back.

She catches his eye, serious now. "Please be careful."

"I will," he says.

After she's gone, he sits at his Paper and starts to edit the beebot blueprint. As he works, he listens to a recording of Clara playing. Music is her gift to him, he thinks, so he will send her something in return.

"This is great, Leibniz," his mother says.

Like Mathew, she feels compelled to thank the robot for the things it does.

"You're welcome," Leibniz says.

"We're getting new locks," Hoshi says to Mathew.

"What's wrong with the old ones?"

"Nothing, but now we can use our bioID to open the doors rather than a hackable digital key fob we might lose."

"Surely our bioID details are freely available to the security services. Doesn't it mean they can march in here anytime they want to?"

"Not with these locks," his mother says, holding her son's gaze and smiling, somewhat mischievously, he thinks. "Anyway, the locksmiths are coming at 2:30 tomorrow afternoon to fit them, front and back of house and all of the windows. Will you let them in and make sure O'Malley doesn't get out?"

"Of course. No problem."

16 THE BEEKEEPER

DAY EIGHT: Monday, 29 November 2055, London

Nan Absolem is sitting in her office. The war has killed her exuberance, or perhaps she thinks it's a more fitting setting to pass on bad news.

"I'm afraid it's no go with Eva and your dragons project, Mathew. I'm sorry."

He considers whether he should tell her that he's already started working with Eva. He thinks better of it and says, "Oh. Bad news."

She doesn't notice how flat his voice sounds. She says, "Yes. I know. I did try. I argued that your project would be a symbol and hope of peace, a beacon in the darkness, but the school board, the regional education board, and the police thought it would be a security risk. I hope you're not too upset."

"No, it's fine. Really."

"I'm afraid it means we still need to find a way to get you collaboration credits. We're scheduling a holophone session on the Nexus with your robotics class."

"Alright."

"Are you okay?" she says.

"Yes. Why?"

"You're unusually agreeable."

"I was bioIDed yesterday," he says.

"Me too."

"The official who processed me said I wasn't British."

"Outrageous! Did you complain?"

"Who to?"

Nan thinks. She doesn't know what to say.

He says, "Don't worry, Nan. I'm going to do some courses on quantum computing and security, if that's okay."

"Sure, that's fine. Do you need anything from me?"

"No. Thanks. Not a thing."

The locksmiths arrive at 2:30 on the dot, a tall, thin, grey-haired man with a moustache, wearing a shirt and tie, and a younger man wearing jeans and a sweatshirt.

While the men are bringing in their tools, Mathew holds O'Malley. "We don't want him to get out," he says to the younger man. "I'll put him in here." He indicates the Darkroom. "The police will shoot him if he escapes, and there's a roadblock at the end of the street now, so the chances are high. Make sure you don't open the door. It's important."

"Are there any doors or windows in your Darkroom?" the younger locksmith asks.

"No."

"Then we won't be going in there."

Mathew fixes the Darkroom with all the things O'Malley needs – food, water, his bed, and his litter tray. O'Malley scratches at the door and jumps and stretches at the door handle, wanting to be freed. Mathew feels guilty, so he starts a natural history holofilm. O'Malley starts to chatter and leap at the birds flying across the room.

Mathew shuts the door tightly behind him and goes to the front room while the men work.

Mathew works on the beebot, turning it into a Blackweb

communications device. Based on a course provided by the school curriculum and a bit of research on MUUT about the quantum security his anonymous friend suggested, he manages to build something he is fairly sure will allow him to have a private conversation with Clara. The first beebot was primitive in design, an off-the-shelf agricultural model. Last night he printed a new beebot for Clara with flourishes. It's covered in tiny gold and black hairs, has iridescent eyes, and long, elaborate, tightly curling antennae. The finished product is like a pendant or a brooch.

He leaves the beebot on the doorstep, waiting for Clara to arrive, and retreats to the Darkroom. The miniature robot is now in the air, circling the streetlight outside, and through its eyes he watches as her car drives up Pickervance Road.

As she exits the car, she looks up at his bedroom window. The shadow of disappointment passing across her face when she realises he isn't there makes him exhilarated, but also slightly ashamed of himself. He flies the beebot behind her, at a low level, avoiding the suspicious, sunglassed gaze of the guard. It zips up and around quickly and lands on her collar, gripping on with tiny carbon-fibre beebot feet.

He puts through a message request. Knowing it will get through to Clara as an unrecognised incoming message, he says,

This is Mathew. I've managed to do what I said I might. I need you to download some software. Please accept the prompt.

She accepts, the software installs, and then he says, "The small insect that just landed on your jacket is mine. It will allow us to talk in private. If you are okay with this, please don't knock it off. Also, could you please wave at the window? I'm not there right now, but then I will know the beebot works and I didn't stay awake all night making this thing for nothing."

Clara raises her hand.

"Thank you," he says.

She smiles.

"I am smiling back. I'll add video for you at some point," he says. "Will you leave it on while you play? I'd like to listen." He isn't going to tell her he's been listening to her for days.

She says, "You'll find it boring. It's classical stuff. Most people our age don't like it. Can you hear me alright?" She smiles at the guard, who she knows will assume she is making a normal e-Pin call.

"Yes, I can hear you, and I will like it."

"How do you know?"

"I hear you playing through our front wall every afternoon."

"Oh, God, really? I'm sorry. I didn't realise the walls were so thin."

"Yeah, they're like paper. But don't be sorry. You are amazing."

"Hardly. But thanks."

They travel into Gen Lacey's house together. He manages to manoeuvre the beebot so it is facing down.

She sits at the piano, and he watches her hands dance.

At the end of her lesson he waits for her to say goodbye to her teacher. As Gen moves into the hallway, Clara whispers, "Don't go. Let's speak when I'm in the car."

She waits for the guard to shut the door on her and for the car to start to drive away before she says "Hi."

"Hi."

"Do you mind if I move?" Mathew says. "From this angle I can't see much."

"Not at all."

He detaches the tiny beebot feet from her collar, flies to her knee, and focuses on her face.

"Better?" she says.

"A bit," he says.

"Is this better?" She offers her hand. He crawls the beebot into her palm, and she lifts it. "Is it too close?"

"The lens is adjustable. There," he says. "Perfect."

"This is different."

"Is it too weird?"

"Yes."

He smiles.

"Are you still there?"

"Yes. I'm smiling."

"I can't see you, remember? I only have the bee. It's sweet but not very expressive. It's different from the other one. Where did you get it?"

"I made it."

"You made it?"

"I got a template on the Nexus. Where are you now?" he asks.

"I'll show you," and she gently grasps the beebot between her thumb and index finger and puts it on the edge of the passenger window.

"You're not going to the river."

"No. I live in Wandsworth."

"You come a long way for a piano lesson."

"It's not just a piano lesson. Gen is a pretty special teacher."

"I know. I searched for you both on the Nexus. You're famous."

"Hmmm . . . amongst those interested in young people who play piano music, perhaps. But yes, Gen is famous."

"I'm not even notable in my class at school. Not in a good way."

"You build things like this bee. That's much more impressive."

"It's nice of you to say so, but any hobbyist would be able to build one of these."

"I've never seen one before."

"Only because you don't live on a farm. Beebots are used as crop pollinators in places where they still grow biofood, because there aren't enough real bees to pollinate crops."

"Do beebots normally talk?"

"No."

"You've done something clever and original with it. I wouldn't know where to start."

"I would never be able to play Bach."

"How do you know I was playing Bach?"

"My dad loved classical music, especially piano music. Bach was his favourite composer."

"Gen told me your dad passed away. I'm so sorry, Mathew." When he doesn't respond, she says, "What do I do with the beebot? Does it fly home?"

"Keep it. If you ever want to chat, say 'Call the beekeeper' to it, and it will call my secure account on the Blackweb. I can't see you unless you accept my call. Keep it locked in a drawer if you don't trust me."

"I trust you."

"You shouldn't. Right now you shouldn't trust anyone. I have to go," he says. "Someone is looking for me. Please do call me, though."

"I will," she says.

17 O'MALLEY AGAIN

One of the locksmiths, the older man, is standing in the doorway wearing a guilty expression.

"Your cat," he says. "It was in the Darkroom."

"Yes," Mathew says. "I put him there because there are no windows or doors in the Darkroom. Your colleague said you wouldn't need to go in."

"He didn't tell me." He says this like it's Mathew's fault. "I thought you were in there. I came to check what you wanted us to do with the old locks. The back door was open . . ."

Mathew scrambles to his feet.

"He rushed past me. I tried to grab him," the locksmith says, following Mathew as he runs along the hallway, through the kitchen, and into the garden. Mathew starts to search frantically. O'Malley is nowhere to be seen.

"Did you see where he went?" Mathew asks.

"He jumped the wall, I think." The locksmith gestures towards Gen Lacey's garden.

"Good. Okay." Mathew rushes back through the hallway, through the front door, and out onto the pavement to Gen's house. He leans on the doorbell. After too many agonising seconds Gen answers, smiling. "Hi, there!" She sees his face. "What's up?"

"O'Malley's run away again."

"Oh no!"

"I think he may be in your garden. Do you mind if I look?"

"Of course not." Gen leads the way through her house. "How did he escape?"

"We're having new locks fitted. The bioID compatible ones. Mum ordered them."

Gen opens the back door, and they go into the garden.

"O'Maaalleeey!" Mathew calls. "O'Malley?" He gets on his hands and knees, peering under bushes, running his hands into the dark spaces at the back near the fence.

"Damn cat," he says. "He's here somewhere. He knows I'm after him. Bloody creature is ignoring me."

"He wants some freedom."

"Yes, but if a policeman catches him, he'll be shot. Okay to stand on this chair?"

"Be my guest."

Mathew gets on the garden chair and peers over the fence.

"He can't have gone far."

"Why don't we go door to door and tell people he's missing? I'll go and talk to the soldiers on the roadblock at the end of the street and let them know."

"Thanks, Gen."

"No problem at all."

Mathew follows Gen onto the street and starts knocking on doors, speaking to neighbours he's never met before. There's no response from number 21, but he manages to find someone in at all the other houses. The All-Day Curfew has grounded most people from their work.

Gen comes back from her visit to the roadblock. "The soldiers were actually really nice. They said if they find O'Malley, they'll bring him back to you. They won't shoot him."

Mathew sighs. "Thanks, Gen." He runs his hand through his hair. "Mum is going to go crazy."

"No, she won't. And anyway, he'll come home. He's stretching his legs. Cats always come home eventually."

It's 8:30 in the evening. Mathew is sitting in his mother's bedroom scanning his neighbour's garden with the night vision in his Lenz. If he hadn't given the beebot to Clara, he could have used it to hunt for O'Malley. He considers the spare in his bedroom and is on the verge of fetching it when he catches movement in his peripheral vision. He turns his head quickly, scanning for the source, his Lenzes taking a moment to refocus.

At first he can't distinguish it. Then a grainy image reveals itself to him. In the shadow of an overhanging tree, on the wall separating the gardens of number 19 and number 21, is a blackbird, flicking its tail, watchful. It's alert to something. The bird stands poised to take off, its head cocked, watching, listening. Even in the poor light the yellow of its beak and the ring around its eyes are striking. It's such a rare sight Mathew is mesmerised.

Then he realises why the bird is agitated.

At the other end of the wall, his chin and chest on the bricks, O'Malley is poised in stalking position, sizing up the bird, calculating a strike. He watches in horror as O'Malley's rump rises and wiggles the way it does before he pounces on something.

Before he even knows what he's doing, Mathew is running down the stairs, through the house, and out the back door. The bird is startled by the noise of Mathew crashing into the garden and takes flight. O'Malley leaps and catches it, disappearing on the other side of the wall.

"Damn," Mathew says. Pushing the garden bench against the wall, he climbs up and peers across the top of the glass roof of the conservatory. O'Malley is sitting in the middle of a pane of glass with the blackbird in his jaws. When he spots Mathew, he starts to growl.

"O'Malley, drop it!" he whispers loudly. But O'Malley has no such intention.

Mathew hauls himself onto the wall and sits astride. The bird may be already dead – it's impossible to tell. O'Malley watches him carefully but doesn't move. Mathew ponders whether the conservatory roof will take his weight. He tests it with one foot and then another, lowering himself tentatively, still bearing most of the load with his arms clinging to the wall.

The roof is sturdy, he decides.

O'Malley is still, but his aquamarine eyes follow Mathew as he edges forward.

"Drop the bird, O'Malley!" Mathew says, lunging forward, and grabbing the cat by the scruff of the neck. Taking a grip of O'Malley's mouth, he levers his jaws open and releases the bird. Miraculously, it flies away.

Mathew pulls the cat to his chest in a bear hug and starts to edge back towards the wall. O'Malley kicks, hard, raking the skin on Mathew's wrists with the long claws on his back feet. Mathew loses his grip and then his footing. O'Malley jumps free, and Mathew topples.

He lands hard on the roof and has a moment to register that it doesn't seem as solid as he thought, before it gives way beneath him.

It takes him only a second to fall, but as is the way of these things, it feels much longer. In that fraction of time, his brain has long enough to register surprise and note that he's falling ten feet to the floor on plates of glass.

When he lands, he freezes for several moments, breathing. Then he lifts his hands off the glass slowly, checking for blood. There's a piece of broken glass stuck to the palm of his left hand, but remarkably he's not bleeding. He carefully picks off the glass and drops it on the floor amongst the rest of the debris, then lifts his arms and comes slowly to his knees, finding a place to put his hand for support. Once on his feet, he examines his trousers, feels his legs. Amazingly, nothing is hurt.

The floor is a mess. Bits of glass are shattered across the tiles. In addition to the section of the roof that's now on the floor in pieces, the blinds are partially torn and hanging, bits of string and canvas and shrilk trailing around him like a broken sail. The orange trees are crushed and the orchids have been thrown from their pots and are lying prone, roots akimbo, in scattered soil. He raises his head. There's a gaping hole in the roof of the conservatory. The night sky is visible through it. Grey clouds cross a bright moon; between them, dim, blinking stars.

He has destroyed Mr Lestrange's conservatory.

He reflects on how Lestrange will react. Somehow he can't imagine him angry.

With all the noise, he's amazed no one has come rushing in. The door into the kitchen is shut, and he worries whether it's locked and he's trapped in the conservatory until Lestrange finds him; but when he tries it, it's open. The kitchen and hallway are in darkness. As he walks forward, the lights automatically come on.

"Hello?" he says, moving towards the front door. "Mr Lestrange? Hello? Mr Lestrange, are you there?" There's no response.

Across the hallway is the door to the library. "Mr Lestrange!" he raises his voice to carry through the house and goes up the stairs. "Hello?" Pushing open each bedroom door in turn, knocking before he does so, he finds the house empty. Each room is as pristine as he saw it through the eyes of the beebot.

Downstairs, he tries the Darkroom and then goes into the library.

Here are the books – the gold leaf on the spines glinting in the bright light hanging from the ceiling.

The table, an antique with veneered surfaces shined to a high polish, has nothing on it. The books he saw Lestrange reading have been cleared away.

Scanning along the shelves, following history around the room, as he saw via the beebot, the books are arranged chronologically starting with ancient history, all the way to modern affairs. *World War III: The First Space War* is on the shelf nearest the door, but it's not the last book on the shelf. It isn't even the last shelf. He sweeps the spines. The titles don't make sense.

There are books on the Second Space War. Something called *The End of Europe and the USA: The Atlantic States Treaty and the Founding of ATLAS* and another called *The Dishonest War: Biological Weapons and Population Control through Manmade Viruses at the End of the Twenty-First Century.*

Kneeling next to *World War III*, he extracts it by its spine and flicks through. There's a chapter on the destruction of the US Battlestars and the subsequent destruction of the Chinese moon base. It describes Russia's push into Europe. All these things have actually happened in the past couple of days. It's strange but not beyond possibility that Mr Lestrange would have written about these things already. But the book appears to describe the rest of the war, the use of robot soldiers and hypersonic planes and the critical role of wireless solar power beamed from space in enabling the US and the Western allies to push an overstretched Russia from Poland. It concludes with a chapter on the cost of victory to the US.

It must be some kind of game, he thinks.

He puts the volume back and browses along to the very last book on the very last shelf. Its title is Fin. It's a thick volume with a blue cloth cover and silver lettering. He stands, opens it, and walks to the table, where he puts it down so he can page through the contents, and skims the chapter titles: 'The Fall of the West', 'The Last Days of Silverwood', 'Evacuation of the Pure', 'Archives and Refuges', 'The Forty-Year Walk of Angel Leventis', 'The Arrival of the Lamplighter', 'The Kind', 'Wormwood'

He looks back at the bookshelves and spies something he hadn't noticed. It's his book – the one Mr Lestrange was reading when he discovered the beebot, a book with his name on the spine. He goes to the shelf to fetch *The Book of Mathew Erlang*. Next to his book is another, with Clara's name. There is also a book of Hoshi Mori, a book of Soren Erlang, a book of Ju Chen.

This is some kind of joke, he thinks. Opening his book, he pauses. *Do I want to know? But this is crazy! It's not real. No one knows what's going to happen.*

He skims through the contents of *The Book of Mathew Erlang*. 'Birth'. 'Early Life'. 'Education'. 'Soren Erlang'. 'Hoshi Mori'. 'Elgol'. 'Ju Chen'. 'Clara Barculo'. 'Silverwood'. 'Eva Aslanova'. 'Yinglong'. 'Hathaway'. 'Death'. 'The Bach Society'.

Staring for a moment at the second to last chapter title, he goes to page 827. It begins:

> On the fourteenth of February 2091, Mathew Erlang delivered his second public lecture concerning Project Yinglong in the auditorium at Silverwood University. It was the greatest day of his career and the last day of his life.

The chapter is long; he's impatient and hurriedly, clumsily flips through to the end. His hands are shaking.

Stupid, he says to himself. *Not real. Not real.*

> In spite of the fact that Erlang modelled the Yinglong on downloads of his own brain patterns, he perversely neglected to record his own DNA and so it was irretrievably lost . . .

The book literally flies from his hand and slams into the wall. He scrambles to his feet.

That did not happen.

Adrenaline is pumping round his body. Though he is gripped by cold terror, his rational mind knows he must have somehow lost control of his muscles and thrown the book. He takes a few steps towards it and bends to pick it up.

It moves away from him.

He is at the front door before he knows what has happened, yanking at the lock and the handle. But it is shut firm.

Who locks a door from the inside?

"Mr Lestrange?!" he shouts, louder again.

The silence in the house swallows his words. The empty, still rooms now seems sinister.

Through the kitchen to the conservatory, picking his way through the hanging bits of blind, he finds the conservatory door and rattles the handle.

Locked as well.

He considers trying to climb through the hole above him, fetches a chair from the kitchen and stands on it, but standing on tiptoes he only just brushes the roof with his fingertips.

He gets down.

It occurs to him to try the Nexus. Perhaps if he logs on to the house network, he might unlock the doors, or summon Mr Lestrange. His Lenz returns a message of

```
No networks found.
```

This is impossible in London. The signal from the house should be available, but he can't even see it, meaning he can't call Gen Lacey and he can't even call his mother.

Going through the kitchen drawers to look for the key to the back patio door, he finds cutlery, plates – all gleaming, clean, and new like everything else in the house. He opens the cupboards and the fridge for good measure. There is food, what you would expect for a single man, but there's nothing going off, nothing mouldy, nothing half-opened. And he realises he hasn't met a HomeAngel in the house. He goes back into the hallway.

"Mr Lestrange?"

It's pointless.

The library door looms beside him, but he doesn't want to go back in there.

There's only the Darkroom.

He pushes open the door.

On one of the chairs there's a naked, coverless skullcap. Reasoning that if he connects to Mr Lestrange's holophone, he'll be able to get a Nexus connection to get help, he puts the skullcap on, half expecting to be rejected by the authentication system.

Then he's standing in a long white corridor.

The doors, ceiling, and floor are all white. There is no obvious source of light, but it's blindingly bright. Turning 360° to see where he came from, there's nothing but a corridor stretching on, apparently endlessly, and door after door as white as the floor, walls, and ceiling. The door nearest him is locked. So is the next one and the one after that. He tries them all.

Standing in the corridor, he tries to quell the rising panic. *It's a game, probably a puzzle. I've played similar.* There's always an exit from virtual worlds. Perhaps you have to open two door handles at the same time. Perhaps only the twentieth door you try opens. He tries both of these strategies to no avail. *Think, Mathew. Think.*

If he keeps walking, the corridor might bend at some point, or end with an opening door. Perhaps an object or a menu will appear to tell me what to do next.

Up ahead he notices something that appears to have materialised out of nowhere, something hanging on a wall, a smudge of yellow, the only coloured object in the monotonous white, and he quickens his pace to investigate.

And there it is!

On a peg on the wall, a parachute hangs by one of its shoulder straps, along with some old-fashioned motorcycle goggles. Is he meant to put them on? He studies the door in front of him. As he turns the handle and leans his weight in, he doesn't expect it to open.

But it does.

Losing his balance, he falls forwards. The instinctive part of his brain responds before he even knows what he's seeing.

It tries to pull him back.

For one wonderful, timeless, elegant moment he teeters on the edge of the doorframe, the self-preserving animal part of him trying to manipulate muscles to do miraculous things, to fight gravity and pull him back towards the corridor. But it doesn't work. Gravity wins, and he is falling forward.

As he does, he raises his eyes, and in that unforgettable second he sees the impossible.

Unfolding before him is a landscape so vast it fades at the horizon. A forest, a canopy of trees stretching away in all directions, a muddy brown river shining in the sun, snaking sleepily through the trees. He is thousands of feet above all of this. Or he was.

Now he is falling.

18 FOUR DAYS

DAY EIGHT: Thursday, 16 June 2472, Chukotka Autonomous Okrug, Siberia, Russia

Pain. Sharp, piercing pain. Something is biting him, and he wakes suddenly. It is light. He checks his Lenz for the time, but the time's not there. He has no clock. It feels like he has been asleep only a short while. The sun is blazing bright. He feels the pain again. There's an ant on his hand. Shaking his wrist, frantically, he knocks it off and examines his skin. There's a red welt, which he sucks and then spits. There are things crawling on him. Sitting, he sees a line of large red ants marching across his legs, clambering over his ankles, sniffing at him. With disgust, he whacks at them with strands of the vine rope he brought up with him the night before.

He rubs sleep from his eyes and recalls his journey here; the long white corridor, the long fall from the sky over the forest, the astonishing view, the plunge into the deep lake. His lungs are still sore from almost drowning. His skin is burnt from lying in the sun to dry. He has cuts and bruises from trying to climb this tree. He has never played a game as real as this in his life.

Shuffling to the edge of his tree house, he peers out. Between gaps in the foliage, the river bubbles away. Carefully, he slides down the trunk, cursing at his screaming feet; he grasps his walking pole from where he'd left it propped against the tree, and goes to the water for a drink. The river is wide and deep here. It runs flat and steady. Branches and leaves are carried along in the swim, washed from the riverbanks by the storm. His stomach rumbles, empty and churning with hunger.

Last night, as he gathered leaves in the rain, he spied something like bananas. Going back to the plant he broke the leaves from, sure enough, a few feet above his head are small, dull yellow bunches. He yanks on a branch and breaks off a fistful. On the ground, legs crossed, he snaps a fruit away and peels it. It's not the best banana he's ever eaten, but it is edible. He bolts the rest hungrily and then goes back to the tree and gathers some more bunches. Grabbing some strips of the bark he used to bind the leaves the night before, he strings the bananas together and hangs them across his shoulder.

He's no longer hungry or thirsty, and he's slept some, but he's tired. Between the gaps in the canopy above him, blue sky. The river is gushing along at his side. The forest is alive with noise. Gripping his stick in his hand, he sets off.

After walking for hours without event, preoccupied by the pain in his feet, he is sitting at the side of the river, eating. The sun is high in a bright blue sky, but there's also the moon hanging over the forest, huge and low. As he stares at it, he hears a distinct snap.

Something is moving along the bank on the other side. Mathew's eyes rake along the forest edge, staring into the dark places between the leaves.

It takes him a while, but eventually he sees it. A pair of almond-shaped, green cat's eyes.

The animal comes further into the daylight. It's not a breed he recognises. It's the size of a large dog, powerfully built, with muscular shoulders. Big enough to fell a cow, a horse . . . a human. It is staring right at him. Brazenly. Not at all afraid. There is no doubt at all where it places itself in the food chain in this particular encounter. Its tail flicks ever so slightly. It yawns. It licks its lips.

Mathew has never felt like prey before, but he does now and finds the experience extraordinary. He is frozen.

You have to move, he says to himself.

The cat goes to the water's edge.

It can swim!

But the cat stops at the water. It paces back and forth, sizing the river. It shies away from it. Then it sits and rages in frustration. Its teeth are formidable.

Slowly, Mathew stands. The cat stands, too. Mathew backs into the forest and walks away. Behind him the cat is growling and, he imagines, cursing, on the other side of the river.

It can't cross, he tells himself. It can't reach me.

If he goes further into the forest, he has no idea how he'll get water. Besides, the river offers a direction. The forest is nothing but confusion, and he might wander around in circles in there for the rest of his life. Even if he doesn't know where he's going to end up, having a definite path forward is better than standing still.

He decides to carry on, trusting that the cat can't cross the river but conscious now of each twig snapping beneath his feet.

He stops when the sun is starting to get low and finds a good tree with vines hanging down, like the one he slept in the night before. The humidity in the air is intensifying; he can sense the rain coming. Gathering banana leaves and bunches of fruit, he hauls the lot into his tree. He has time to gather more comfortable bedding and to make the roof of his tree house good and waterproof before the rain starts.

Safely in his small bedroom, he takes off his shoes and socks. His feet are white and wrinkled with the constant dampness, and red and oozing on top where his boots have rubbed his sunburn raw. He dries the white parts with some of the forest moss he managed to gather for his bed but daren't touch the red parts. He takes off his top and his trousers to dry. Sweat clings to him. He stinks. *I need a bath*, he thinks. The last thing passing through his mind before he falls into a deep dreamless sleep is I hope the cat can't climb trees.

.

Friday, 17 June 2472, Siberia

In the morning, life seems better. He has slept in; he doesn't know how long, but through the leaves he can see the sun blazing high in the sky.

When he gets down from his tree, the cat is nowhere to be seen. A few feet away there's a bend in the river where the water filters off and slows into a shallow pool. Wading in, he washes himself and his clothes and hangs them on sticks to dry in the sun while he eats his breakfast. A sunny rock provides a place to dry his sodden boots and he opens the fronts, pulling at the laces. He tosses the banana skins into the swim of the river.

As he eats he tries the Nexus and the Blackweb once more, booting Charybdis. He thinks about Clara and wonders if she's wondering why he hasn't called. He thinks about his mother and what she must have thought when she came home and he was missing. She must have called the police by now. Someone will search Mr Lestrange's house, and they will find him. But then he realises, although he's in Lestrange's house, he's in a game and time passes differently in games. Perhaps in the game, his mother still hasn't come home from work.

He wants something other than bananas now, fairly badly. Wondering what else in the forest is edible, he packs moss on the top of his wounded feet in his socks and boots and laces them, wincing as he tightens.

Less and less focused on finding the door back to reality, more focused on the cat, he carries on.

He senses it. He's sure it's nearby, on the other side of the thin strip of water. His mind cycles feverishly through ways to get away from it – climbing trees, running further into the forest. Occasionally, as he walks along, he comes across felled trees, their thick trunks lying across his path, so he has to clamber over them. It crosses his mind that if he rolls one of the smaller trees into the water, he might ride on it like a boat down the river and away from the cat. He casts around for the right kind of tree.

Hours later, he thinks he's found one. It's a little way from the water's edge, but he guesses it won't be too hard to drag it. He wedges his stick under it, to help dislodge it from the undergrowth. It takes the next couple of hours to snap off twigs and branches. His hands are cut and sore when he stops to wash and drink in the late afternoon. He glances at the sky. The big low moon is still his companion, but it's obscured by gathering clouds, and he realises he needs to prepare for the night. Hunting about, he finds a tree to climb and banana leaves, but no bananas, which unnerves him. Up in his tree, wedged between thick branches at the top of the bowl, unable to lie down, he listens to the night and falls asleep hungry.

Saturday, 18 June 2472, Siberia

When he wakes, he lies for a few minutes wondering how many hours in his real life amount to hours in this virtual world. He's trying to work out if his hunger is real-world hunger or if, as is often the case in these games, he has only been playing a few hours and his rumbling stomach is a trick of the VR.

Now he's sleeping as long as his body needs, distrusting the sunlight. The nights seem very short.

Sitting in his treehouse, he examines his hands, arms, and feet. They're sore, really painful. It's a remarkable simulation. It's reassuring that, back in real life, Mr Lestrange is sure to discover him in his Darkroom soon and end the game.

He climbs down; the tree trunk boat is where he left it.

When he goes down to the river to drink, he scans for the cat and concludes it's moved on, at least for now. He's torn about whether he should keep walking and leave the tree trunk boat where it is or finish it and make his escape while he can.

Hunger drives him further into the forest in search of breakfast, and he finds another banana tree. After he's eaten, he loads a bark rope with bananas and hangs it over his shoulder. On his hunt he finds berries, nuts, and fungus but has no idea what is edible and what is poisonous, so he daren't eat them. After breakfast, he becomes preoccupied by the idea that there might be fish in the river. Some of the rivers on the Elgol estate have been repopulated with salmon and trout. This place is wild enough not to have been overfished. Indeed, as it's just a game, and the forest is crawling with life, it follows that the river would be full of fish. Perhaps he could fashion a fishing rod from a sapling and use some of the abundant forest insects as bait. But he lacks the skill to build a fire in this damp place and, even if he caught something, the thought of raw fish makes his stomach churn. His grandmother would be ashamed of him.

If he gets killed in the game, he imagines, as in all games he'll be ejected, back into cold, hard reality – or in this particular case, gentle, safe reality. Perhaps, then, he should get himself killed. Incredible as this world is, it's frustrating and he's growing tired of it. With that thought in his mind, he heads back to his tree trunk boat.

Having loosened the trunk some more with his walking stick, he makes a long rope with the bark strips, ties it around one end of the tree and pulls, stopping periodically to clear the route of stones, branches, and plants.

After forty minutes of hard work, he manages to drag the trunk to the edge of the riverbank and pushes it in with a great splash, then jumps in after it, just managing to catch hold of the slippery bark as the trunk is turned and grabbed by the river.

It catches the flow and starts to travel down sideways. Mathew gets behind it, throws his arms and his chest over the top, hauls himself up and hugs the wet wood to him, in the still fast centre of the river now. The riverbed is far from the reach of his feet. The force of the water pushes him and the tree on, and they gather momentum. Then, as the river bends, it suddenly narrows, and the tree gets jammed between the bank and a rock. He hauls himself along the trunk, the current rushing beneath him, dragging at his legs.

When it's shallow enough for him to touch the rocky river bottom with his feet, he stands and pushes at the wedged tree. It won't move. In front of the tree, on the bank, branches and other debris have got tangled against a jutting rock. His tree is caught on this mess. Reaching across the trunk, he manages to clear away the debris and push the front of the log to face down the river. Taking a firm hold as the log-boat starts to move again, he uses the momentum to drag himself chest-first along the top. Lying face-down, he precariously manages to balance and he thinks that when he stops again, he'll try to find two smaller logs to tie to the trunk with bark rope, to form a raft.

The river widens and deepens again, and he hangs on harder still as the force of the water gathers, but he feels more vulnerable and wonders how he might turn the trunk so he's behind it again. He slips off and gradually edges it around in the water, pushing against the current.

Staring ahead to where the river narrows, he spots a large stony beach on the right-hand side. The water becomes shallower, his feet bang and drag on the riverbed, and he lifts his legs. Near the beach, the water gets shallower still, the tree gets stuck, and he wades around to push it free.

Something large and powerful hits him from the side, throwing him onto the shore.

He's so dazed, it takes him a moment to realise it's the cat. He scrambles to his feet – there's a searing pain in his shoulder, but no time to think. The cat is between him and the river. He tries to move further along the beach nearer the water, but the cat has him covered and cuts him off. Slowly, he backs towards the forest, all the time expecting the creature to pounce. He somehow scrambles over a bank, gripping roots, grass, plant stems – anything. There's a vine hanging by his face – he grips it and pulls, testing it, and quickly gets a foothold and swings towards the trunk of a tree, throwing his leg and catching it on a branch, levering himself with his arms and his wounded foot. The cat comes bounding up the bank. Mathew gets clear just as the cat launches itself at the tree, leaving a great gash mark in the bark. Struggling crazily, Mathew kicks and scrambles and climbs desperately, until he's sitting on a sturdy branch. The cat makes one more attempt to get at him, leaping and falling with a crash.

For a long time it sits at the base of the tree, roaring at him whenever he peers down.

It starts to rain. The branch becomes slippy, and he retreats slowly to the heart of the tree. His shoulder is numb with pain. Touching it with his hand, he finds that it's wet and sticky. When he looks at his fingers, they're covered in blood.

Thunder shakes the tree, and then rain is beating down all around him, bouncing off the shiny leaves. He notices a bank of moss growing on the side of a thick branch, scrapes off a handful and holds it in the rain until it's sodden, then presses it against his shoulder.

He finds a way to lie down securely without danger of falling from the tree and rests there miserably, the rain pounding down, relentless. When it finally stops, he cranes his neck over the side of his refuge. The cat has gone, but night is closing in, and he's too tired to go down and gather things to make a decent bed. He sleeps fitfully where he is, his shoulder throbbing.

Sunday, 19 June 2472, Siberia

In the morning, there's no sign of the cat. He lets himself down and goes to the river to drink. His arm aches. At the water's edge he takes off his shirt and examines his shoulder. There's a large gash, red and gaping. He cleans it in the river, then gathers some more moss, and tears a strip off his shirt to bind the wet moss to his wound. His shirt is now in tatters. He considers putting it back on and then ties it around his head to keep off the sun and catch the sweat that constantly drips down his face.

He spends a long time searching for food in the forest, distracted by the wound inflicted by the cat. The day before, he left his walking pole on the bank of the river and moving in the undergrowth is harder without it. Hunting around, he finds another buried in a tangle of sticky clinging vines and low broad-leafed growth. As he pulls it carefully from the leaves, he thinks about snakes and spiders. This new stick is a better one. He sizes it, balancing it in his good hand. His other arm is throbbing, and his skin is stained with his own blood, but he tries to put that from his mind.

Heading to the river, he hears an animal noise, a growl, coming from across the water, but it isn't close enough for him to be sure it's the cat. He scans around for a tree to climb, but he is in amongst small shrubs and banana trees. Taking another route, he walks deeper in the forest for a while, until finally he turns again towards the river and hears the cat, distinctly this time. He's forced to retreat, trying to stay parallel to the river from a distance.

The river is his compass, and he doesn't want to lose it.

As the day goes on and he gets thirsty, he wonders how he can find clean, fresh water. Searching amongst the low-growing plants, he finds one whose centre is full of rainwater. Cautious, he tastes a small amount first, worried the plant might have poisoned it, but the water is sweet and clean, better than the river water. When he's finished drinking, he examines his bandage and thinks about washing the wound in the water, but when he touches the moss, the pain is so bad he decides to leave it alone.

The ground is becoming stony, and he realises he's climbing and getting further away from the river. Straining his ears, he can no longer hear the rushing sound of the water. He clambers across a rocky outcrop on the side of the hill, bare of plants, and, standing on a boulder, takes a breather and surveys his whereabouts. Down below the treetops the river gleams silver in the sunlight. He sighs with relief. It looks like if he walks down at a diagonal, he'll meet the river, so he slides off the boulder and sets off again.

There are a few taller trees to use as landmarks and a rocky peak on the other side of the valley atop a flat-sided cliff next to the river. It's hot. The sun burns without the shade of the forest. He arranges the hat he's made with his shirt to cover his neck and shoulders. The large moon in the blue sky hangs over him.

He moves on quickly, starting off with purpose, but he hasn't gone far when he hears a snapping of branches. The sound is close. The cat is walking through the undergrowth directly ahead.

Once again he searches frantically for somewhere to hide. He's surrounded by tall trees, but they have straight, smooth trunks with no low branches to grip hold of. Striking a slightly different path, to his right, along the contour of the hillside rather than directly down, he glimpses a flash of the cat between the trunks of trees. It does not come directly at him but crosses his path, through the dense foliage ahead. It's gone and then appears again, some way down the hillside.

It's sitting. Waiting. It yawns.

He climbs slightly higher and tries to walk forward along the hillside again, but the cat is there.

Is it playing with me? he wonders. Cats do that with their food before they make a kill.

His pulse hammers away, but he doesn't experience the rising panic he's felt before in encounters with the cat, even though, this time, he seems to have nowhere to go. They continue. The cat, he realises, is pushing him higher up the mountain. It's herding him. They climb. There are more and more rocks, fewer trees and shrubs. A high stone cliff rises above him, penning him in on the cliff side.

Is it taking me to the place it wants to kill me?

This is a game, he reminds himself. A highly realistic, rather horrifying game.

Then the mantra: *This is not real. I cannot die.*

He is at the base of the cliff. The cat has come from the forest. It's standing in front of him. As he moves to go the other way, fluidly, free of the least effort, it moves into his path. In every physical way this animal is superior.

Carved into the cliff, there's a cave. Its black mouth gapes at the daylight. The cat is weaving backwards and forwards now, pushing Mathew into the cave. *This is where it brings its prey to die.*

The gunshot rings pure and clear, the sound bouncing off the cliff side and echoing down the canyon. The bullet was aimed at the cat. It misses and takes down a tree instead, which cracks and breaks and falls. The cat is gone in the blink of an eye. Air shudders in Mathew's lungs. He breathes out.

He is saved.

There are men coming towards him.

19 DRAGOMIROV

"Стой!"

A human voice. A foreign language but a human voice. Mathew doesn't understand the words, but they have the international sound of a command. The game clearly doesn't allow ordinary Nexus simultaneous translation. The sound of people approaching. Rocks disturbed, branches broken. Conversation. There's an urgency and aggression to the exchanges that make Mathew think these people are not out on a Sunday stroll. The language is familiar, though. It sounds like Eva. It sounds like Russian.

They break through the trees and start climbing the rocky slope towards him. Four soldiers in jungle camouflage carrying strange-looking guns. Two of the soldiers have their crosshairs trained on him as they approach. Slowly, Mathew puts down his walking stick and puts his hands in the air.

"Как тебя зовут? Откуда вы? Вы понимаете меня?"

The man who has spoken to him, and who appears to be in charge, indicates to the others to lower their weapons. Mathew feels only marginally safer when they do.

"Говорить!" snaps the man in charge. He has a blond crew cut, a two-day beard and the distinctive deep-set eyes of Russian people; he's glistening with sweat, dark patches under his arms and across his chest.

"I don't understand," Mathew says. "I don't speak Russian."

The man smiles, clearly pleased, like he has found something he was searching for, like he has struck gold. He looks around at the other soldiers, who grin back at him, and then says to Mathew in heavily accented English, "You come with us."

They walk for an hour at a military clip Mathew barely keeps pace with, down to the river and along the bank until they reach a broad rocky shore, like the one where the cat pounced on him. At the edge, on the river-smoothed stones, is a camp in a cleared area. There are shelters, tarpaulins stretched between posts, hammocks, equipment and supplies hanging from the beams of the shelters, a fire tended by another soldier, the smell of food.

Mathew thirstily drinks clean, fresh water from a beaker offered to him by the crew-cut Russian who refills it for him from a hanging barrel fed from a water filter. He indicates to a makeshift bench made from forest wood. Mathew sits down. Crew-cut shouts at the man tending the fire. The man is fat, with curly greying black hair, the bulbous nose of a heavy drinker, a red face, and smiling dark eyes. He brings something to Mathew – a metal bowl, a spoon, food, some kind of stew. It smells amazing. Mathew delves in ravenously, unquestioning. It is food. It is hot. Crew-cut smiles at him indulgently, is patient, lets him eat.

The fat man watches him eat, too. "I am Evgeny, Evgeny Shukshin," he says, touching his fingers to his chest. "Who are you?"

"Mathew," he says between mouthfuls, spooning the last bits of gravy into his mouth. "You speak English?"

"Little bit," the cook says, grinning. "I wish more." The cook notices his shoulder. "You are hurting."

Trying to escape the cat, meeting the Russians, Mathew has forgotten his shoulder, which has started to bleed again. The shirt and moss bandage are hanging off him.

"I hurt my arm. And my feet." He puts the bowl on the floor, bends down and loosens the laces of his boots, slowly drawing out his feet, removing his filthy, sodden, blood-stained socks and picking off the wad of moss covering his weeping skin.

The cooks says something to crew-cut, who calls to another soldier who's hanging water carriers on one of the tent poles. A young man with a shaven head and a missing front tooth comes and takes hold of Mathew's arm. He flinches. Gap-tooth says something to Evgeny.

Evgeny says, "It's okay. He will help you."

Mathew nods and turns to the soldier, who's looking at him expectantly.

"Okay."

Gap-tooth unwinds the remains of the makeshift bandage and picks away the moss. Mathew turns away and grits his teeth. The soldier whistles, goes to one of the hanging bags and comes back with a medical kit. Rummaging inside, he pulls out a tube, removes the top, and squeezes a transparent cream directly onto the wound. Then he sets to work pulling the wound together and binding the skin with adhesive strips. He wraps the whole thing in a clean bandage and then a waterproof dressing; he then turns his attention to Mathew's damaged feet.

"Thank you," Mathew says.

"Спасибо," Evgeny says to Mathew. "It's thank you in Russian. Spaz iba."

"Spaziba," he repeats back to Evgeny.

The soldier grins and says something. Evgeny translates. "He says you're welcome."

Another, older man holding a telephone receiver attached to a box speaks to crew-cut, who gets up, takes the receiver, and starts speaking into the receiver in Russian, looking at Mathew.

The cook stays with him, offering him more food and water. No one points a gun at him now.

After he has eaten, Evgeny gives him soap and nods at the river. "You smell bad. Get clean." He mimes scrubbing himself and washing his face.

Mathew gratefully goes down to the water's edge, strips down to his underwear, then looks around, shrugs and takes them off as well. Wading thigh-deep, he scrubs himself with the soap and a cloth, scouring off days of grime and sweat. The soap pools around him and forms a line as it's slowly taken down the river. When he comes into shore, Evgeny offers him a towel and fresh, dry clothes, jungle camouflage like theirs, too big for him. He rolls up the legs of the trousers and his sleeves and ties the waist with some rope Evgeny gives him. Evgeny also finds him fresh clean, dry socks, and Mathew is more grateful than he has felt in a long time.

Evgeny puts out his shoes to dry. Mathew expects them to throw his old clothes on the fire, but crew-cut washes them, dries them in the sun, and then puts them in a bag like they are evidence.

In the afternoon, in his fresh-smelling, clean clothes, no longer hungry or thirsty, he watches the soldiers fish in the river. They score a fine dinner, which they slowly smoke above the fire on greenwood sticks. The light starts to fade.

As they sit around the fire, waiting for the fish to cook, Evgeny teaches Mathew all the soldiers' names in turn. The gap-toothed man, cleaner and fixer of his wounds, is Abram Salko. There's a grim-faced man with a well-bushed low brow and a half-day beard, hunched by the fire carving wood with a survival knife. His name is Vladimir Klokov. The soldier who handed crew-cut the phone is older, small, wiry, with greying hair and a lined, sad face, but he smiles at Mathew. His name is Yakov Zarubin. There's a good-looking blond boy, trying to grow a moustache, called Pavel Folkin, who stands and tests one of the cooking fish.

"Andrei . . ." Evgeny says, pointing to crew-cut.

Crew-cut says something sharply to Evgeny. "His name is Kapral Churkin. Churkin, not Andrei."

"He wants to be known by his last name?"

"Yes. Only rank and last names here, he says. But I am Evgeny. I have son. Your age. Far away. You understand?"

Mathew nods.

Later, as the fire crackles, some alcoholic liquid is passed around. Mathew takes a sip. It is strong and makes him cough. The soldiers laugh, but not unkindly. He's a boy, after all.

They string a hammock for him under a mosquito net.

His eyes grow heavy watching the embers glow in the fire.

Monday, 20 June 2472, Siberia

In the morning, there is more fresh water and food: a kind of porridge with something sweet in it. Churkin the crew-cut is on the strange old phone again. The soldiers get busy packing camp. The camp is put away in bags and boxes with military efficiency. It's all stacked neatly on the stony shore. Then they sit and wait. Salko gap-tooth and Folkin the boy wrestle to pass the time. Others sit around and yell abuse or encouragement; it's difficult for Mathew to tell which.

Then Zarubin shouts and points. A boat is coming along the river. It's a military vehicle, wide and flat-bottomed, big enough to carry Churkin's small outfit and all their stuff, pushed along by a powerful engine. It is also sheltered, with a canvas canopy, a necessity in the climate.

Once they've loaded and pushed off, Mathew sits at the front watching Evgeny preparing lunch for the others while they travel. Evgeny hands him some cans and a can opener.

"Here," he starts one off.

Mathew nods, "I know." He has done this in an old game loosely based on a twentieth-century war. As he opens the cans, he passes them to Evgeny, who's spreading paste onto biscuits, which he puts in metal bowls and hands round the men. Klokov takes a bite and spits his mouthful over the side of the boat, complaining loudly at Evgeny. Evgeny says something back to the man, who takes offence and stands. Churkin yells at him, and he sits down, reluctantly.

Evgeny glances at Mathew and grunts. "Hard ass," he says,

meaning Klokov.

Mathew grins, eating his biscuits happily, still grateful for anything not banana.

"Where are we going?" Mathew asks.

"Home," Evgeny says. Then he thinks. "No. Not home. Base camp."

"Where are we?"

"You don't know?"

Mathew shakes his head.

"How did you get here?"

Mathew shrugs. How to explain?

"You better have story when get to base camp. You better have good story."

"Why?"

"Dragomirov."

Churkin bawls something at Evgeny, who replies deferentially and turns to deal with the empty tins.

"But how do I compose a good story if I don't know where I am?" Mathew says to Evgeny.

Evgeny puts his finger to his lips and indicates that Churkin is watching them.

For the rest of the journey, Evgeny won't do more than grunt at Mathew, passing him water and food, but speaking loudly only in Russian, glancing all the time at Churkin like a dog waiting to be kicked by its master.

As they round a bend, on a wide stretch of water, a clearing, a small village, comes into view, smoke billowing from fires and chimneys in thatched-roof wooden houses. People working on the bank spot the boat and start to call. Others gather on the wooden jetty, where a number of other boats are secured. In the boat, Churkin starts giving orders. Klokov and Folkin come to where Mathew is sitting. They pull him to his feet and roughly turn him around.

Metal circles his wrists. He's being handcuffed. They stand with him at the front of the boat as it draws in to shore. Zarubin hops onto the bow, carrying a rope. He jumps onto the jetty, pulls them in with the rope, and ties it fast. Klokov and Folkin push Mathew forward. He nearly slips and falls without arms to balance. Klokov holds him up and all but lifts him onto the jetty. They wait while Churkin gets off. Evgeny comes ashore carrying a case of food. Bending to put the case on the floor near Mathew, he whispers as he stands, "We're in Chukotka. We're in Siberia."

Klokov gives the cook a shove, says something, and Evgeny goes back into the boat to continue to unload. Churkin arrives, and they start to walk along the jetty.

As they go into the village, people stop and peer from their work. All the people here are men, and they're all in uniform.

The base camp is in a clearing in the jungle. They walk along a makeshift runway with a windsock at the end of a tall pole and a helipad. There's a large, open-sided building with benches in it and a number of wooden huts with banana-leaf thatches.

Mathew is taken to one of these smaller huts and hustled through the door, boots loud on the raised wooden floor. There's a short corridor with a chair in it and two rooms with their doors open. Klokov shoves Mathew inside the second room, shuts the door and locks it behind him.

There's nothing in the room but a low wooden bed pushed against a wall. The walls are lime-washed mud and straw. The floor is wooden, dry and clean. The room is spotless. There's one narrow window letting in bright sunlight, but it's too high up to see out of. It's cool in the room, and Mathew is cold. He hasn't felt cold in days. He grabs the thin blanket off the bed and wraps it around his shoulders.

Then there is nothing to do but sit and wait.

He uses the time to think of a story, like Evgeny told him. Why would he be in Siberia?

This is the strangest game I have ever played. Siberia isn't anything like this. I saw on the news only a few months ago that it's uninhabitable because of all the methane from the melting permafrost. But this is a game, and the game requires me to invent a story.

Thinking hard, he starts to invent.

Later, the door unlocks, a man comes in, and the door locks behind him. He is balding, with a salt-and-pepper moustache, and wears a uniform with a red cross sewn on his sleeve. He is carrying a medical bag, which he puts on the floor and opens. Without comment or introduction, he gets straight to business, unwrapping the dressings around his shoulder. Brusquely gripping Mathew's arm, he examines the wound. He pours liquid onto some cotton wool, and Mathew gasps and flinches as the doctor swabs the weeping skin. The man grips his shoulder more tightly and holds it in place as he continues to work, using a device unfamiliar to Mathew to stitch the wound, and redresses it.

Once he has finished with Mathew's injuries, the doctor takes an electrical device from the bag on the floor. Pushing Mathew's head forward, he runs the device across the skin at the back of his neck. There is a beep. The man stands back, punches keys on the device, reads something, looks at Mathew suspiciously, and then peers at the device again, punching some more buttons. The machine beeps again. He repeats the exercise, pushing Mathew's head down, frowning at the screen, displeased. Doing the whole thing one more time makes him no happier. Standing and stepping quickly across the room, he briskly bangs on the door. The door is unlocked, and the doctor leaves. Mathew is alone again.

Much later, the light from the high window is still bright. The guard comes into the room and places a chair in the middle of the empty floor, a few feet away from the bed, and leaves the room without having once looked at Mathew, slamming the bolt behind him.

Several minutes pass before the door opens again.

A new man comes into the room and sits down on the chair, facing Mathew. Short in stature, he is slight, not muscular, but something in his body language carries such aggression and malice that Mathew is immediately on his guard. He has a thick mat of dark hair, the type that forms into springy curls if it isn't kept short, small black angry eyes, and an expression of utter contempt. Leaning forward, his elbows on his knees, he assesses his prisoner like a spider contemplating breakfast, finally saying in accentless English, "So, you are Mathew Erlang?"

"Yes," Mathew croaks. His throat is terribly dry.

"I am Polkovnik Grigory Dragomirov. Colonel Dragomirov." The man's eyes are hard, unblinking. "You don't speak a word of Russian?"

"Not without a simultaneous translation plug-in to my e-Pin, no."

"We don't use simultaneous translation devices here," the man says, leaning back, getting comfortable. "Firstly, they tend to break easily because of the extreme humidity. Secondly, we don't need them, because we all speak Russian."

Dragomirov sits back in his chair, stretching his neck, gazing at the ceiling. He closes his eyes and sighs.

"Why would an English or Japanese boy . . . what are you again?"

"I'm English."

"I'm surprised you didn't try to say you were Chinese, which would at least make some sense. So why would a boy with English credentials be wandering around in the jungle in northeast Siberia?" He seems to be genuinely engaged in puzzling this out, trying to glean the answer from the ceiling. Then he drops his head and stares directly at Mathew. "Do you know?"

"I was – I am – travelling with my father. He's a research scientist." Mathew hears the question in his tone. It doesn't sound convincing even to himself.

The man smiles indulgently. "And where is your father now?"

"We got separated. I got lost. I fell into the river and got swept downstream. I was trying to find him, when a big cat attacked me. Your soldiers saved me."

"Yes. How nice of them." He smiles, waits for Mathew to smile, and then hardens his face. "So if we all go back upstream and hunt, we will find an English scientist working in the jungle, presumably now searching for his son?"

"Yes."

"Does he have a permit to do research in the jungle?"

"I . . . I don't know."

"You don't know?"

Mathew shakes his head. The man sighs again.

"It is odd. We have no record of any English scientist working here. Nor does anyone in the Federation government. It's strange, given there is a war on. Why would an English research scientist be working in Russia in the middle of a war?"

The war! He'd forgotten the war.

"But do you know what is even more puzzling?"

Mathew blinks.

"Do you know?" He really wants a response.

"No," Mathew croaks.

"Your father is dead," the man says.

How could they know? Did they get it from my chip?

"But that is still not the strangest thing of all. The strangest thing is . . ." – Dragomirov is leaning forward again – "you have been dead for 381 years."

20 MATHEW ERLANG IS DEAD

"What do you mean I'm dead?"

"Major Lapin, the doctor who came to examine you before, scanned you with a chip reader. It found your bioID. We have international records – they're easy enough to get. It says you are who you claim to be. You are Mathew Erlang. You were born in London."

"So?"

"London hasn't been populated since the late twenty-first century. It also says you died in Silverwood."

"Where is Silverwood?"

The man laughs. "But you aren't Mathew Erlang. It upset Dr Lapin because he believes in these systems and thinks they are infallible. I don't agree. I don't believe any system is infallible. Nothing humans build, anyway."

The door opens, and Evgeny brings in food.

Dragomirov doesn't move but watches Evgeny hand a bowl and a spoon to Mathew with the same unwavering expression of contempt. Evgeny doesn't speak to Mathew, doesn't even look at him, and backs away through the door, as if afraid to turn his back on the colonel.

"What did you eat in the jungle?" Dragomirov asks.

"Bananas."

"And what did you drink?"

"Water."

"Where did you get the water?"

"From the river."

"Then you should be dead. The river is full of disease. Have you taken malaria medication?"

Mathew shakes his head.

The man gazes at him with mock admiration. "Remarkable. A medical marvel."

"I have medibots," Mathew says.

The man's face pales slightly. "Do you?" he says. "You know those are illegal for the non-Pure in 206 sovereign states around the world. And you are non-Pure, you know. We'll have to have the doctor examine you properly later; perhaps he will help you and kill your medibots."

"What do you mean, non-Pure?"

"I mean you are imperfect like most of the rest of us. Not whole. Unable to contribute to the continuance of the human race. It's a pity for you, because it might have saved you. Even I won't kill the Pure."

"I don't understand."

"You don't understand much, do you? How many days did you say you were there on your own, after you lost your father, as you say?"

"I've lost count."

"Roughly?"

Mathew thinks and then says, "Four nights. Five if you count the night I spent with your men in the jungle."

Dragomirov indicates the bowl of food in Mathew's hands. "You're eating that disgusting bile like it's something special. You're either a good actor, or what you're saying is at least partly true."

"It is true," Mathew says.

The man sniffs, watches Mathew finish his meal, stands abruptly, walks to the door, and leans his back against it, his legs crossed at the ankles, observing Mathew.

"You know, in all my years in the military, I've never come across a successful chip hacker." He says this with genuine admiration. "ATLAS may be close to annihilation, but it still has one or two clever people. It's a shame." He bangs on the door, which is promptly opened. "We're taking the boy to the medical block," he says.

Dragomirov gives Mathew his spider smile and gestures with an open hand through the door.

"Shall we?"

Dr Lapin is waiting in the examination room. It's a hut like the prison block, but the walls are hung with white cupboards, and it's equipped with an array of strange machines. The doctor gestures towards the tall bed on wheels on one side of the room.

"Sit," he says.

Dragomirov stands in the corner, his arms folded, speaking to the doctor in Russian. The doctor nods and turns to the counter underneath the cupboards, where he selects something, takes off a wrapper, and comes to Mathew holding a syringe with a long needle.

"Blood sample," he says in stilted English.

Then he says something in Russian to Dragomirov.

Dragomirov says to Mathew, "He wants you to roll up your sleeve."

The doctor takes the syringe full of blood to the side of the room and drops small amounts into various tubes sitting on a tray attached to a machine. Unrolling a kind of thin, transparent Paper, he snaps it to a frame. Then he presses a couple of buttons on the machine, and numbers and words start to scroll onto the Paper. The doctor stands in front of it, apparently issuing voice commands in Russian. Dragomirov stands beside him. Lapin points, and they talk in Russian. By the tone of his voice, the colonel is displeased. The doctor raises his hands defensively. Dragomirov walks to the door, opens it suddenly, and barks an order at the guard.

He says to Mathew, "Okay, we're done in here. You go with him."

The guard waits for Mathew on the other side of the door. Mathew leaves the room, blood trickling down his arm. The doctor doesn't notice.

There's no way of telling what time it is in his cell. The daylight is endless. Since the guard brought him back from the medical block, he has been alone in the room for what seems like several hours, although it is difficult to say for sure.

He marvels at this game he's in and wonders how Lestrange created it. What kind of advanced tele-existence and haptic technologies produce such a persistent sense of reality? It must involve brain-altering chemicals delivered somehow via that innocent-looking skullcap in Lestrange's Darkroom. Although, he thinks, as with the crudest video-and-audio-only virtual reality, the longer you're in them, the more accustomed you become to the sensory experience provided, and the more convinced you become of their reality. There are probably some obvious scams in the program he's not registering. But these thoughts will do him no good, when his priority should be to discover how to play and win the game. Right now, he has the distinct idea he's losing in every conceivable way.

There are noises in the corridor. The door opens, and Evgeny comes into the room with a tray; the door is shut and locked behind him.

"Evgeny! What time is it?"

"Dinner time. I am not allowed to speak to you."

"Please. I have no idea what is going on. You have to help me."

"I can't. They will know."

"Why are they keeping me here? Why are they taking blood samples? What's wrong with my bioID?"

"I don't know." Evgeny is harassed. His hands shake as he passes Mathew a bowl of roasted fish and steamed vegetables. Pressing a fork into his hand, he says, "Eat."

He puts a jug of water and a cup on the floor. "You must drink," he says.

He stands to go.

"What is ATLAS?" Mathew says.

Evgeny gapes at Mathew like he is stupid. "It is our enemy. It is where you are from. England. The United States. Europe."

"What year is it?"

"You are a crazy boy. You must have fallen from the sky."

"Yes. I fell from the sky. What year is it?"

"2472."

The soldier bangs on the door.

Evgeny is frightened. "I must go. You drink." He thuds back, signalling he is ready. As the door opens, the guard exchanges sharp words with him. The door closes with a bang.

2472.

Mathew is in the future. That's why he's dead.

21 BORODIN THE CAT

Whomp, whomp, whomp.

They hear the chopper before they see it. It comes in low over the treetops, creating a mini-cyclone, flattening and splaying leaves, bending boughs.

Dragomirov hurries from his hut, still pulling on his jacket. Major Anatoly Rostov, his second in command, is with him.

"Who the hell is this man?" Dragomirov is asking.

"He's the district governor of the Chukotka Autonomous Okrug. This is his territory, and he wants to understand what you are doing here."

"Didn't you send the authorisation through?"

"Yes."

"We have clearance from the head of the FSB. What else does he need to know? What's his name?"

"Polkovnik Konstantin Borodin."

"What do we have on him?"

"Not much. No one seems to know anything about him."

Dragomirov laughs. "He can't be anyone then, can he? Let's get this over with quickly."

They walk towards the helipad.

The district governor is already climbing from the copter, his head bowed out of the way of the blades, walking directly towards

Dragomirov. He's a big man with a broad chest, well-muscled; he moves in a confident, curiously fluid motion. The sinews in his neck are so defined under his skin they seem like they could be plucked. His face is chiselled, his jaw strong, and he has strange green eyes. They salute each other. They are of equivalent rank. This is a problem, Dragomirov realises.

Dragomirov's private hut has a sitting room with armchairs, a rug, and a makeshift fireplace with a mantelpiece, a painting of an old-fashioned Russian dacha above it. In front of the armchairs is an antique coffee table. There's a hot samovar in the corner of the room, a tea service on the table. Dragomirov has poured the tea himself. Half a fresh lemon sits in a saucer, and a china bowl decorated with painted violets contains lumps of brown and white sugar. Dragomirov is sitting with his legs crossed, relaxed in his armchair, sipping his tea.

"So, Borodin, what brings you this way?"

Borodin's voice is deep, guttural, a purr. Sitting in the armchair, he is a bundle of contained energy and loaded, poised muscle, as though he might leap up at any moment. He makes the chair seem like a toy. He doesn't seem to belong in the room, or any room. He says, "You have a prisoner."

"Yes, we do. How do you know?"

"I was tracking him myself."

"Why were you tracking him?"

"He is a foreigner in Russian territory and doesn't belong here."

"Yes, well, you don't need to worry now. We have him. All is well."

"But I do have to worry. This is my territory. A foreigner from an enemy nation has fallen from the sky into Siberia. It's concerning to me. Teenagers don't usually wander unaccompanied around rain forests, not for long, anyway. I need to know what you know."

"You saw the communication from my staff?"

"Yes, of course. Which is why I came here."

"Then you know I am here on classified business."

"I thought you would say that," Borodin says. He is bored, Dragomirov thinks. "Check your Paper."

"What?"

"I said, check your Paper."

Dragomirov unfolds the portable Paper he keeps in his chest pocket. There is a flag on the screen. A message from Central Command. Classified. The usual bureaucratic language, but the gist of it: Give Colonel Borodin your full cooperation.

"How did you do this?" Dragomirov asks, flabbergasted.

Borodin fixes him with his steady green eyes. "We are at war. I am in charge of a highly strategic territory. I want to know what's going on. Have you interrogated him?"

"I interviewed him yesterday. His story is inconsistent. His bioID is giving a strange readout."

"In what way?"

"He has the bioID of someone who died 381 years ago."

Borodin doesn't show any sign of surprise, doesn't laugh or even raise an eyebrow. Not a muscle on his face moves.

Dragomirov asks, "You don't think it's odd? Have you come across this before, Polkovnik? This kind of anomaly?"

Borodin ignores the question. "Why are you interested in this boy? Why are you here in my territory? Why does the government think it a good idea to send you here?" He says this with such direct rudeness that Dragomirov is amazed. "You were tracking someone else, weren't you? You weren't searching for the boy."

Then Dragomirov smiles, a spider again. "For weeks we have tracked ATLAS terrorists across your territory. I am surprised, frankly, that your people weren't aware of this. I'm amazed they failed to notice us."

"You lost the terrorists, Dragomirov." The word terrorists is accented with his fingers. "You found this boy accidentally. You think he's like the one you had but lost. He isn't."

How does he know this? Dragomirov is open-mouthed. Before

he regains his composure, Borodin is on his feet, the coiled energy suddenly released.

"I am taking the prisoner."

"What? No. You won't take the prisoner." Dragomirov scrambles from the armchair, putting his teacup down with a clatter.

"I will take him. You read the orders. Full cooperation."

Dragomirov gathers himself. His eyes are barely level with the buttons on the chest of Borodin's jacket. There's no way for him to look this man in the eye, unless he stands on a ladder. It makes him angry. He says, "I want authorisation on this matter from the Security Council. I want them made aware of a reference to a specific FSB case."

Borodin gazes down at him with what Dragomirov imagines is an indulgent expression. "Go and check with your committees. If you don't have an answer by tomorrow morning, I am taking the boy with me." Borodin goes to the door of the hut. "But if you want my advice, I would give up. The war is coming to its climax. Go home and be with your family."

Livid with anger, Dragomirov spits, "You will get communication from the director tonight."

Borodin half-shrugs, as if the response was inevitable. "Don't concern yourself with hospitality for me and my men," he says. "We brought our own shelter and supplies." He pushes open the door, and then he is gone.

Dragomirov is in the briefing room with Dr Lapin and Major Rostov. He's agitated. "Doctor, what do you need from me to complete your tests?"

"We need to get the boy back to Moscow to test him thoroughly, but I told you the blood tests I ran yesterday were normal. There was nothing like the anomalies we saw with Lamplighter. His blood is pedestrian, with the exception of the medibot, which is, of course, illegal. There was one strange thing, though."

"Yes?"

"His medibot is exactly like the type in common use at the outbreak of the First Space War. He is wearing a Lenz and an e-Pin, but they are also of an old design and use protocols long defunct."

"You are telling me you think this boy is 433 years old?"

The doctor smiles and shakes his head. "No, no. As I said, it's impossible. I'm saying the technology is consistent with the identity he is assuming. It's consistent with the data in his bioID."

"Meaning this is an elaborate hoax?"

"Why would the ATLAS secret services send a sixteen-year-old secret agent deep into enemy territory unsupported? Why on earth would his cover be time travel?" Rostov asks.

Dragomirov says, "He is part of the group of maggots with the Lamplighter. I am sure of it. Doctor, you need to keep working on this boy. Maybe they've found a way to mask his biological anomalies."

"Then I need to get him back to Moscow. There's no more for me to do with the tools I have here."

"We need to get this man Borodin off our backs. He knows far too much. It's strange," Dragomirov says.

"Perhaps he was briefed by Central Command Centre. Their communication did indicate he has the highest clearance," replies Rostov.

"No one knows about this mission but us and the director of the FSB. This whole thing with the authorisation is odd. I don't believe it," says Dragomirov.

"I've taken a look at it myself. It's genuine. I even requested and received a confirmation. But he's on the same side as us. Shouldn't we bring him in?" asks Rostov.

"No. I want him gone." Dragomirov stares at his shoes. He says, "Get me a meeting with the director in Moscow as soon as possible. We need to make sure we control the prisoner. Let's get Borodin off our backs, and then we'll get authorisation to send you back to Moscow with the prisoner, doctor."

"What about you?" Lapin asks.

"We're going to stay and continue to hunt down Lamplighter," Dragomirov says.

Rostov stands, ready to go and execute orders.

Dragomirov looks at him. "There's something else, Major. We have a weak link. Someone is leaking information, and it's getting back to Borodin. Let's make sure it's no one here."

"I'm on it," Rostov says.

22 THE SILENT PRAYER

The night falls suddenly in the forest, like a heavy cloak being thrown over a lamp.

A few miles from base camp, an odd group of men and women sit around a fire. There are a few grey heads and wrinkled faces, some much younger, too. They are the strangest army in the world.

A priest, one of the grey heads, dressed in a threadbare dog collar, leads the group in prayer. They hold hands. The tall, gaunt man they call Lev, short for Angel Leventis, opens his eyes during the prayer and winks at an elderly woman with garishly dyed red hair and skin so gnarled her face is like one of the trees surrounding them. She sits next to a heavy man with a skinhead and a scar on his face. A wizened old man whose head nods slightly watches them, and beside him sits a man in his late thirties with a massively well-developed upper body, arms the size of most thighs, and no legs. His face is set in an expression of concentrated piety, and he holds the hands of his wife on one side and his teenaged son on the other.

Oblivious, the priest gives thanks for their food, for their lives, for their opportunity in history. The priest asks for God's protection on one last mission before they and all the other rejected peoples of the earth go underground to save themselves from Wormwood.

"May we humbly try to emulate the ways of the first Tekton. May we follow his advice. Because we believe his ways were consistent with the ways of God."

"Amen."

The prayer finishes.
Not a word is spoken, but everyone hears.

23 EVGENY

Klokov is searching for the cook.

Kapral Churkin says there is a mole in the camp. All the other men in their platoon think if anyone's a squealer, it's the soft, fat cook, Evgeny Shukshin. Speaking English, after all, is deeply suspect. The way he behaves with the foreign boy prisoner is odd. Plus, he makes them eat those disgusting biscuits. They are all ready to serve him up to Dragomirov, but they have to find him first.

He's not in the cookhouse or in the mess. He's not down at the wash block or in the barracks. He's not in the open-air shelter or where the men play cards at night near the fire. Or down by the boats.

There are not many other places he might be.

Klokov stops, his hands behind his head, scanning. Not far from the helipad, on the cleared land next to the edge of the forest near the water, the district governor's men have set up camp. They have a roaring fire going under a fish-laden spit. They have tarpaulins and hammocks. A couple of the men are cutting wood at the edge of the jungle with machetes. Another is gutting and washing more fish in the river.

Then Klokov spots the cook walking across from their camp, with one of the governor's men, in plain sight, running a hose from the base camp well to their temporary camp. They are deep in conversation. They run the hose all the way to a cauldron hanging above the fire.

Klokov is convinced Evgeny is the mole. But he wants to hear what he's discussing with the soldier. He quickly retreats to base camp and then slips into the forest, taking a circuit all the way around the boundary of the settlement, until he's next to Borodin's camp. The fire is on the edge of the clearing. The fat cook is still talking to Borodin's soldier. His name is Yolkov. Their voices carry. Standing with his back to a large kapok tree, Klokov listens.

"I like to put thyme inside the fish skins. These river fish have a strong taste. It takes the edge off," says Evgeny. Delving into his pocket, he pulls out some leaves. "Here, I took the liberty of bringing you some from the cookhouse. Shall I show you?"

"Please do."

Evgeny uses a knife to make pockets in the sides of the cooking fish and stuffs in the herbs.

"Thank you, Evgeny. And thanks for the potatoes and the water, too. The colonel thinks we ought to be self-sufficient, but he's not the one cooking for fifteen men in the jungle with no provisions. We have a proper camp thirty miles north. We were only meant to come down here for the day. In and out, was what he said. I'm not even a cook, but suddenly like that" – he clicks his fingers – "I'm meant to know how to do all these things."

Evgeny nods sympathetically.

"Do you always camp in the jungle? I would have thought Borodin would have a more civilised base camp."

"Oh, he does, back in Uelen. A proper barracks, parade ground, a nearby town with restaurants and shops. It's civilised. But we're hardly ever there. Borodin likes to tour his territory. Recently, we've trekked over every inch of this godforsaken snake and spider pit of an ant-infested excuse for a strip of jungle, looking for god-only-knows what."

"Is it true they call him the Cat, your colonel?"

Yolkov nods. "We all do."

"On account of?"

"His eyes. The way he walks. And the fact he'll track any living thing in the jungle. If it's here, he will know it." Yolkov grins. "The men say at night he doesn't sleep but wakes and goes a-hunting. Comes back in the morning with bloody teeth."

"Ha!"

"Of course, it's nonsense."

"Of course it is! Pot is full." Evgeny switches off the hose using a nozzle at the end, lays it on the ground and checks the fish, then selects a potato from the bag on the floor and starts to peel it with his pocket knife. Handing a potato to Yolkov, he says, "Here. I'm not doing all the work."

Yolkov starts to peel. "Five months in this hell-hole," he says.

"We've been on the road a year."

"A year!"

Evgeny nods. "We started in the desert, would you believe it, and then we went everywhere there is to go on the Federation map."

"Do you have a family?"

"Yes. A wife, Marta." Evgeny digs into the inside pocket of his shirt, pulls out a crumpled, faded photograph. "And Edik, my son. See, he is fifteen. Getting so tall! Do you have kids?"

"I have a wife, Bria. No children."

Evgeny holds Yolkov's eyes, sorry to have made so much of his son.

"Don't you miss them? All that time on the road! A year!" Yolkov says.

"Of course I miss them! Like missing limbs. I wish we'd finish this crazy mission Dragomirov is on. Then I can go home."

"I want a hot shower, running water, a cold beer, dry socks, a proper bed. Even though it would mean certain court martial, I would walk back to town now if I thought I had a cat-in-hell's chance of making it five hundred yards through the jungle alive. . . . It is odd the boy survived."

"It's a mystery how he got here in the first place. Doesn't speak a word of Russian. Luckily, I speak English."

"You spoke to him?"

"I was with the group that found him."

"Is he what Dragomirov was hunting for?"

"No. I don't think so. Dragomirov is searching for a girl."

"A girl?"

"They call her the Lamplighter."

"Who does?"

"The maggots. The non-people living beyond the city walls. They think she's some kind of sign. I don't know. It's all crazy stuff. Anyhow, she caused several rebellions amongst the maggots, whether she intended to or not. Dragomirov caught her at one point and took her to a lab for Dr Lapin to examine with his machines. Some of the men say Dragomirov thinks she's some kind of weapon."

"A weapon?!"

"Yes, some kind of hyper-tech advanced, enhanced human. But the men talk nonsense most of the time. Half of them think the world is about to end."

The two men laugh.

"What happened to the girl?" Yolkov asks.

"She escaped. God knows how. We have the tightest security imaginable. Now the man is obsessed with trying to get her back." Evgeny stops talking suddenly. It occurs to him he's doing what he has been told many times he shouldn't do, shooting his mouth off. He says, "I should be getting back."

Still with his back pressed against the tree, Klokov is soaking up this conversation with a surging glee. He has caught the traitor red-handed and can hardly wait to get back to Churkin and tell him what he's heard. Dragomirov will praise him for his vigilance. He thinks about the promotion he'll surely get and all the benefits that go with it. No more damned mouldy biscuits.

Then without warning, without sound or the faintest disturbance to alert him, something cold and sharp presses against the skin of his neck. Cold like metal. Sharp like a knife. Straining his eyes down, he sees it. There is a hand and an arm, holding a blade to his throat.

A voice says, "Don't move. Don't even breathe. I will kill you right here, drag your body into the forest for the night creatures to clean, and never give it a second thought." It's a deep, growling kind of a voice. The knife slowly lifts from Klokov's skin. Breathing out with relief, he staggers forward. Borodin comes from behind the tree, sheathing his knife. "Why are you spying on my camp and my men? Why are you creeping around? I could have killed you."

Klokov scrambles to salute. "I wasn't spying on your men, sir. I was spying on one of ours."

"Who?"

"Our fat cook. I'll show you." Hard-ass leads Borodin the few steps from the undergrowth to the fire with the spit and the cooking pot.

Yolkov is tending to the roasting fish and peers through streaming, smoky eyes as Borodin approaches and salutes. Evgeny has disappeared.

Dragomirov's face and neck are red. He's having a terrible evening.

First, Rostov came to tell him that the FSB director isn't available for a conference call, but he sent a message to say that Borodin is one of the best trackers in the Russian army and Dragomirov should make full use of his skills and resources in his search for the Lamplighter, and he must respect Borodin's rank and authority. In other words, Dragomirov is going to have to bow and scrape to the overgrown animal.

Now, before Rostov has even finished, Borodin himself has come bursting into his private quarters, shoving ahead of him some cretin from the lower ranks, bringing in all sorts of jungle debris on the bottom of his boots.

"I found this man hiding in the trees beside my camp. By his own admission he was spying."

Klokov is shaken. This isn't how he imagined things at all. "I wasn't spying on Colonel Borodin's men, sir."

Rostov, smarting from the dressing-down he's just received on account of the failed attempt to organise a call with the FSB director, yells at Klokov, "Did anyone ask you to speak, soldat?!"

"No, sir!"

"Then shut up!"

"What were you doing in Colonel Borodin's camp?" Dragomirov asks.

Klokov hesitates.

Major Rostov yells, "Speak when you're asked a question!"

"Sir! I was following soldat Evgeny Shukshin."

"What? Why?" Dragomirov asks.

"Following orders, sir!"

"Whose orders?"

"Kapral Andrei Churkin."

Dragomirov sighs and says to Rostov, "Major, go and get Churkin." Rostov moves towards the door. "Actually, hold on, Rostov." Dragomirov turns to Klokov again. "Do you know why Kapral Churkin wanted you to follow – who is it again?"

Rostov and Klokov both say "Shukshin" at the same time.

Dragomirov nods. "Do you know why you were ordered to follow this man?"

"We thought he was a spy, sir!"

"A spy? Who was he supposed to be spying on?"

"Us. For Colonel Dragomirov, sir."

Dragomirov, confused, frowns at Rostov. "Any idea what's going on here?"

The penny drops for Major Rostov, with a cold, creeping horror. He says, "Sir, I'm not sure we want to discuss . . ." He tries to indicate Borodin with his eyes, but Dragomirov snaps impatiently. "Say it, whatever it is, Major."

"I briefed Churkin and other section leaders yesterday, sir. I asked them to be vigilant and not discuss or share classified information. I also asked them to search for weak links in their ranks."

"Why did you ask them that, Major Rostov?"

"Because you asked me to, sir."

"I did?"

"Yes, sir. You said you thought we have a leak."

Dragomirov remembers and coughs, not daring to even glance at Borodin, who's standing silently in the corner of the room, observing. He turns to Klokov. "Well, what did you find? Is . . . What's his name again?"

"Soldat Evgeny Shukshin."

"Is Shukshin a spy?"

"Yes, sir," says Klokov.

Rostov says, "You're sure? This is a serious allegation."

"Yes, sir!"

Borodin speaks from the shadows, his low growl of a voice making Klokov noticeably paler. "What is your evidence?"

"Evidence, sir?"

"On what basis are you accusing your fellow soldier of treachery?"

"I heard him speak to your cook, sir, and he passed on classified information."

"What did he actually say?" Dragomirov asks.

"He spoke of cooking and his family."

"What did he say relevant to your accusation?" Rostov says, impatiently.

"It is relevant. It's context."

"Context?"

"His character. What sort of man he is, soft and weak. A liar and a blabbermouth, stealing food from our kitchen to give to Colonel Borodin's cook. And he lied about his family."

"Giving army food to members of the same army is not stealing. Arguably, it's helpful behaviour and commendable," Borodin says. "How did he lie?"

"He showed your cook a photograph of his family. He's always showing his photo to strangers. Anyone who will listen, boasting of having a son."

"How is that lying? Does he not have a son?"

Rostov clears his throat. "He did have a son. His entire family died in a wildfire five years ago while he was away on active duty, but it won't go in here," he says, violently tapping his own forehead in a way that must have hurt.

"It sounds like the man is due sympathy and understanding more than condemnation," Borodin says.

"It is a dangerous thing to fight with weak-minded men," Dragomirov says, focusing on Rostov, who looks uncomfortable.

Borodin says, "Presumably, you have been aware of these things for a while and have found him able to perform his duties – otherwise, he wouldn't be here. This isn't a revelation to you, surely?"

Dragomirov was barely aware of the cook's name and rank before this moment, but he isn't going to give Borodin the satisfaction, so he inclines his head in a gesture that might be interpreted as agreement or might be stretching, and turns again to Klokov. "Well?"

"I meant he's not alright in the head, not to be trusted. He said other things to Colonel Borodin's cook. Classified things."

"Like what?"

"I don't know if I should . . ." He glances at Borodin and then back at Dragomirov.

Borodin says, "If this information was passed to my cook, it will be passed to me later anyway."

Klokov glances at Dragomirov, who nods.

"Your cook was complaining because you are constantly in the jungle," he says to Borodin.

Dragomirov smiles, but Borodin is poker-faced.

"Shukshin told him we've been on the road for more than a year, told him of the Lamplighter. He told him we'd lost her and were trying to find her again."

"We already know about the Lamplighter," Borodin says. "Is that all?"

"Yes," Klokov says.

Borodin turns to Dragomirov. "You must judge your own men, but it sounds like nothing to me. Do you have any news on the authorisation you said you would have tonight?"

Dragomirov says, "We will have it later this evening." Rostov and Dragomirov exchange glances, giving Dragomirov away to Borodin, but it doesn't matter because he already knows Dragomirov is lying.

"Let me know as soon as you get it through, won't you? And please do brief your people not to snoop around my camp while we're here. I am sometimes over-sensitive on the matter of intruders and may accidentally slip with my knife next time. Goodnight." He nods at Dragomirov and is gone.

There is a special punishment cage beside the prison block. It's made of wood from the forest, and the door is barred with a thick pole. It isn't possible to stand in the cage, and jungle grass and earth serve as the floor, making it easy for any snake, spider, or insect to crawl in. It's rarely used. The last time was when Osin drank a day's worth of his section's ration of vodka, getting sick drunk and resulting in his comrades missing their daily allocation. No one argued for him.

No one argues for the mad fat cook, either, as he is dragged by Klokov and Churkin across the yard, with Rostov overseeing and Dragomirov taking it all in from the door of his quarters. Evgeny begs and sobs and grabs at the doorframe. Klokov merely stamps on his hands and pushes him inside with his foot. When he won't stop crying, he pours a bucket of water over him.

"Next time it will be a bucket from the shithouse," he says.

"That's enough," Rostov says, and sends Klokov and Churkin back to their barracks.

But Dragomirov lingers in the doorway, wishing Rostov hadn't stopped them.

24 THE NIGHT RESCUE

Tuesday, 21 June 2472, Siberia

In the dead of the short night the forest is never still. A million life-and-death battles are fought. Things crash through the undergrowth, fall from branches, splash through water, dislodge rocks on the mountainside, and scream in warning or pain. Nocturnal insects leap from leaf to leaf or flutter in the moonlight, singing to find mates, and reptiles with strange, giant, unblinking eyes hunt them and make meals of them. The alert and the paranoid could be driven mad listening to noises in the forest at night.

On this particular night, it is not just the animals on the prowl. People move with soft, sure feet, communicating without speaking, moving as one, without the need of light. They come down from the side of the mountain with such stealth, even the hunters and the hunted do not see them go. They pass through thick undergrowth and then suddenly disappear as if they were never there at all.

Mathew is in a fitful sleep, tossing on the hard bench that serves as his bed, shivering under the thin blanket. He is woken by the sound of his name being called in an English voice.

Half-asleep, he thinks, *It's Mum saying she's leaving for work. No… It's a man's voice! Dad?*

His father had an accent. He hears the voice again, distinctly, and it fully wakes him up.

A hand covers his mouth. Someone is crouching beside him. They have two fingers pressed to their lips. In his head, clearly, not aloud: "Be quiet. Don't make a sound."

Whoever it is is speaking to him via his e-Pin.

It's pitch-dark, but there is a dim light source from somewhere, and he sees that the door to his cell is open. *Are my Lenzes working now?* He has night vision! In a blue-and-white wash of light he sees a man with wild grey hair, a tumbling grey beard.

In Mathew's head, not aloud, the man says, "My name is Lev. I am a friend, and I've come to get you away from here. It's important you are as quiet as possible. Do not speak. Think loudly if you want to say something. We have adjusted your Lenz and e-Pin so you can use them in this way. Be quick now! We need to leave. You'll be able to ask all the questions you like when we get to safety. Come quickly now. It will not be dark for much longer."

Mathew gets off his bench and goes from his cell into the corridor. The guard is in a dead sleep, slumped in his chair, snoring, catching flies. "Don't worry, he will not wake for several hours," the grey-haired man says in his head.

The door to the guardhouse is open. A bank of clouds covers the moon. He follows the man, bending low, keeping to the shade cast by the guardhouse.

Then Mathew spots Evgeny. He has seen them, too, crouched on the ground, holding on to the wooden bars of his cage, his eyes wide. Mathew knows he wouldn't say anything to anyone about their escape, but he doesn't want to abandon him.

Mathew tugs on the shirt of the grey-haired man called Lev, thinking hard. "He's my friend."

Something must have got through to the man because he nods. "Alright. Stay here. Do not move for now. If someone finds me, crawl under this building and wait for them to go. When it's clear, head for the biggest tree, right ahead at the edge of the clearing. People will meet you there. Okay?"

Mathew nods.

Lifting the wooden pole locking the door of Evgeny's cage, he sets it aside silently. As he'd done with Mathew, he puts his fingers to his lips. Evgeny appears to understand, crawling from the cage, and joining Mathew in the shadows of the prison block. They follow Lev to the end of the building.

"This will be the most dangerous part. We need to get to that tree." Mathew immediately understands he means the tallest, thickest one on the boundary of the clearing. "Your friend can't hear me."

Mathew nods. Touching Evgeny on the arm, he points at the tree, making a running gesture with his fingers.

Lev walks silently into the twilight. Evgeny and Mathew follow close behind. Evgeny grabs the back of Mathew's shirt, and Mathew guesses that Evgeny is effectively blind, walking straight into darkness. Low clouds cloak the lightening sky until they are at the edge of the clearing and under the shade of the trees. It's still the middle of the night, but the sun is coming up, breaking golden light brilliantly across the camp. Mathew glances back, but Lev taps him on his shoulder and indicates they should keep moving.

They walk no more than thirty feet. Lev bends down and lifts some banana leaves, revealing a deep hole in the ground, a vertical tunnel, just wider than a man's shoulders.

"Quickly," he says.

There is a ladder. Manoeuvring himself carefully, Mathew gets his feet onto the rungs and starts climbing down. Evgeny follows. When Mathew reaches the bottom and raises his eyes, Lev is at the top, pulling the leaves back to hide the hole. Coming down after them, he collapses the ladder into a kind of portable stick and puts it in a bag on the floor at the base of the hole, which he slings over his shoulder. Light spills across the hollow from a lantern on the floor. Lev grabs this and uses it to light their way. Darkness folds behind them.

They're walking along a narrow tunnel. Lev is tall, and his wild grey hair brushes the roof. Evgeny barely fits through. The tunnel is cut from the bedrock of the forest. The sides are polished smooth. They walk in silence for what feels like a long time, perhaps twenty minutes, and then the tunnel starts to slope upwards. Lev stops, puts the lantern on the ground, takes the ladder stick from his bag and throws it at the wall. It unfurls all the way to the top of a shaft directly above their heads. This time he goes first, telling them to wait. He hauls himself out at the top, disappears for a few moments, and then comes down again.

"Okay, Mathew, you first."

Mathew climbs the ladder, pokes his head out at the top, and peers about. Standing around him are four men in their twenties and thirties. They're dressed like the bearded man in strange civilian clothes. One of the men takes Mathew's hand and hauls him from the shaft. With lips closed, he says, "Hello, I'm Tristan. These are my brothers, Bren, Liam, and Kell. We still have some way to go, and we must be quiet. We will speak only through your e-Pin. Okay?"

Mathew nods.

The other men smile at him, and he grins back. One of them rushes to the shaft Evgeny is having difficulty squeezing through. Lev quickly explains Evgeny's unplanned presence to the others. Once Evgeny is clear, they bury the shaft under leaves.

They are immediately on their way, swift and quiet through the undergrowth. They stop a few times for Evgeny to catch his breath. They are patient, Mathew notices, and not at all critical of Evgeny's weight or poor level of fitness.

Eventually, they arrive at a cliff face. It's sheer, rising above them a hundred feet or more. Lev walks to an outcrop of rocks sitting to one side of the cliff, lifts some leaves and holds them up for the others to pass under. The leaves are attached to a rough-fashioned door, made from wood. Inside the door is a cave.

Tristan goes in first. Lev hangs behind to help them all in and then shuts the door behind them.

They stand in darkness for a few moments while someone lights a lamp, and then lamps go on all around and a cave is revealed. One of Tristan's brothers hands Mathew a lantern.

They start to move off again.

The cave is low and wide at first, the roof slanting at either side, so they have to move in single file and bend as they walk. Their lamps cast strange phantoms on the roof and into the corners of the cave.

Towards the back the roof dips. Tristan gets down on his hands and knees and indicates that Mathew and Evgeny should do so too. They crawl through a narrow space. Mathew thinks about the weight of the entire mountain above him. The stone is wet and cold where it brushes his skin.

They shuffle along for thirty feet or so and come into a much larger cavern, the roof high above their heads. They're standing on the shore of a large underground lake that glistens in the lamplight but becomes black where the light runs out.

"We have to swim for a while," Lev says.

There's a wooden crate against the wall of the cave on the shore. Lev goes to it and collects small mouthpieces, goggles, and headlamps, which he hands around. He offers Evgeny and Mathew life jackets and helps to fit Evgeny's. Tristan shows them both how to use the breathing equipment. Mathew puts the small mask to his face. It grips him like a living creature, soft and sucking against his skin. There's no strap at the back. Taking in a shuddery breath, his eyes wide, not expecting to be able to breathe, he finds he can do so well and fluidly, and he relaxes.

"Good," Tristan says. He turns to Evgeny and makes sure his mask is secure. "Okay?" he asks.

Evgeny puts up his thumb.

Tristan's brothers gather the lanterns, turn them off and stack them in the crate. The cave is lit only by their wavering headlamps.

"Ready?" Lev puts on his breathing mask and wades into the dark water. The others follow.

The water is ice-cold. Mathew gasps as it reaches his stomach, and he has to fight his instincts in order to keep pace with the others. Gripped by fear at the thought of getting further into the dark water, he continues to wade and watches the brothers begin to swim away, only the backs of their heads visible in the inky lake. He starts to swim out but fears going beyond his depth.

Sensing his fear, Tristan says, "Put your head under the water. Look down."

Mathew does so, and he's transported into a different world. They are floating in a cathedral. Their lamps seek and illuminate strange majestic shapes: underwater stalagmites like the ruined columns made to support the roof of a once great and ancient church, the rocks carved by water and formed by minerals over millennia into wonderful natural sculptures. The water is fresh and clear, and it's possible to see a long way. Mathew is stunned at the beauty of it. He treads water, gapes, and forgets where he is. Lev taps him on his shoulder. The others have moved off and are disappearing into a narrow tunnel ahead.

"We must keep going," he says, turning

Mathew nods and follows. Now when he lifts his head from the water there's only a couple of feet of air above him, but beneath, the water is a vast open space. The tunnel widens and narrows periodically as they go along, and then finally they stop and put aside their breathing equipment. It's a dead end. There are no more tunnels for them to swim down.

Mathew bends back his neck and is once again aware of the crushing weight of rock above their heads and now how deep inside the mountain they are. If anything happens, there's no easy escape. He's starting to feel chilled.

Lev speaks aloud for the first time, using his voice for the benefit of Evgeny. "We need to dive and swim underwater for a while. Straight in front of us, under that wall, is a lip and a narrow underwater tunnel. Your breathing equipment will work. You have to trust it and follow the man in front. It'll be fine." He glances between Evgeny and Mathew. "Okay?"

They both nod. Evgeny is shivering. Lev takes their life jackets from them and passes them to Tristan and one of his brothers. Then he dives.

Tristan takes Mathew to the wall at the end of the cave and pulls him underwater with him. Looking in his eyes, he speaks through his e-Pin: "Breathe normally like you were doing all along. Look ahead. Resist the temptation to panic." He waits until he sees Mathew take a few unsteady breaths, then he says, "That's it." Pointing, he shows the way to a tunnel, lit by Lev's headlamp. Up ahead, Lev is swimming on. "Pull yourself through with your hands," he says, indicating the stalactites hanging down from the roof.

Mathew says, "Thank you. I'm okay. Help Evgeny."

Tristan nods and swims to the surface. Mathew follows Lev into the tunnel. Taking Tristan's advice, he pulls on the protruding rocks to give himself momentum. His hands and feet are numb with cold. He hears music, and he thinks he must be hallucinating, but then he realises Lev is humming down his e-Pin.

Lev disappears from view. Mathew swims after him. They have come into another cavern. The water now stretches out below and beside him and far above his head. Raising his eyes, he can see Lev swimming at the surface, silhouetted against the light. Following, pulling with his hands, he kicks and then bursts through. Lev is there beside him.

"Take off your mask," he says. "You can breathe." Treading water, he helps Mathew, who takes a grateful, shuddering gulp of air.

His eyes are drawn upwards.

The roof of the cavern is two hundred feet above his head and brightly lit. They are swimming at the bottom of a cliff in an underground lake. Water cascades down the rock side, the terminus of another underground stream. Ferns grow on shelves and crevices nourished by spray from the water. Lev swims strongly to the shore and wades out, climbing steps to dry land. He beckons to Mathew. All around, lining the lakeside, there are people – women, men, children, young people, elderly people, people of all ethnicities, dressed like Lev in strange civilian clothes. Two of Tristan's brothers break the surface with Evgeny between them. They swim him to the water's edge and help him to the shore.

Mathew follows them, shivering. A tall, bulky elderly woman with wild, dyed red hair comes towards him with towels. "I'm Rose," she says. "You need to get warm. Come this way."

Carved into the sides of the cavern are thousands of steps zigzagging to higher levels. They provide ways to balconies, walkways, and landings, which he later discovers lead to yet more staircases and passageways carved into the rock. Rose climbs steadily, and Mathew, Evgeny, Lev, Tristan, and his brothers follow. The shallow, deep steps are carved with precision, as if machine-made, cross-hatched on top to prevent slipping, with high edges and railings made from some kind of material Mathew doesn't recognise.

Rose leads them to a landing and then into a corridor and from there into a cave or room carved into the rock. Here there is a steaming bath.

This cave has tall windows overlooking the larger cavern. Rose checks the temperature of the water and then says, "I'll leave you to it," and disappears back the way she came.

Lev and the others strip from their jungle clothes, wash under a shower to one side of the pool, and then get into the hot water. Mathew and Evgeny step in after them. Mathew feels his bones thaw, and the blood returns to his hands. He gazes across at Tristan. He and his three brothers are grinning. They reach across the water and high-five each other.

Even Lev is smiling.

"Welcome to our home, Mathew and Evgeny," he says.

25 FRIENDS UNDER THE MOUNTAIN

Tristan is giving them a tour of the place he calls the Theseum.

Mathew and Evgeny are wearing the clean, dry clothes Rose put aside for them, made of the loose light fabrics Tristan and the others wear. Mathew takes a bit of the cloth in his hand and examines it. It looks like linen, but it doesn't feel like linen and it's surprisingly warm.

"It's made of a special type of material made partly from carbon nanotubes," Tristan explains. "Something we've developed ourselves over the years. It's intelligent. It generates and stores energy. It maintains optimum body temperature whether we're in the jungle or in the cave. It's also waterproof, but breathable, and lightweight so it doesn't get in the way of physical activity. And it's self-cleaning, and self-repairing, so we need few changes of clothes. Our boots are hyper-lightweight but tough."

Evgeny has been fitted with a kind of e-Pin, a clip-on device that sits inside his ear providing simultaneous translation and allowing him to join in any silent conversation. Mathew has already discovered that even when they're speaking aloud, Tristan's people use mind speech and a subtle kind of super-fast mind communication, a sort of inter-brain emotional gesturing.

Tristan is now talking aloud in plain speech. "In this cave we use geothermal energy for heat. That's what heated your shower and your bath. We've rigged solar power through trees in the forest with a liquid we paint on the leaves. It doesn't harm the trees. The liquid contains nanomachines that capture energy from sunlight and disseminate it via a secure coded wireless transmission system, which is, of course, encrypted and masked from the various military populations that pass through. The energy collection device is embedded on the side of the mountain and we have a system to route the energy inside, even when we are in lock-down. We don't use real fire down here because of smoke pollution and because any chimney would give away our location. We have ample water from the underground supplies, although we use a filter. For fresh air circulation we have drilled vents that open high on the mountain. They should be hard to detect for outsiders, and they can be shut as required. We have a system to recycle air when the refuge needs to be airtight."

Mathew, Tristan, and Evgeny walk past an area where a group of men and women are preparing a large meal. They raise their eyes when Mathew and Evgeny pass, smiling and saying hello.

Tristan says, "We are self-sufficient in food. We grow a lot of vegetables using hydroponics, and we get what we can't grow through the advanced replicators we have. Our waste is recycled to produce fertiliser for our hydroponic gardens."

A large terraced garden is cut into a wall. The terraces are filled with a brown water solution and filled with plants. Hanging above them are sets of hot lamps.

"We grow salads, fresh vegetables, and even flowers under high-energy light."

They climb one of the many sets of stairs and walk down a brightly lit corridor carved out of bare rock and polished to a high sheen.

"These are my quarters," he says.

He takes them into a simple room, with a comfortable, neatly made bed, a table with a vase and real flowers, a product of the hydroponic gardens. Above the bed, hanging on the wall is a large, thin Canvas, which is showing various images of rocky, dusty, arid landscapes and deserts, thin, parched shrubs all surrounded by aquamarine waters.

"I'm terribly nostalgic," he says ruefully. "I miss home. So I have all these memory images, probably idealised. It's a human failing," he continues. "Nostalgia. But then, I am human . . ."

"Memory images?"

"The images on the walls are made from my memories."

"How?" Mathew says, amazed.

"I don't understand the tech in detail, but like everyone's here, my brain is connected to our central computer system. Parts of my brain, mainly images, can be downloaded, if I choose, for storage or sharing, or in this case, for decorating my room with images of my childhood home."

"Where is home?" Evgeny asks.

"England, of course," Tristan says.

"That is England?" Mathew says incredulously.

"Yes . . ." Tristan says, for a moment not understanding Mathew's horror. "To me it is beautiful. Of course . . . you wouldn't. . . . I'll let Lev explain." They leave Tristan's quarters and head back towards the main cavern, pausing to observe it from the stairwell. Tristan says, "We have only been here six months, so our build is crude but adequate for our purposes."

"Six months?!" Evgeny says, astounded. "You have only been here six months and you have built this?"

"Yes, this is the most basic type of facility we've made, but we didn't have much time to do it."

"There are others?"

"Hundreds."

"Where?"

"Everywhere Lev managed to get to and was successful in persuading people he wasn't a crazy man. He mostly failed, it has to be said. He walked all the way from Britain to Tierra del Fuego, via continental Europe, with some detours into Scandinavia, through Russia, sailing across to Alaska, then on foot again down through the Americas and back again, covering territories he missed on his way down. We believe his message has spread further via people he met on his travels – he was walking for forty years. It's why we call him the Pathbreaker. People not so keen on him have other names for him, but you'll have to ask him yourself."

"How old is he?" Evgeny asks.

"Sixty-five."

"He's amazingly fit."

"He's not especially youthful amongst the Kind, which is a shame, because we wish we could have him around forever. However, he's surprising healthy, given his adventures, the dangerous territories he's travelled through, the physical privation of his journeys, the battles he's fought. A necessary evil in his line of work, and more recently ours."

"What is the Kind?" Mathew asks.

"It's what we call ourselves. I believe the name was first used in irony by people who thought we murdered people put outside the City walls. However, we think it accurately describes behaviour we aspire to, so we're happy to adopt the name."

"You are non-people," Evgeny says with a shocked expression.

"We say Non Grata. Strictly speaking, we're a branch of the Non Grata. There are many different types. The term originates from your time, I believe, Mathew."

Mathew is puzzled.

"It comes from persona non grata. People not welcome, who are put outside; people who, as Evgeny suggested, are legally non-existent. We are all people who have been ostracised or are descended from the rejected. We live beyond the reach of the main cities protected by government. We don't live by their rules and laws. We have our own."

"And you all live like this, underground?" Evgeny asks.

Tristan shakes his head. "No. Only the Kind and those willing to listen to Lev and take our technology. And we wouldn't live like this if we didn't have to. The proper place for people is under the sky, not in tunnels and caves."

"So why do you do it?"

"I will let Lev explain. Come on, breakfast is ready, and there are all sorts of people to introduce you to."

26 THE EMPTY CELL

Colonel Borodin's camp is packed up. His pilots are checking the engine of the chopper. It's early morning, and the men in Dragomirov's camp are waking, taking showers, preparing to go into the mess hall. Borodin decides to go to Dragomirov directly to check on the status of the authorisation he knows will never come and to collect his prisoner.

Churkin, experiencing a rare pang of conscience, has gone down to the prison block to check on Evgeny. He stops dead. The wooden cage is empty. The door to the prison block is ajar, and he strides in. The guard is still asleep. Kicking him awake, Churkin rushes past him to the cell, which he also finds empty, and raises the alarm.

Borodin reaches the prison block in the middle of a scene of some chaos.

Dragomirov is interrogating the sleeping guard.

"You are wasting your energy hitting him, Colonel. He doesn't know anything," Borodin says.

"This is not your command, Colonel," growls Dragomirov.

"No, it's not. But you've lost my prisoner." Borodin walks into the prison block and slowly examines the cells, the locks on the door, then goes outside to examine the wooden cage Evgeny was locked in.

"There was a man in here?" he asks.

No one responds.

Smiling wryly, shaking his head, he says, "Of course, your spy."

At the edge of the prison block he crouches down, touching the ground gently with his fingers.

Dragomirov and his men stop paying attention to Borodin and go back to interrogating the guard.

Borodin moves along the edge of the prison block and scans across the cleared land to the forest edge. Slowly, he paces towards the trees, stopping every now and then to stoop and examine the ground. Then he disappears under a canopy of leaves.

Standing next to the chopper, in what remains of Borodin's camp, Yolkov watches his colonel walk towards the forest and calls to another soldier hauling their rations into the back of the chopper.

"Don't bother, Istomin," Yokov says. "The colonel will be a while. Let's brew some tea."

Borodin stands on the edge of the jungle, his keen eyes raking about with a hunting look. Dead ahead, under the cover of a low-growing palm, he spots something not quite right. He walks directly to it, lifts a branch and then the banana leaves, and peers down into the shaft.

He doesn't need a torch. He sees in the dark perfectly.

.

27 KINDNESS

Mathew is starving, and the food is the best he has eaten since he left home. There are all kinds of breads, jams, pancakes, yoghurts, and fruit, even. Tristan's people sit around large tables to eat. The food is served buffet-style. People load up their own plates and find a place. There are coffee, teas, fruit juice, and fresh water on the tables. Evgeny is tucking in to a huge plateful of practically everything. He is glowing with happiness.

"I haven't eaten like this since I left Moscow," he says. "In fact, we didn't eat this well in Moscow."

They are sitting with Tristan and all of his brothers. It turns out he has a lot more than the three Mathew had already met. There are twelve in all. Gower, the oldest, is nearly forty; Dom, the youngest, is eighteen. Only half of them are married with children, but they still have a formidable extended family. Some of the smallest members are playing under the tables, crawling about between the legs of people who are getting their breakfast.

"The rest of us would like to get married," Tristan says, "but there is a shortage of women."

"Speak for yourself," Dom says. "I don't want to get married."

"Okay, the rest of us, apart from Dom."

Evgeny, between mouthfuls of muffin, says, "There was never a man with so many sons. These days a person is lucky if he has one child, girl or boy. Who is this fertile man?"

Evgeny is expecting to have some hulking, virile-looking man pointed out to him, but the sons all indicate the next table, where their father sits.

"That is Peter, our father," Tristan says.

He is a small, thin, delicately framed man, who appears far too young to have produced so many children. In fact, he appears younger than some of his sons. His wife appears to be considerably older, and no wonder, thinks Evgeny. The father of twelve smiles at them and raises his hand in a half-wave.

"How old was he when the first one of you was born?" Evgeny asks, shocked.

"Dad was in his early twenties when Gower was born. He's sixty-two now."

"No! You are pulling our legs," and Evgeny starts to laugh, muffin spraying everywhere.

Nothing the sons say convinces Evgeny.

Mathew gapes at Tristan. "You're serious, aren't you?" Tristan nods, and this sends Evgeny into more spasms of laughter.

"He's messing with you, Mathew."

Tristan shakes his head slightly and shrugs.

Mathew says, "How do you talk to me through my e-Pin?" He touches the earring in his left ear. "You don't have them."

"We all have implants. They're more advanced versions of the communications technology used in your e-Pin. The technology we use allows us to intercept brain signals."

"You're reading my mind?"

"No. Properly reading someone's mind requires a more advanced set of technologies than we're able to leverage reliably right now. Plus, there are ethical issues, and human brains aren't yet evolved enough to handle the psychological impact.

"We're intercepting the brain signals for speech. We create public conversations inaudible to anyone outside of the group, or we create private conversations between two people. It's very useful in situations where we need to communicate but speaking aloud would be dangerous, like when we rescued you. We hijacked the more primitive technology in your e-Pin to enable us to talk to you and for it to intercept and transmit your speech signals, as you experienced."

"How do you do that? If I want a machine to read my brain signals, I need to wear a synthetic telepathy cap full of electrodes and a signal amplifier."

"Nano-technology," Tristan says.

"Tiny invisible flying machines," says Dom. "We sent them to rewire your e-Pin and a tiny bit of your brain."

Evgeny is stricken.

Tristan says to Mathew, "Implants are enhancements banned by most governments."

Evgeny says, "Why are you explaining this to him? He must know this. Doesn't the ATLAS government ban enhancements, too?"

"I don't know," Mathew says.

"People in the Atlantic states, or ATLAS, where England is now, and the Federation of Free Republics, where Evgeny is from, are allowed wearable technology like yours, but it's considered an abomination to do anything to actually amend your body. We don't agree with this. Most of us have amended our eyes to allow us to enjoy improvements in vision and also augmented reality, a bit like the Lenzes you're wearing, Mathew. We all have biobots, like you, although several generations more advanced. Most of us have enhanced cognitive functions, hearing, physical fitness, mental health, and general wellness. We have daily access to technologies across a range of areas outlawed in most of the so-called more civilised world, and we have spent the last forty years developing them."

Dom says, "Not all of us need enhancements."

Frey, one of Tristan's older brothers, says, "But it's a long story and not one for breakfast."

Evgeny asks, "What are a bunch of ATLAS people doing in a mountain in Russia, anyway?"

"We're not ATLAS people," Dom says. "We're Non Grata. The Non Grata aren't part of your war. We don't care about national boundaries."

"But why come here in the first place?"

"We were escorting someone on a journey. Then we bumped into your Mr Dragomirov, Evgeny."

"You are the maggots we were tracking!" Evgeny says. He gawps wonderingly. "Do you have the girl here?"

"No. She's gone. She left Russia four months ago with some of our party."

"Left Russia?"

"She crossed the Bering Strait. She's now in ATLAS territory. She'll be settling down underground like us for the duration, and then when everything is clear, she'll be completing her journey. She still has a long way to go. We'll follow her eventually."

"You know where she is?"

"Of course."

"By using your technology? Your enhancements?"

"Partly."

"Why did you stay? Why didn't you go with her?"

"To distract Mr Dragomirov and take him off our friend's scent. He was tracking us for several months. We send parties to take him on long detours. The majority of us stayed here to build this place. Mr Dragomirov followed us to this region. We were out on one last patrol before retreating to the mountain when we discovered Mathew."

"How did you find Mathew?"

Tristan turns to Mathew. "We came across you and the big cat. We were watching when one of Mr Dragomirov's men fired his gun. We decided to wait until the fuss died down and made the plan to rescue you."

Mathew asks Evgeny, "Why were you chasing this girl?"

Evgeny glances at the others, looks uncomfortable, and says, "Dragomirov captured the girl a year ago. There are routine tests of identity run on people. You experienced them yourself. When these were run on her, there were strange results. Like you, this girl was supposed to be dead. She was a former citizen of an ATLAS city, cast out and deleted. They checked for enhancements. She didn't have any obvious technology implants. She didn't have a medibot, like you, but many of her results were very strange. Her brain scans revealed extraordinary activity, and her body seemed to have an endless capacity for regeneration and self-healing. Dragomirov thought she was some kind of highly secret advanced military technology developed by ATLAS. None of our intelligence found anything like this, but ATLAS always has the capacity to surprise. Dragomirov was taking the girl to Moscow when she escaped."

"She is not military technology," Dom says.

"I never thought she was," Evgeny says.

Tristan says, "Mathew, I hope you don't mind, but when we were bathing, I noticed you have a dressing on your arm. You have an injury."

Mathew puts his hand to his shoulder instinctively. "Yes. The cat scratched me."

Evgeny says, "Some scratch! We stitched it at the camp."

Tristan says, "Our father is a healer. Why don't you let him examine it?"

After breakfast, one of Tristan's brothers takes Evgeny for a tour of the kitchens.

Tristan speaks to his father, who turns and beckons to Mathew. He smiles as Mathew approaches, and the three walk together towards the back of the large cavern, through groups of people standing and talking after breakfast, and then up a few steps to a room carved into the rock.

The floor of the room is decorated with brightly coloured rugs and cushions. Tristan stands by the door, leaning against the frame, his arms crossed, looking out, as if giving them some privacy. Peter gestures to Mathew to sit on one of the cushions, and he does the same. There's music playing faintly in the background, piano music Mathew recognises but can't name. He glances with surprise at Peter.

"What did you expect?" Peter asks, and he smiles, his eyes sparkling.

Mathew smiles back, but he is unnerved. In spite of what Tristan said earlier, Peter has read his mind.

At close quarters, Mathew is able to observe Peter properly. He appears no older than Tristan, perhaps even younger, and has an incredibly calm, slow manner. Mathew imagines he's never rushed or harassed. It's relaxing to be in his company.

Peter asks him to loosen his shirt and take his arm from one of the sleeves. He examines the wound. Mathew peers down at his shoulder. It's red and swollen around the stitches.

"There's a slight infection," Peter says. "Normal in this jungle. The army doctor's medicines were not able to cope."

"But I have a medibot."

"Your medibot isn't working. Like your e-Pin and Lenzes, it requires software updates and needs to be connected to a network to properly function. It shut down the moment you came to the jungle. It would not be able to access modern Russian networks."

"Then why didn't I get sick in the jungle?"

Peter smiles gently. "Because you have a guardian angel."

Mathew is amazed. "Did you send your nanomachines after me?"

But Peter is focusing on his shoulder. He hovers his hands close to, but not touching, Mathew's skin and closes his eyes. Mathew is disappointed. This behaviour reminds him of some of the wacky healing videos his grandmother is always sending him, which have no scientific basis and which he considers irresponsible. But as he sits there feeling slightly cheated, he looks at his shoulder and sees the stitches unwind and disintegrate. The wound actually opens, and the yellow pus bubbles and then disappears. The wound is left red but clean. It starts to close, and the split skin cleaves together until there is just an angry red line running across his shoulder.

Peter opens his eyes, peering closely at the wound. "I'll remove the scar tomorrow. Let's give a tiny bit of time for nature to help us, shall we?"

"But . . . how did you do it?"

Peter's gaze is very direct. It's like he's delving into Mathew's mind. "Don't look so worried. It's not magic or anything supernatural. I promise. We are all scientists here."

"But how. . . ?"

Tristan says, "It's a long story. If you stay, I will tell you, but not now, not today."

As they're still sitting, Lev comes into the room. He greets Peter and Tristan and says, "Hello, Mathew. How was your breakfast?"

"Delicious, thank you," Mathew says.

Compared to Peter, Lev looks old, with his lined face and greying beard and thick head of hair. Yet he is fit enough to have led a dangerous mission to rescue him.

Peter says to Lev, "Mathew has a lot of questions. I think you are the better person to answer them."

Lev nods and says to Mathew, "Come on. Shall we have a walk?" He helps Mathew to his feet. Mathew turns to thank Peter, but Peter is now sitting cross-legged with his eyes closed, apparently meditating.

Lev and Mathew go back into the cavern and slowly cross the main floor. "Not what you expected?" Lev asks him.

"I don't know what to say. What I saw is not possible."

"But think, Mathew. How might he do it without violating the scientific laws you hold so dear?"

"He would have to be able to control matter at the molecular level."

Lev nods slowly. "So, it is not impossible."

"It may not be impossible, but it is unlikely."

Lev raises an eyebrow. "What a fixed point of view. For a boy who is 433 years old and who dropped from the sky from London into tropical Siberia, you are strangely keen to hang on to what you think you know. Are you able to explain any of those things?"

"I'm in a game. The most amazing virtual reality game anyone has ever created, but this isn't real."

"If you think you're in a game, a simulation, why are you so surprised and concerned by what Peter did to you? Surely anything is possible in a game?"

Mathew frowns. "The game is so real, I keep forgetting it's not real."

"I see. So I am not real?"

"No."

"That's upsetting. But it's quite a philosophical point of view. Some people actually think the universe is a giant computer simulation made by the ultimate programmer, you know. But then people believe all kinds of things. It's no crazier than gods, monsters, or ghosts."

Mathew says, "How do you think I got here?"

"Oh, Mathew, I've no idea. But I have met stranger strangers in my time. When I was young, I was like you. I thought I was rational, but my mind and ideas were fixed. My life has since taken me down some extraordinary paths, and I've learned to accept that I might not always have the answer. But the Kind aren't in any way a mystical group. As Peter says, everything we do obeys the laws of science. It's just the means may not always be transparent to us. What is the famous quote? 'Any sufficiently advanced technology is indistinguishable from magic.'"

Mathew grins. "Arthur C. Clarke."

Lev smiles and nods.

"So do you know how Peter healed me?"

"You have explained it yourself. He is able to manipulate matter at the molecular level."

"But in detail, how do you explain how he does it? Are you able to do it yourself?"

Lev shakes his head. "No. The Kind have many advanced technologies, but we did not invent Peter's abilities. They were gifted by a much greater technologist we both used to know."

"Where is he, this great technologist?"

"He has other lives to lead."

"Where did he go?"

Lev thinks. "He is still here in this world and is working through a small number of people like Peter and especially now the Lamplighter. She is his agent. And indirectly through me, and he is waiting, like we are."

"What are you waiting for?"

"For history to end. It's why we are here in the mountain. It's why I have walked across the world. When we emerge again from under this mountain, there will be a completely blank sheet, and we will start again. Perhaps we will do it right next time."

"I don't understand."

"The man I told you of, the technologist, he wasn't from the past like you; he was from a time way into the future and was able to tell us many incredible things. But he also warned us. In the world beyond this mountain right now, there are two great armies fighting a war, the remnants of the old nations, expressing ancient tribal behaviours using technologies they are ill-equipped psychologically to control. The way things have gone, it's a vastly unequal war. The Federation has more resources than ATLAS, and it is on the verge of crushing that collection of ancient nation states. But it is making a tremendous error of judgment, because ATLAS knows it is going to be crushed. It is desperate, and it will deploy a weapon they call Wormwood, more awful and destructive than anything human beings have ever managed to create before. We have spent the last forty years learning to build shelters to protect us from this weapon and developing the means to survive while we wait for it to be safe to emerge back under the sky again. My role was to travel as far as possible to tell our story to those willing to listen and to provide them with the means to protect themselves."

"When will this happen?"

"It is imminent."

"Do you know precisely?"

"Yes."

"Is it happening now?"

"It is under way. It will reach here later tonight."

"But Evgeny's camp, the people there?"

"When he eventually goes back, the whole place will be as he left it. The barracks, the prison house, the cookhouse. The food, the supplies. But there will be no people. Not a trace of them. Not a shadow on the ground or a pile of dust. Every human molecule will have been dismantled."

"Shouldn't we warn them?"

Lev smiles. "If only it were so easy. They will not believe what we tell them, Mathew. Beliefs kill more humans than all diseases and weapons combined, an inevitable tragedy because it's the hardest thing there is, knowing what to believe."

"What do you believe in?"

"Science and the future. And that although humans are the most violent, destructive animal ever to have polluted the face of the earth, there is something sublime in every one of them, and one day perhaps the intelligent and good will become preeminent."

They walk to the lake. Some children are playing, swimming in a shallower part at the edge. They stand watching them.

As they do, a man surfaces at the base of the cliff. He has come from the tunnel.

People gasp. Men shout. Mathew watches Tristan and the other brothers run down to the lake. Frey has a kind of rifle pointed at the intruder. Unperturbed, the intruder starts swimming to the shore with strong steady strokes. He stands where it is shallow and wades ashore, his hands raised. Frey comes down towards him, still pointing his gun. Lev walks down to them both.

Lev puts his hand on Frey's shoulder, "It's okay, brother. Not necessary."

The intruder stands there, bare-chested and dripping but not shivering. Mathew knows him, even though he's never seen him before. He'd know those green eyes anywhere.

"I've come for the boy," Borodin says.

28 THE DOOR

Lev, Peter, Rose, and a few people Mathew hadn't met previously – two priests, one of them elderly; a middle-aged woman called Lilly, who's holding the hand of the younger priest; a man with robotic prosthetic legs; a youngish man they call Carey; and a grizzled giant of a man with a nasty scar on his face introduced as Gentle Mick – all sit around a table staring at Borodin. Mathew sits to one side.

"We shouldn't have the boy here," Borodin says.

"It's his fate we're deciding. He should have a say, at least," Lev says.

"He should make the decision himself," Rose says.

Peter says, "I think Mr Borodin might have good reason for what he's asking," and Gentle Mick and Carey nod. "Mr Borodin is somewhat . . . like us."

Lev is surprised and then says, "We have told the boy many things already, Mr Borodin."

"It's unfortunate." Borodin studies Mathew, frowning. "This is a delicate matter. A mistake was made. A significant mistake. The boy shouldn't be here. He's not incidental to history – to all our fates. He shouldn't stay here. To be clear, unless this boy lives his own life in his own time, there will be no Kind; there will be no Tekton."

"And you will take him back, to where he came from, Mr Borodin?" Gentle Mick asks.

"Yes, I will take him back. I *must* take him back."

Peter glances around the table at Lev, Rose, Lilly, and the two priests and says, "Borodin is speaking the truth."

"Agreed," says Gentle Mick.

Carey nods.

Lev asks, "Are we all comfortable with placing Mathew in Mr Borodin's care? Peter, Gentle Mick, Carey?"

"I am," Peter says.

"Me, too," Gentle Mick says.

Lev goes around the table. They all agree.

"But what if I don't want to go?" Mathew says.

Lev turns to Mathew. "We will get you ready."

The only exit from the mountain is through the cave system. Mathew stands at the side of the lake, saying goodbye and thank you to Tristan, Peter, his many sons, Rose, Lev, and Evgeny, who is especially distressed to watch him go.

"I don't understand why I can't go with him," he's saying to Tristan.

"I will explain. I promise."

"So you keep saying," Evgeny grunts.

Borodin is keen to be on the move. Mathew is provided with breathing apparatus, a headlamp, and a life vest. Borodin refuses even the breathing mask.

"Crazy," Dom says.

"He got here alright, didn't he?" Tristan says.

Wading into the lake, Mathew finds the water more pleasant to be in, now he is wearing his strange new clothes. Borodin takes Mathew's life jacket and dives first. Mathew dives but finds it hard to swim down to the required depth. He bobs up, unable to fight his own buoyancy, so Borodin swims back to him, grabs him, and takes him down and into the drowned tunnel.

Borodin's headlamp picks out the way ahead. Mathew hauls himself after Borodin, grabbing rock protrusions to give himself momentum once again. Following the man in front, he starts to swim upwards, and they emerge in the place where there's a foot or two of air above them. Borodin doesn't wait. He starts to swim along at the surface.

The route is familiar to Mathew, less frightening, less eerie. But Borodin doesn't talk to him, in his head or otherwise. He's grim and purposeful, urging Mathew on, helping him when he struggles as they retrace their steps leaving the mountain. In total silence they wade from the water onto the shore. They follow the cave and the tunnel to the makeshift door, and soon Mathew once again finds himself in the jungle.

He had been in the mountain less than a day, but he had adjusted to the comparative silence, even the bustle of the people of the Kind being absorbed in the cathedral-like vaults underground. Now the noise of the forest assaults him, deafening. The birds and insects and unknown mammals are mostly invisible but audible all around.

Borodin retracts the ladder and shields the hole to the shaft with leaves. He does a better job than Lev, Mathew notices. He briefly wonders why a senior Russian soldier would want to conceal the whereabouts of outlaws.

Only then does Borodin speak, the words crystal clear to Mathew, though his lips are closed. The strange green eyes observe him coldly, objectively. "We have to be quick and stealthy. Dragomirov will be hunting for us. It doesn't matter if they find us, they are trivial to handle, but I would rather not kill anyone."

Mathew thinks back, "I thought they were going to die anyway."

But Borodin just starts walking.

They hug the mountainside. Mathew follows in Borodin's steps along a stony path. The man moves with supernatural fluid grace, unnerving Mathew. He's not comfortable in Borodin's presence the way he was with the Kind. They stop for Mathew to drink water

Borodin finds for him in the heart of a plant. Borodin doesn't need to drink and is patient, but only to the extent that he seems to instinctively understand Mathew's physical limits.

The higher ground they are walking on has fewer trees and less wildlife. Mathew recognises the terrain. It's the same landscape the cat chased him into.

Then he spots the cave and the gaping black mouth in the side of the mountain and stops dead in his tracks.

Borodin turns back to him. "This is the way," he says.

"No," Mathew says. "I'm not going in there with you."

Borodin walks back towards him. Mathew turns to run, but Borodin has him – grabs him around the waist and lifts him over his shoulder. Mathew pounds on Borodin's shoulders and kicks, but the man's body is like iron, and he has a grip like a vice.

What has Lev done? This man is the cat! He tricked them.

They are in the cave. It's cold and dark. Borodin keeps walking, gripping Mathew to him. Mathew is blind. He is terrified, certain that at any minute Borodin intends to kill him. Then they pause. Borodin is reaching forward, struggling with something. Opening a door. They burst through into the light. Borodin lets Mathew slump to the floor and turns to shut and lock a door behind him. Mathew blinks in the bright light and gazes around.

He is in Mr Lestrange's Darkroom, sitting in a chair. Borodin has gone.

29 REALITY

Monday, 29 November 2055, London

Relief floods through him. Relief at not being murdered by Borodin. Relief because it was a game, after all – the world is not ending – he is back home.

Looking around the Darkroom, he breathes deeply, his heart still racing in his chest. Now he's safe, he is able to marvel at how true to life the experience was, and he wants to tell someone, anyone. Lestrange, or whoever he works for, has invented full-immersion virtual reality!

Issuing voice commands to his Lenz, he's still unable to get a network connection, but he connects to his Lenz interface. He checks the time. And checks again. The evidence of his eyes defies his senses. It's nine o'clock.

But nine o'clock on what day?

He checks the date. It's Monday, 29 November 2055. Of course it is! It was a game he was playing; he wasn't away for days. But even if he was playing a game, hours must have elapsed, surely? According to the clock, no time has passed at all. Rising from the chair, he walks to the door and into the hallway.

The house is in darkness. Lights flicker on as he moves around. Still no one is home.

"Mr Lestrange?" he calls.

The door to the library is open. A book is open on the table. It's the book called *Fin* that he had been studying before he went into the Darkroom and forgot to put away. Then he remembers *The Book of Mathew Erlang* with a shudder.

He picks up *Fin*. The page it's open at reads:

Through 2472 and the last days of human civilisation, Polkovnik Grigory Dragomirov tirelessly attempted to track the Lamplighter across Russia and into Siberia. However, he was actually following a breakaway section of the Kind, and the Lamplighter escaped to the American continent four months before Wormwood. The breakaway group, which included Angel Leventis and Peter the Sleeper, built a refuge inside a mountain in Chukotka Autonomous Okrug, where they waited for the end of history.

The streetlights are blazing. The curtains are drawn, and he pulls them to one side and peers out at the little street and the row of silent houses. The road is just as it was before he fell through the conservatory roof. It's night-time. All the curtains and blinds in the windows of all the other houses are drawn. Above the rooftops grey clouds travel across the sky. Stars twinkle in between, mysterious, far away.

Going over to the shelf, he puts *Fin* back in its place. It's the strangest thing he's ever come across to have self-writing and rewriting books linked to a game. He trails his hand across the covers of the books until he finds *The Book of Mathew Erlang*. His fingers grasp the spine, and he starts to pull at the book and then stops.

This is weird stuff, and it will mess with your head. None of it is true. What does Lestrange want with me? Does he work for the government, or is he some genius crazy man?

Mathew sighs. It's inevitable that Mr Lestrange will come home and find him unless he finds an escape route. In the hallway he steps to the front door and, not expecting it to open, tries the handle once more.

It opens. He's free to go.

Standing for a moment, he gazes into the ordinary London street, not sure of himself. Then he steps out, pulls the door shut carefully behind him, and turns to his own front door a few feet away. Standing there, he realises he left the house in a rush and of course failed to take his key fob with him. Knowing he won't find it, he searches his pockets anyway. The back door is open, but the houses are terraced, and there's no way for him to get to it. He supposes he could knock on Gen's door and climb her fence. But the door lock clicks open as he moves slightly towards it. Of course! The locksmiths changed the locks. The door now opens to his bioID. He'd forgotten.

The house is silent. Walking straight through to the kitchen, he pulls the back door closed.

Then he remembers.

"O'Malley!" But he doesn't expect his cat to appear.

His mother will kill him. He closes his eyes and runs his hands through his hair.

Leibniz, idle and charging in the corner of the room, wakes, alerted to his presence.

"Hello, Mathew. It is late, and you have not eaten this evening. Would you like me to cook you dinner? Your medibot says you have a remarkably balanced metabolism. Congratulations! You can have anything you would like from our stores. Should I display the menu in your Lenz?"

"No, thank you, Leibniz. I'm not hungry." The meal with Tristan only a few hours ago was enormous.

What am I thinking? He catches himself. *I haven't eaten since lunchtime.*

All the same, he isn't hungry.

Then O'Malley comes into the kitchen from the direction of

the front room, crumpled and sleepy-looking. Stretching, he lazily saunters to Mathew, rubbing against his ankles and purring. Mathew bends down and scoops him into his arms. He seems like he's been settled and asleep for hours.

"*You* are a horrible cat!" Mathew says. "Bad, bad, bad cat." But he holds him to his chest and hugs him, incredibly grateful he isn't lost.

A wave of exhaustion washes over him, and he wavers on his feet.

"Are you not feeling well?" Leibniz says. "Your health indicators all show you to be in remarkable health. Is there incomplete information?"

"No, Leibniz. I'm fine. I'm tired. I think I need an early night. Will you tell Mum I'm sorry I missed her, but I decided to turn in?"

He heads upstairs, carrying O'Malley with him, strips down to his t-shirt, and gets into bed.

"System. Lights off," he says to the household control centre, and the room is plunged into darkness.

For ten minutes he lies awake, vivid images from the game churning through his brain. As he's falling asleep, it crosses his mind to wonder whether tomorrow Mr Lestrange will come calling to complain about his conservatory.

30 BAD HEAD

DAY NINE: Tuesday, 30 November 2055, London

Mathew is underwater, trying to swim towards the light. It's dark and cold. There is luminescence on the surface of the water, but no matter how hard he tries to swim towards it, it gets farther and farther away. He needs to open a door. Someone is banging on the door, but he is so far underwater it's beyond reach.

"Mathew! Are you awake? Mathew!"

Waking suddenly, sitting, gasping for air, disorientated, he realises he is in his bed. The bed sheets are sodden with sweat, and he has twisted them around him so his legs are bound together. Pulling them off his legs, he swings his feet to the floor. His head feels awful. He gets to his feet, staggers to the door, and opens it.

"Mum!" he says, peering round the door.

"Don't seem so surprised – this happens every morning. I'm running a bit late. The car is here. Are you okay? You look terrible. . . . Did I wake you?"

"Yes. Overslept," he murmurs. "Bad dream," he clutches his head. "Headache."

"A headache? Your medibot must be faulty. Better make an appointment with Dr Girsh."

"Don't worry," Mathew says. "Probably nothing. If I still have it at lunchtime, I'll make an appointment."

"You shouldn't have a headache."

"No . . ." He couldn't remember the last time he'd had a headache. Or when he'd slept so deeply. He feels drugged.

His mother says, "Let me know if it doesn't go away." She moves to go. "Oh and thanks for helping with the locks. They're working fine. They let me in without a hitch when I got home last night."

"The locks!" Mathew says, remembering. "O'Malley. . . . Oh, god. Where's O'Malley?"

"He's there," his mother says. "He's stolen your bed."

Mathew turns his head gingerly and glances back into his room. O'Malley is curled in his bed, asleep.

"Did something happen?"

Mathew is confused. "I'm not sure."

A horn sounds on the road. "Okay, now my driver's pissed off with me," his mother says.

Mathew raises an eyebrow, and his mother grins. "Language," he says.

"Caught red-handed. But I don't think you're well at all. Make the appointment. Better safe than sorry."

She leans towards him and kisses him on the forehead. "Take it easy today, okay?"

Mathew nods. She turns. He watches her walk down the stairs and hears the door slam, the strange sound of the new locks bolting in place.

Slowly, he makes his way downstairs. Leibniz is in the kitchen, cleaning up after his mother.

"Good morning, Mathew. Should I fix you breakfast?"

Mathew sits down at the table. "Yes, please."

Leibniz isn't surprised at this change in the routine, but then why would it be? It's a machine.

"What would you like?"

"Hot rolls."

The lights on Leibniz's chest interface flash on and off for a moment. "We have the ingredients for hot rolls. Breakfast ETA four minutes. Do you want butter and jam?"

"Yes please, Leibniz."

"Coming right away, Mathew."

The Canvas is on, tuned in to the news channel. There is film footage of a young woman in handcuffs being bundled into the back of a police car by uniformed policemen. The headline scrolling along the bottom of the picture is: "Seventeen-year-old Reagan Feye arrested on suspicion of being a member of dissident Blackweb group Psychopomp."

"Breakfast is served," Leibniz says.

Mathew sits at the table. "Thank you, Leibniz," he says.

He starts to eat, watching the screen. He increases the volume of the Canvas via voice control.

Prime Minister Saul Justice is being interviewed. He says, "I am sensitive to the arguments concerning freedom of speech. We live in one of the oldest and most advanced democracies in the world and, unlike our enemies, we respect the right of our citizens to express opinions. But this must be balanced with the need for national security. We are at war, and at times like these the people of this country need to understand who the enemy is. We don't have time to squabble internally. If we do, we will lose this war. Psychopomp, as many of you will know, has a history of leaking state secrets.

"We cannot afford to allow this organisation to exist beyond the laws you and I obey each day of our lives. So we are shutting it down. Reagan Feye is accused of being a member of this organisation. She will have a fair trial. But if she is found guilty, we will use the new powers Parliament has given us to bring the full weight of the law down upon her and any other members of this group we find. Let this be a warning." Saul Justice is staring dead at the camera. "We will not tolerate traitors and dissidents. We will find you, wherever you are."

The journalist is flustered and disturbed. The commentators in the studio talk all at once, trying to explain what has just happened. Mathew turns off the Canvas.

He finishes his breakfast and allows Leibniz to clean.

His head is pounding. He goes upstairs, finds his Paper and checks in to his medibot. There is an alert. It says:

```
Unidentified chemical disturbance prefrontal cortex,
neocortex, parietal lobe, and hippocampus. Recommended
remedy: two paracetamol. Select print to send request to
edible carbon compound printer located in room: kitchen.
```

Mathew accepts.

The medibot interface says,

```
Request sent. Thank you. Please make an appointment with
your GP if symptoms persist.
```

A text message comes through on his Paper via the Blackweb network asking if he'll accept a call. He gets the usual security warning. He thinks it might be Eva or Wooden Soldier, No Right Turn, or whatever he is called today, but it's his grandmother.

"Did you see the news?" she says.

"Yes. Briefly. How did they catch her?"

"Ironically, she's the daughter of a senior politician in Saul Justice's government. The SIS put surveillance on him to protect him and caught her accidentally."

"Do you think she'll betray the others?"

"I hope not. We live in frightening times. Have they chipped you yet?"

"Yes."

Ju Chen is silent for a few moments.

"Hello?" he says.

"Sorry. I'm shocked they've done it so quickly. Are you okay?"

"I feel a little strange today, I have to admit. I had an incredibly vivid dream. You know those dreams that are so vivid they feel real?"

"Yes, I do."

"It was extraordinary. But I can't remember it. It's bugging me. I played a new type of virtual reality holovision game yesterday. I think it has messed with my head."

"I keep telling you those holo-things are bad for you."

"Yes, you do," he says.

"But you should trust your dreams, Mathew. Sometimes they work in mysterious ways."

"I might consider it, if I'm ever sure of the difference between dreams and reality again. Things are so weird here I don't think I know the difference."

"You need to play fewer Darkroom games," his grandmother says.

Mathew has worn Soren Erlang's spare Lenz and e-Pin ever since his father's death. Lenzes are made to personal specifications to exactly match eye colour and retina pattern. When he disappeared, Mathew's father was using his corporate communication equipment, and he left his personal devices at home. Mathew adopted them, and for some reason, even though it was obvious he was wearing his father's Lenzes, his mother never objected. However, she gave him a new pair for his last birthday, to match his own eye colour, with a fashionable e-Pin. Now he removes his father's Lenzes and replaces them with the pair his mother had made for him, peering into the mirror, into his own brown eyes for the first time in two years.

Downstairs he collects his paracetamol from the printer and takes them with a glass of water from the kitchen. He stares out of the kitchen window at the garden. Finding himself staring at the garden wall, the one separating their garden from Mr Lestrange's, something flashes in his head – a series of images: a blackbird with a bright yellow beak. O'Malley with a bird in his mouth.

I climbed over the wall last night.
The conservatory . . .
I fell through the conservatory!

Running upstairs, two stairs at a time, he bursts into his mother's bedroom and goes to the window. Mr Lestrange's conservatory is as it ever was. It isn't broken. His mind bends.

In the bathroom, he starts the shower running, undresses, and examines himself in the bathroom mirror. His ribs are a little more visible than normal. He tells himself he must try to eat more. Food is always the last thing on his mind.

On his shoulder he notices a tiny red line he's never noticed before, like a scratch or the scar of a scratch. Running his index finger along it, he has another one of those flashes.

A cat, he thinks. *A cat did this.*

A vivid image flashes into his mind of being knocked off his feet by a large wildcat, being chased through a jungle. *It was in the game. A game, Mathew*, he says to himself. *It's a coincidence. O'Malley must have scratched me in the night.*

He's had O'Malley on his mind for days. His head is pounding, and he closes his eyes and leans against the sink. *I need something stronger than the paracetamol. Maybe I will make an appointment with Dr Girsh.*

After he showers, he goes back to his room and logs in to the school register on his Paper. He remembers he initiated some courses on quantum computing and security. It seems like a long time since he has considered these things. His mind wanders, and he feels restless.

Opening Charybdis, he logs into the Blackweb and starts a MUUT session. MUUT is ugly and difficult to use, deliberately so, he guesses, as he starts a search on military virtual reality programs.

Leaving it to run, he goes downstairs again, to the Darkroom. O'Malley runs inside in front of him, straight for his litter tray. For a moment Mathew is confused. Why is O'Malley's litter tray in the Darkroom? But then he remembers the locksmiths. The locks did get changed, and he did put O'Malley in the Darkroom, after all. O'Malley finishes in the box, and Mathew takes it back to the utility room, where it's normally kept. Leibniz immediately sets to work cleaning it. O'Malley's water and food bowls are also locked in the Darkroom. The poor cat was probably hungry and thirsty. Mathew puts them in their usual place and tops up O'Malley's food bowl himself, giving him some enviro-chicken from the fridge to apologise for the delay to his breakfast. O'Malley eats gratefully. Mathew stands thoughtfully watching him. In his mind he's retracing the events of the day before. The locksmiths came, he locked O'Malley away, and sent the beebot to Clara. Did he do this?

He decides to call Clara on the beebot and goes back to the Darkroom where he starts the control software and makes his call. She answers immediately.

"Hi," she says. She sounds pleased to hear from him.

"Is this a bad time?"

"No. It's a great time. I'm halfway through a music theory video lesson and bored to tears. It's probably something you'd like. It's on mathematics and music."

"Sounds interesting."

"I wish you could take the test for me at the end. Do you have video activated on your end? Here, I'm going to move the beebot, so you get a better picture."

"I did a voice call. Hold on. It's activated."

"Is that better?"

"Yes. You're still in your pyjamas."

"My parents are both in town supervising some group project work, and I have virtual school. I'm being lazy. I'll get dressed in a bit. I do feel at a disadvantage, though. When are you going to fix the beebot so I have video on my end?"

"Working on it," he lies.

"I was going to call you."

"Sure."

"No, for real I was. I wanted to ask you if you would come to Gen's later this afternoon to watch me play when I have my lesson. I've cleared it with Gen. I told her you are a Bach fan."

"Yes. I'd like to. Thanks."

"Great. What are you up to today?"

"Oh, you know. School."

"What are you studying? I probably shouldn't ask. I won't understand it."

"Quantum computing and security."

"I knew I wouldn't understand it."

"I'm not sure I do, either, to be honest. My head's all over the place today."

"Why, has something happened? You sound a bit strange. Are you okay?"

"I have a cracking headache. And I had peculiar dreams. Something weird happened last night . . ."

"Oh, hold on, Mat! Sorry . . . my supervisor is calling me. I have to go. See you at four? Let's talk then, alright?"

"Absolutely. Keep your security guard on a leash, though."

"I promise no one will wrestle you to the ground and point a gun to your head."

"Good. Later then."

"Wish me luck with my mathematics course."

"Good luck."

"Thanks. Bye!"

So he *did* send the beebot to Clara.

31 THE DREAM SCENARIO

In the Darkroom, he pulls on the skullcap, summons the location of Eva's virtual world, and logs in.

He is standing at the gate. Checking the bricks, he finds the key, takes the knife from the belt now tied around his waist, cuts his finger, and draws gamma on the door with his blood. The lock appears, and he turns the key in the lock and walks into the forest clearing.

The empty crates are still there. There's smoke coming from the chimney in the hunting lodge, and he walks down the hill in the clearing between the trees. Everything is beautifully rendered – he even smells pine needles and senses the soft ground underfoot – but it's not like Lestrange's world. Not even close. He experiences a strange sense of disappointment, of loss.

The dragons have long since left the area. He knows he can summon a menu to jump to their location in order to observe them, but he doesn't.

There's snow on the mountains, but it's a warm, sunny day. Spring. Wildflowers grow on the meadow. The deciduous trees growing amongst the conifers have new green leaves. Birdsong comes at him from all directions. There's the sound of a rushing river somewhere close, which reminds him of the river in Siberia.

How much was in the game, and how much did I dream?

Perhaps it was *all* a dream. The jungle may be a transmogrification of Eva's virtual-world forest, made tropical because he was hot and sweating in the night.

A twig snaps behind him. He jumps and turns quickly – sudden, irrational fear pulsing through him.

"Sorry, I didn't mean to sneak up on you," Eva says, walking towards him. "I saw you'd entered the world and decided to come for a chat."

"Is your dad still in St Petersburg?" Mathew asks, normally enough, although his heart is beating fast.

"Yes, thank god."

And the jungle was in Russia.

"Are you okay? You seem distracted."

"I had a strange, vivid dream, and it's been bugging me all morning."

"You've probably been cooped up too much in your house. Too much virtual reality, not enough reality. I'd go for a walk if I were you. In the real world."

He nods. "You're probably right, but we've been under All-Day Curfew since the Thames flooded."

"Try doing some meditation. I do it when I'm not in touch with myself."

"You meditate?"

"Yes. Why is that surprising?"

He shakes his head. "No reason."

Eva says, "Do you want to check in with your dragons? I've tracked them. They're somewhere above Chukotka. They're having fun melting snow. They're going to cause global warming all by themselves."

"Chukotka… Did you mention that name before?"

Eva thought. "No, I don't think so. Why?"

A bolt of pain strikes in his head. He winces.

"Wow. You know you shouldn't be in the Darkroom if you're not well. You should go and lie down."

"I'm fine," he says. "What is this place, this Chukotka?"

"It's a region in Russia. In Siberia. My model will be of the whole world when I've finished it. I'm still geo-forming. I started with the bits closest to home. I've completed Russia now, and I'm halfway through China."

"What are you going to do with your world model when you've finished?"

"My main project is to run different climate scenarios. There'll be a world where humans never existed, a version with human-made climate change analogous to our own, then iterations where humans, or the climate impact of humans, suddenly disappear at various points in time. This scenario is of a 5-degree Celsius temperature rise compared to the beginning of the century – pretty much like we have now, which is why there's forest rather than tundra. Of course, I've left out all the oil wells."

"And what do you think it'll be like in three or four hundred years?"

"The point of the experiment is to discover that exactly. But millions of years ago, when carbon dioxide concentrations in the atmosphere were high, palm trees were growing in Antarctica. We're heading for a similar level of carbon dioxide in our atmosphere. So under that scenario this would be a tropical jungle. Crazy, isn't it?"

"Are you sure you haven't told this to me before?"

"I may have. I've no idea. Come on, I have some eggnog in the cabin. You have to try it. It will be like we're actually drinking."

After lunch he goes back to his room to check on the MUUT search. There's a list of results, and he starts scrolling through them when an advert for technical support pops up. He accepts and waits.

"Hello, I'm Ship of Fools. You're Conjurer. Acknowledge."

"Acknowledge Ship of Fools."

"How are you, Conjurer?"

"Good, thank you," Mathew lies.

"Good, good. I wanted to alert you. You're leaving a trail around you as bright as an elephant's paint fight.

"Wow. Okay. I didn't realise."

"I assumed as much. Suggest you shut the search down. I'll help you."

Mathew terminates his MUUT search.

"Have you moved on from Ithaca?"

Ithaca? Mathew searches his tired, sore brain. *He means Lestrange!*

"No. This is related."

"What do you want to know exactly?"

"Whether there are any full-immersion virtual reality projects in prototype?"

"And the military connection?"

"I've no idea, to be honest. Yesterday I think I got shut in Ithaca's house. I logged in to his Darkroom and experienced a VR so real I couldn't tell it from this world."

"You *think* you got locked in his house?"

"I got locked in."

"Are you sure?"

"Yes."

"What was this full immersion like?"

"Like I said, so real it was indistinguishable from this world. Is it even possible?"

"I don't know. It must be if you experienced it. If you did."

"*I did.* But technically, do you know of any companies or any projects producing this technology? Because I thought we were years from being able to do these things."

"There are lots of experiments. Of course, all sorts of governments and corporations are working on VR technology, but there's nothing commercially available, and I'm not sure any of the technology is complete. How did you access the world?"

"From a Darkroom seat."

"And did you wear anything else? Use any other equipment, drink anything, or inject anything?"

"I put on a skullcap and logged in."

"Just a skullcap? You used nothing else?"

"No."

"It isn't possible. Your body would have to be crawling with nanobots, repressing all the signals from this world and replacing them with information from the virtual world. A skullcap won't do it. You'd need to be in a lab or something."

Mathew's vision clouds, and a static speck appears in his left eye. His head explodes in pain.

"Thanks for your help. I have to go."

"Okay. Don't do any more wild searches, though. Let me know if you want help searching for anything. This is crazy shit, and I think you may be a little bit bonkers yourself, but it's also pretty damn cool. Okay if I send you another ad? I have some friends investigating Ithaca's network."

"Yes," Mathew manages, but he's hardly able to think or speak.

He teeters to his bed, collapses, and immediately falls asleep.

In his dream, he's back in Mr Lestrange's library, sitting in an old armchair. Borodin and Mr Lestrange are standing on either side of him. They are all staring at the table, at two books laid open. Lestrange is leafing through the pages.

"It's not what we expected, Borodin. Who would have predicted it?"

"It was pure laziness on our part. We are too easily distracted, too complacent. We are all guilty of too much play. All of us. This is what comes of never being challenged."

"Guilty of too much play! What a strange idea. But what is to be done?"

They both focus on Mathew. Borodin places his huge hand on the top of Mathew's head. "We can't go delving around too much inside here. If we remove what we don't want, we may accidentally delete what we want to keep."

"So true, so true. Such a simple structure, but there's so much that could go wrong. It's so fragile!"

"We have to be careful with it. He's had headaches all day."

"I agree. We agree. We all agree. Now we're involved, we have to be careful. So then, the dream scenario?"

"It'll have to do."

"It's the best option."

"We all agree."

When he wakes, he feels lighter, refreshed. His headache has gone, and he experiences a flush of well-being and optimism. Remembering that he's going to see Clara, he's happy and checks the time. It's nearly four o'clock.

When Clara's car turns up, he's standing in the window waiting. He waves and then goes down the stairs and into the porch.

Cold rain is driving down the street. He momentarily steps back to keep dry. The guard eyes him warily but shuts the door to the car and does not comment. Clara doesn't speak but she smiles at him and he smiles back. The rain is in her eyes. As she walks up the path, he makes a dash for it.

Gen Lacey comes to her front door, and Mathew, Clara and Gen huddle inside, shutting the door against the weather.

"Hello, Mathew! I hear you're a Bach fan," Gen says.

"An amateur one, but willing to learn."

"Any friend of Bach is a friend of ours," Gen says cheerily. "Don't you think, Clara?"

"Absolutely."

"This is a teaching session, not a concert, so I hope you won't be too bored."

"Not at all. I think it'll be fascinating," Mathew says.

Gen leads the way into her front room. "I did make some tea, and I have some cake. Help yourself while Clara and I get started,"

Gen says.

Mathew sits down on the sofa. Clara takes her seat at the piano.

Gen says to him, "How is O'Malley?"

"He's fine. . . . Why?"

Gen frowns. "You and I spent part of last night hunting high and low for him."

"Yes. . . . Yes! Thanks for your help . . ."

"No problem at all. Anyway, all's well that ends well. I'm glad he's okay."

"Yes. Me, too," he says.

Gen turns to Clara. "Right, shall we try Prelude and Fugue No. 2 in C minor?"

"Sure," Clara says, grinning at Mathew.

Mathew smiles back, but his eyes are drawn momentarily away from her face by something glinting. She has pinned the beebot to her collar. She raises an eyebrow at him quizzically, responding to the strange expression on his face. Gen wonders if Mathew is going to be a distraction. In fact, he sits patiently, absorbed, listening as she begins to play.

He's remembering the beebot and how he flew it down Mr Lestrange's chimney into his front room and the books, his book, *The Book of Mathew Erlang.*

Since the headache cleared, his mind, if anything, feels sharper than it has in months. But when he tries to recall the events of the past few days, it's like he's attempting to conjure a particularly vivid dream that evaporates on waking. Dissolving sequences of images he experienced as concrete reality seem bizarre on reflection, when he can remember them, leaving behind a strong residue of feeling – but most of it is maddeningly just out of reach. He knows some of the fragments are real. What else has he forgotten?

As he sits, a message comes in directly via Charybdis. He opens it and reads:

This message responds to signals in your Lenz registering as you read and eating the words as you go.

These words immediately fracture and disappear.

This comes to you from your friend in technical support. Further investigation finds your virtual reality experience unique given current state of technical capability. No known project in existence that could do what you described, but will keep looking. Could be something highly classified.

On the other matter, my friends say Ithaca's network is impenetrable. This is extraordinary.

Simultaneously had a slow, deep MUUT search running. Found this in the British Library archives, of all places. Seems to have been judiciously wiped from all other locations. It regards Ithaca. Enjoy.

The Times, *London, Monday, April 11, 2038*

Soho Easter Miracle As Stabbed Man Comes Back from the Dead

Paramedics are claiming it as an Easter miracle. A man they found slumped in a doorway in Kemps Court in Soho last night "came back from the dead." London Ambulance Service veteran Martin McInnery told reporters that when they arrived at the scene, they found forty-five-year-old August Lestrange, a Reader in History at King's College London, lying in a large pool of his own blood, after a vicious knife attack by an unknown assailant.

"There was no pulse," McInnery, who has served as a paramedic for fourteen years, told us. "It was clear from what he was lying in that he had bled out, and we concluded he was beyond resuscitation. We put him in a body bag, zipped him up, loaded him into the ambulance, and called through to the morgue to expect us.

"He was such a certain gonner that we shut him in the back and went into the front part of the vehicle. Neither of us like riding with the dead. I was the one to open the back of the truck to take the trolley out when we arrived. I nearly had a heart attack when I saw him sitting up on the stretcher."

Mr Lestrange is said to be recovering at home. He declined to be interviewed.

"Mathew, are you okay?" It's Gen's voice. She is bending over him, her hand on his back.

He realises that as he was reading, the music stopped. Clara is standing. She has her jacket over her arm, ready to leave. Mathew scrambles to his feet.

"Yes! Yes, sorry."

"You were miles away," Gen says.

"Must have been my sublime playing," says Clara.

"It was lovely."

She raises an eyebrow. "My car is here. Do you want to walk me out?"

"Sure."

They leave Gen on her step. Clara's guard stands stiffly by the open car door, eyeing Mathew.

Clara says, "You're really not okay, are you?"

"I'm fine."

"You seemed fine when you arrived. Did something happen while I was playing?"

Mathew smiles to reassure her. "No. Nothing. Everything's fine."

She squints at him sceptically but gets into the car. "Speak later?" she says.

He nods. The guard slams her door shut, gets in himself, and they drive away.

Mathew turns to his own house. Instinctively, he glances at the bay window of number 21 as he passes through the gate and walks along the short path. The message has been deleted, but the date is burnt into his memory.

Monday, April 11, 2038. The year before I was born.

No one is at the bay window, but Mathew knows for sure now. He's being watched.

THE END

Thank you for reading *The Boy Who Fell from the Sky*

If you enjoyed it, please leave a review on Amazon or the website of the retailer of your choice. Reviews help me write more books.

Mathew's adventures continue in…

SILVERWOOD

Book Two of the
House Next Door

trilogy

By

Jule Owen

Read the first chapter of *Silverwood*

1 THE BEST AND BRIGHTEST SCIENTISTS

DAY TEN Wednesday, 1 December 2055, London, England

"Eva Aslanova!" he shouts. "Eva, if you can hear me, I badly need a door!"

A roaring column of furnace-hot flame blasts the tree for five, ten, fifteen, twenty seconds – leaves, bark, branches, and trunk all igniting and burning ferociously. Mathew, scrabbling and clinging precariously to the higher branches, feels the heat blast towards him, toasting the soles of his dangling feet. The tree slumps and gives beneath him. He's falling. Then somehow he's on his feet. Yet another in a series of near-death experiences survived, he knows, only due to the fact that in this world his body is an avatar. Presumably, Eva doesn't see the need to programme into his virtual self the means to die a hundred horrible different ways, mostly by fire. She thinks his project childish. She wouldn't have put that much effort into it.

Or so he hopes.

He gets up from the scorched and smouldering earth beside the tree and gives himself a moment to glance back.

Two dragons, as tall as London double-decker buses, shift on their feet, flex their claws, flick their long, serpent-like tails ridged with spikes and plates. The power of a tail-swipe brings another tree crashing to the ground. It gets skewered by a cluster of spines, and the dragon thrashes its tail around until the tree, now uprooted and spraying earth and rocks and bird's nests, is pulled loose.

They are trashing Eva's world.

The larger dragon belches, and smoke billows out of her enormous nostrils. The male yawns, displaying a mouth full of splinter-sharp white teeth the size of large bottles and the blue tongue Mathew had been particularly proud of when he'd designed them.

They have grown enormously. They are huge. And now, completely oblivious to the fact that he created them in the first place, they think he is dinner, and they are very hungry.

He is fairly sure that he can't die in Eva's world, but just in case, he runs.

He is dodging trees as he goes, stumbling over tree roots. A hot blast of air funnels past him with such force that it blows him sideways. He dares not stop to look, but as he steadies himself, the rough bark of a redwood scraping the skin on the palm of his hand, out of his peripheral vision he catches the image of a red glowing cindered tree crumbling into a pile of charcoal and ash.

Up ahead, on the crest of a small bank, is an unusually large trunk, the width of several men standing shoulder to shoulder. In front of the tree he sees a young woman with very straight, thin, white-blonde hair and paper-white skin. She's small anyway, but she seems tiny, dwarfed by the giant conifer. Behind her is a door.

"Eva!" he gasps, lurching forward.

He scrambles up the bank, yanking at saplings to pull himself up, his feet slipping on the loose earth and stones. His leg muscles are burning.

"Thank god!" he wheezes, bent over double before her, grasping his knees.

She grabs him, pulls him inside the tree, and shuts the door.

He's back in his Darkroom. The blackened bare walls and floor seem less real than the forest. He sits down heavily in the chair behind him, still catching his breath. In a large armchair in front of him, Eva is curled up in her pyjamas.

"You do realise it's four hours ahead here?" she says. "Bedtime. You were lucky you caught me. I was just brushing my teeth. Fifteen minutes later, I'd have been asleep."

"I hope I didn't get you into trouble with your dad?"

"No, no, don't worry. He's not here. Off again on his travels, immortalising the story of our great and glorious army to anyone who will listen."

"St Petersburg again?"

"St Petersburg is done and dusted. Not sure where this time. He wouldn't say. No doubt, we'll see it all on the news soon enough."

"You're sure you're safe talking to me like this?"

"As safe as anyone is these days."

"That's not very reassuring."

"Best I can do. Look, Mathew, I think we need to talk about these dragons."

"It's not turning out quite as I'd planned."

"Yes, well, that's what's confusing me. How did you plan it, exactly?"

"I'm not sure I did that much, to be honest. Beyond getting them into a world where they could evolve."

"But in your programming, what did evolution consist of exactly? Growing endlessly larger?"

"They are quite big, aren't they? They should stop, though. I made them what I thought was dragon size."

"Which is? Forgive me, I've never seen a dragon."

"Oh, you must have, in films."

"I don't watch those kinds of films."

"About twice the size of a large dinosaur."

"Right. Why did you do that?"

"Because I could?"

"What I mean is, what are you trying to achieve with this project?"

"I was just trying to make dragons, using the new genetic coding programme I had. And I wanted them to be able to interact with their environment and evolve their behaviour over time."

"You succeeded. Congratulations. So we can close the server down then?"

"No. They were meant to breed."

"They can breed?"

"Yes."

"You want more of those things crawling about in that virtual earth of yours?"

"Obviously, I don't now, but when I coded them, I did."

"Wow. I don't wish to put a downer on things, but a few more of those things and you won't have much virtual earth left."

"Yes, I know."

"It seems a bit . . ."

"What?"

"Pointless . . ."

"I know."

"You can still code them, can't you?"

"I'm not sure. I packaged them. Doesn't that seal off the creation?"

"Just go back to the source code, amend, repackage, and then redeploy."

"Won't that overwrite them?"

"Yes."

"It will kill them."

"They're not alive, Mathew. Besides, they are fairly unpleasant, destructive creatures the way they are."

"I suppose."

"Why don't you have a think about how you might make their behaviour a bit more interesting, rather than just predatory and destructive?"

"Such as?"

"For instance, if I was interested in creating fauna-type

programmes rather than creating worlds, I wouldn't be interested in making stupid animals. I would see if I could make a mind more interesting and better than a human mind."

"But the best and brightest scientists alive aren't able to do that."

"So?"

"So how on earth am I meant to do it?"

"Mathew, I thought you and I were training to be the next generation of the best and brightest scientists."

"Uh-huh."

"Shouldn't we be cleverer than the last generation? Shouldn't we be able to do things they can't? Shouldn't we at least be trying to do those things?"

"I'd never thought of it like that."

"My father is always saying that the West is degenerate, and your schools and universities aren't a patch on ours. I'm always arguing with him that he doesn't know what he's talking about. Please don't let him be right. Look, why don't you at least try and concentrate on improving the dragons' minds and behaviour? Give them some higher reasoning, a personality, even? You must have done some personality-typing courses?"

"Yes, but I hated them."

"There's a surprise. Anyway, what do I know? They're your dragons, and it's your world, for however long it takes them to burn everything to a cinder. Next time you decide to go in there, can you make sure you check the time difference, though?" Eva yawns. "You wouldn't want to be toasted while I'm asleep. It could be an uncomfortable eight hours. I'm off to bed. Night, Mathew."

"Night, Eva. And thanks," he says, but the armchair has gone.

END OF CHAPTER ONE

To be continued…

SILVERWOOD

When Mathew's mother, Hoshi, becomes seriously ill, he'll do anything he can to save her and he knows his future self would too. Breaking into the house next door, the one belonging to his peculiar neighbour, August Lestrange, he activates his holographic games room, which doubles as a time machine, to hack into his own future. Alone in an England afflicted by extreme weather, biological warfare and civil war, Mathew needs to find his older self before Lestrange catches up with him and takes him back to his own time.

Silverwood is available to purchase as an e-book and as a paperback.

Visit my website www.juleowen.com to find out more about *Silverwood,* for offers, news and giveaways.

ACKNOWLEDGMENTS

NOTES

The Boy Who Fell from the Sky and the other books in the *House Next Door* trilogy represent my version of the future, inspired by non-fiction books by Michio Kaku, Martin Rees, K Eric Drexler, George Friedman, Alan Weisman, James Lovelock and James Hansen, amongst others. My full list of sources can be found on my website at http://juleowen.com/futurology-resources

We are now living in the Anthropocene age, the first period in geological history when humans have had a significant impact on the earth's ecosystem. One direct result of this is climate change. We are also living in a time of exponential technological innovation. It is an extraordinary and frightening time to be alive. My stories are my way of coming to terms with this by exploring possible futures. Find out more about the background to my stories here http://juleowen.com/futurology/

WITH THANKS

I think the point when I realised that I needed others help to complete this book was the point when it became possible.

Thanks to my editors Jill Mason and Lynda Thornhill. You have saved me many blushes. Any blushes I consequently have are entirely of my own making.

Thanks to Tommy Nakamura, Amy DuBoff, Marc Weldon and Lorna Barker for reading and offering useful comments on this book. Thanks also to others who were generous with their time, by reading my book, supporting me on Wattpad or helping with my launch, including Emilie MacMullen, Akvilė Štuopytė, Caroline Juricic, Caroline Bertin, Rita Liotisaite, Lara Hayward, Mark Klein, Jennifer Wirth, James McCarthy, Henry Blanchard, Adam Masojada, Pilar Knoke, Nativ Gill, Lizzy Arnold, Camille Rougié, Jonathan Hulse, Victoria and Nigel Webb, Ruanne Cluer, Lydia Foulkes, Kim Huggins, Triin Kambek, Natalie Waser, Rory McNeice, David Sorsoli, Christina Hegele, Emily Brett, Simon Darby, Heather Allen, Lindsay Charman, Ailsa McLaren, Elizabeth Garnham-Jong, Stefanie Wai, Julie Walsh, Eilis Kerr, Mauro Doni, Rob Crossen, Sam Martin, Cynthia Crossley, Max Beckmann, Rae Dowds, Anna Fullerton-Batten, Peter Bell, Bridget Beirne, Daren Pickering, Cassie Condon, Zuzana Dobrovolna and Laxmi Hariharan.

I'm lucky enough to be part of a few awesome communities that have eased my way. Thanks to the Alliance of Independent Authors and to the extraordinary Escape the City community. Thanks especially to Alexis Garnaut-Miller, Bella Zenesco and the my12for12 crew. Your friendship and support this year has mattered more than you could possibly know.

I owe a huge debt of gratitude to Mark Speed, who was kind enough to read early versions of this book, edit and offer invaluable feedback. He took me under his wing and has been a constant source of encouragement and useful advice.

Mark is the creator of the wonderful Doctor How series, the real story behind the Doctor Who myth. For those of you who like some comedy with their sci-fi, Mark's books are a tonic. The first in the series, *Doctor How and the Illegal Aliens* can be found on Amazon.

Thanks to my Dad for always being there.

Most of all, thanks to Lauren for your endless patience, support and kindness. This book would never have been written without you

ABOUT THE AUTHOR

Jule Owen was born in the North of England and now lives in London. She spent many years working in online technology, latterly in the video games industry and is fascinated by science, technology, futurology and equally terrified by climate change.

She can be found online and would love to hear from you. Look her up here:
www.juleowen.com
@juleowen

THE BOY WHO FELL FROM THE SKY

Lightning Source UK Ltd.
Milton Keynes UK
UKOW04f2249250216

269103UK00002B/15/P